IMPERFECT

RILEY EDWARDS

Imperfect
Triple Canopy
Book 3

Riley Edwards

Copyright © 2021 by Riley Edwards

Cover design: Lori Jackson Designs

Written by: Riley Edwards

Published by: Riley Edwards/Rebels Romance

Edited by: Rebecca Hodgkins

Proofreader: Julie Deaton, Rebecca Kendall

Imperfect

Paperback ISBN: 978-1-951567-16-3

First edition: April 27, 2021

Copyright © 2021 Riley Edwards

All rights reserved

To my family - my team – my tribe.
This is for you.

In memory of
Senior Chief Petty Officer Shannon Kent.
Until Valhalla sister.

CONTENTS

1

"Luke," Lauren happily chirped my name as soon as I walked into the reception area at Triple Canopy.

I felt my eyes narrow at her happy tone. Sure, Lauren was friendly, but not overly so, and usually, she saved her cheeriness for clients. Today, she was overly so toward me. I searched my recent memories for a reason for the pretty receptionist's joyfulness and I came up empty. Not that Lauren shared. She came to work, did her job—most of the time with a smile—then left. But she'd never been overly cheery toward me. Logan sometimes, but I figured it was mostly to get under his skin. Like pulling a tiger's tail to get a reaction. Lucky for her, Logan didn't bite—ever. He simply ignored her.

"Lauren," I returned. "What's up?"

"Your one o'clock is here," she informed me.

"My one o'clock?"

"Um. Yeah," she drawled slowly like I was an idiot. "Your one o'clock with Shiloh Kent."

"I don't—" *Shit, damn, and fuck.* "I forgot I was taking over Brady's classes while he's on his honeymoon."

"We can reschedule." A feminine voice came from behind me.

A very smooth, husky voice that sounded like sex. Not empty, superficial sex that left your balls drained but your soul cold. A sweet promise to warm you from the inside out. The sound of it rich and soothing.

I felt my body grow tight and I turned, ignoring Lauren's dirty look. Then I had to look down, *way* down—the woman was no taller than five-four. A pixie face, pale blue eyes that were so light they were pastel. The stark contrast to her sun-kissed skin made them look luminescent. Blonde hair that was so shiny it looked like she'd oiled it up then brushed it smooth.

Christ.

No, Shiloh Kent was not rescheduling.

"Has Miss Kent signed in?" I asked Lauren and held my breath waiting for a correction on her marital status.

None came and Lauren was back to smiling. The receptionist would be on the phone with Quinn before I made it to the range.

"Yeah, all her paperwork is on file and current."

"You've been here before?" I asked Shiloh, and the sexiest fucking smile tipped her lips.

Lauren snorted and I felt like I was missing a joke.

"A few times," she confirmed.

"This is *Sunny* Kent," Lauren informed me.

"I'm sorry—"

"Don't be." She waved me off. "It was nice seeing you, Lauren."

"You, too, Sunny."

I glanced down at the rifle case and that sexy-as-all-hell voice floated through the air and slammed straight into my chest.

"Fair warning, if you offer to carry my rifle, I'm gonna kick you in the shin."

"Come again?"

"Again?" Sunny tipped her head to the side and a playful smirk lit her face. "Hadn't realized I'd come at all."

It took a moment to get it. But when it hit, for the first time in a long time I roared with laughter. When I was done, I gave her another once-over. She was cute, no doubt. But that wicked dry humor did it for me.

"All right, Sunny Kent. I won't offer to carry your rifle. Do you know where we're going?"

"Yes."

"Lead the way." I swept my hand toward the hall.

"You just wanna stare at my ass, don't you?"

Who the hell is this woman, and where has she been my whole life?

"Yep."

"Well, at least you're honest."

She gave a saucy wink and started down the hall.

Damn. I think I'm in love.

2

"That's a miss."

I clenched my teeth, slid my finger out of the trigger well, lifted my cheek off the stock of my custom 6.5, and hung my head in frustration.

Third missed shot in a row.

"Call your shot," Luke continued.

"Left." I begrudgingly told him something he very well knew since he was looking down range through his spotting scope.

Of all days for me to be off my game it had to be in front of Luke Marcou. I should've canceled my range time. Not because my normal spotter when I came to Triple Canopy was on vacation—actually Brady was on his honeymoon which I guess was still a vacation. Not that I'd know anything about honeymoons or vacations since I'd never taken either.

No, I should've canceled when I woke up after four hours of sleep and knew today was going to be another shit day. And it was going to be a shit day because I'd had only four hours of sleep after working all night. Work that included being shot at. That wasn't the shit part—that was par for the job.

The paperwork that went along with discharging my taser and getting my ass chewed out was the shit part. The ass-chewing was the result of me pulling a hotshot move that not only put me in danger but my team as well. I should've waited, but the skinny, nineteen-year-old kid who'd barricaded himself in his parents' house after he'd robbed a grocery store had run out the front door guns-a-blazin'. He'd practically ran into me and I made my move without thinking. Lucky for him, his parents weren't home and he was in the house alone so there were no hostages. Unlucky for me, my captain was unhappy. As in displeased I'd bum-rushed the kid, and took him to the floor while he was still armed. As they say, all's well that ends well but it could've ended a different way—with me being shot or someone on my team taking a round because my head was jacked-up. That last part was according to my captain and he was giving me a short leash to untwist myself before he took action.

I thought some time at the range would help clear my head. And normally it would've helped but today I had two things working against me. I was a little banged up from last night's activities. Just because the kid was skinny didn't mean he didn't fight before I got him to his stomach and J.D. "Gordy" Gordon got to my side to help subdue the suspect. Again, par for the job, so I couldn't blame my crappy shooting solely on my bruises.

Luke was the more likely cause of my poor concentration. Technically, my concentration wasn't lacking. I was hyperaware Luke was close. I was acutely cognizant of Luke's presence and had been for the last hour. But it was just in the last thirty minutes since we'd left the pistol range that my focus wavered. It was a strong possibility this shift happened when he told me to "assume the position and get yourself right." He gave the order in a light-hearted, teasing manner which seemed to be Luke's way. It also wasn't an abnormal order, as Brady had also issued the same with a slight variation—minus the teasing tone—when it was time for me to get on my belly in the dirt and square up with my rifle.

I couldn't deny it; Luke's way of delivering the command made me feel all sorts of tingles in places that shouldn't be tingling. Not only because I was supposed to be practicing my long-distance shooting skills but because the tingle had long since stopped tingling.

That was by design. I worked in a male-dominated field with uber-alpha men and I had to be on top of my game at all times. Deviation from that could be fatal. I worked my ass off to be taken seriously by my fellow officers. I'd worked double-hard to make it to SWAT. Nothing was going to derail my dreams. And feeling the tingle would be a distraction I couldn't afford. So I no longer felt it. I was solo-sexual. Meaning I only had sex with myself. The unfortunate part was I sucked at it. So I'd given up that, too. So really, I was a practicing nun. That was if nuns worked in law enforcement and shot people, which I didn't think they did.

"Shiloh?" Luke called.

"Huh?"

"Where's your head?"

Without thinking I answered, "I was wondering if nuns masturbated and carried weapons."

"Come again?"

Shit.

Side note: growing up with three older brothers, no mother, a shitty father, and working in—as mentioned—a male-dominated field, I had a bad habit of blurting out stupid stuff. Blame my faulty filter. I cursed too much. I had a dirty sense of humor and a competitive gene that could get ugly when I lost. Not because I had a chip on my shoulder and had something to prove to my male counterparts. This was hardwired in my DNA as a result of growing up with three older brothers who were high achievers. I hadn't worked out which one specifically was responsible for my overactive competitiveness.

So needless to say, my shitty performance in front of Luke didn't make me happy. And now my minimal filter was on the fritz.

"Never mind. I spaced out for a second. Sorry."

"Yeah, no." Luke chuckled and my gaze went from the rock in the dirt I'd been staring at to Luke.

Boy-oh-boy, the man was good-looking. Strong masculine features that screamed he had superior genes and would one day pass them down to his kids, which would mean the mother of his children would not see herself in her sons or daughters but instead she'd be blessed her children looked like their father.

"I pulled to the left," I told him unnecessarily, seeing as I missed the target completely and debris plumed to the left of the metal disk.

"You did," Luke confirmed. "And I'll tell you why after you explain to me why you're wondering if nuns diddle themselves."

"Diddle?"

"I already have an iffy rapport with the man upstairs. No way in hell am I saying masturbate and nun in the same sentence. That's asking to be sent to the dark place," he told me.

"And you came up with diddle?"

"Shiloh!"

"Sunny," I corrected. "No one calls me Shiloh."

"Woman, just answer the question." He smiled.

Good Lord Almighty, he was hotter than Hades when he smiled.

"I'd rather not."

"Yeah, I bet you wouldn't." He stepped away from his spotting scope still smiling which led me to take an unsteady breath as he closed the distance between us.

I lost sight of his smile seeing as I was on my stomach and he was standing at my hip. Even with my neck craned, with his height it was no use.

"You're leaning on your left hip," he continued and went into a crouch before he grabbed my hips and twisted them the way he wanted.

I bit back a groan as my bruised right side made contact with the hard ground.

"Normally I prefer dinner before the groping commences," I quipped.

"Sunny. Sunny. Sunny," Luke clucked. "That breaks my heart."

"What does? That you can't cop a feel until we've shared a meal?"

I'd lost my mind. What the hell was I doing flirting with Luke? I *was* flirting, wasn't I? It'd been so long I couldn't remember if I was doing it right.

"No, babe, breaks my heart knowing you've never properly been groped."

That didn't cause a tingle—it sent a thrill straight between my legs, which was way more dangerous than a tingle.

"I've been properly groped," I said haughtily.

"Right."

"I have," I continued to defend myself.

I belatedly realized he was teasing and I was protesting way too much. Likely because I had a feeling he was right and I'd never been properly groped. If I had, I doubted I would've been able to give up sex without much thought.

"Maybe you're right," I grumbled stupidly.

"I know I am."

I felt my eye twitch and I rolled to my side in an effort to engage in a suitable staredown.

"You don't have to be smug about it," I snapped.

Luke's gaze traveled down the length of my body then came back to meet mine. Something flashed in his eyes before it cleared, but not before he shook his head in what looked to be like an attempt to knock his thoughts from his head.

"Roll back, Shiloh, and make ready."

Crisp.

Sharp.

No more taunting and teasing.

Playtime was over and Luke was making that clear. I shifted back to my stomach, bent my left arm, wrapped my left hand around the dropdown of the buttstock, and pulled my Tikka tight against my shoulder. I lowered my face to the cheek rest, and finally, I ejected the spent cartridge out of the chamber and slammed the bolt closed.

Once I had my rifle cradled I took a moment to slow my accelerated heartrate—courtesy of sexy-as-hell Luke The Spotter. With an exhale I made ready.

"Call it," I told him.

"Hold at six-hundred yards. Red target."

Looking downrange through my scope I found the target.

"Yellow dot center. Number two low right corner," I returned.

"Correct." There was a pause then, "Get your hips right."

Momentarily my mind flashed back to how his big hands had fit nicely...

Down girl. Playtime's over.

I was grateful Luke couldn't read my mind or see the wince when I gently eased my hips into the correct position.

"Ready."

"Hold one mil right for wind," Luke instructed.

I adjusted my aim, slid my finger onto the trigger, and on an exhale pressed.

The crack of the projectile leaving the barrel. Then the snap of the bullet, and finally the faint ding of bullet meeting steel.

"Center," I belatedly called the shot.

"Good hit. Do it again."

That was how the next twenty minutes went. All business. Luke calling targets, me shooting. Just as I was feeling good and relaxed my pager beeped and that was all it took for tension to suffuse my body.

I cleared the chamber, dropped the magazine, and double-checked my rifle was safe before I rolled to my side then sat up.

"Sorry, I gotta run. Call out."

Luke did another body sweep but this time there was no heat behind his gaze. And when his eyes settled on mine I knew he didn't miss the exhaustion.

"Do you need help?"

Yeah, I needed mental help but I didn't think that was what Luke was offering.

"Help?"

"With your kit? Do you need me to lock your weapon in the TC safe?"

I was on my knees collapsing the bipod when I answered, "No, but thanks."

Luke jerked his chin and started packing up his spotting gear.

We were hoofing it back to the office when Luke broke the silence.

"How often does SWAT get called out?"

"Well, the weather's warm and there's a full moon. It feels like we've been doing double call-outs all week. Last week was slow—three warrants and four barricades. Hopefully next week we can go back to that."

We made it to the back door. Luke held it open and smiled. "After you."

"Back to checkin' out my ass?"

"Yep."

"See you around, Luke. Thanks for today."

"Yeah, Shiloh, see you around."

Now that light-hearted, teasing Luke was back, I wished I had time to stick around and flirt. But alas, I did not.

Sweat trickled down under my helmet, rolled down my temple, down the side of my face, dripped off my chin. Some might think the physical training on the road to becoming a Special Weapons and Tactical Operator was hard. And it was—totally. But you want to know what the hardest freaking part was? Not wiping the sweat off your face. No joke. When you're in full kit with the hot sun beating down, humidity so thick you actually debate the necessity of your body armor and contemplate tearing off your vest, and the annoying dripping starts, it takes some serious self-control not to wipe the bead of sweat off the tip of your nose.

"Sir. Think about your family. We have you surrounded!" Chip, our loud hailer, yelled. "Come out the front door with your hands up."

Chip had been at this for an hour. The dude was not going to come out with his hands up. If he were, he would've done it already.

"I have movement," Mereno radioed. "Window A three."

My gaze snapped to the third window from the left side of the house and I saw the blinds pulled apart and someone peering out. I brought my M4 up and went to glass.

I see you, asshole.

With the blaring sun at my back through the magnification of my scope, I could see a pair of brown eyes peeking out the blinds shifting right to left. Probably weighing his odds of escape.

There were none. The dude was surrounded. Entry Team Charlie was at the rear of the house. Alpha Team had the front covered. He wasn't getting out of the house without being apprehended.

"Pump gas," Lieutenant Ocala radioed from the command patrol vehicle parked three houses down.

"About fucking time," Gordy muttered from beside me.

It would seem I wasn't the only one impatient.

"Six-thirty on the move," Mereno returned.

Two seconds later the thunk of the less-than-lethal munitions weapon deploying the CS ferret went off and glass shattered.

"Damn good shot," Gordy continued his commentary.

He wasn't lying. Mereno's aim was true.

"The only move you can make is to come out with your

hands up," Chip said into the bullhorn. "The gas is only going to get worse."

White powder from the gas canister barely wafted out the broken window before Ocala ordered, "Entry teams go."

Go time.

Gordy shuffled from our position and like the well-trained machine we were Gordy and I met Riddle and Watson near the front door. Riddle swung the battering ram and the front door splintered. Riddle tossed the ram to the side like it weighed nothing when in actuality the bitch weighed a ton. Behind a riot shield, Watson took point and made entry. Riddle followed, I was in next, and Gordy had my six.

I could hear Charlie Team coming, shattering a window, when the suspect ran straight at me and dipped his shoulder.

No weapon.

Thank God.

Thank you, God.

I side-stepped and swung the butt of my M4, catching the guy in his jaw.

Then the dude was no longer standing. Mereno had him belly to the ground with his arms twisted behind his back.

"And that's how it's done," Riddle whooped. "Suspect in custody."

The room filled with men and now the slow, meticulous processes of clearing the structure began.

Six hours later I was finally on my way home.

3

"I heard you took Sunny out the other day," Jason Walker said and stopped next to the weight bench I was using.

"What?"

"Sunny Kent. You took her out to the range."

Shiloh.

Yes, I indeed had taken the beautiful police officer to the range. And in an act of award-winning self-control, I'd left it at that. Shiloh Kent was the total package—the type of woman who crawled under a man's skin and felt so good there he worked his ass off to make sure he never lost the feel of her there.

I wasn't sure what I was attracted to more, her glossy blonde hair, light baby-blues, pretty face, legs that, even encased in denim, couldn't hide their length and shape, or the fact that on her feet were a pair of combat boots and her sense of humor was wicked sharp. It would be a crying shame for a woman who looked like Shiloh to wind up dull and boring, but two minutes in, the pretty cop's presence told me she was anything but.

And since she wasn't dull or boring and had a face that

fueled fantasies—and I'd know because I'd dreamed about her last night—it had taken an ungodly amount of effort to let her walk away.

"I did," I confirmed.

"You know who she is, right?"

I knew I wanted her in my bed, but beyond knowing she was a police officer on a SWAT team I knew nothing else.

"No. Who is she?"

"Her dad's Lester Kent. He's doing life for killing a cop."

"No shit?"

I ducked my head under the bench press bar and sat up, not believing the carefree, teasing woman I met a few days ago had a father serving life. Not that I knew how a woman whose father killed a cop would act, but Shiloh's sunny disposition wouldn't have been my guess.

My friends call me Sunny.

The nickname fit. She was like a ray of sunshine on a cool day.

Okay. Full stop. Now I was poeticizing about the woman and that shit needed to stop. One, because I was a man whose testicles were in good working order therefore I didn't spout off poetic anything, *ever.* Two, I wasn't on the market for a morning-after-type girl. And Shiloh was the very definition of a woman you woke up next to. Not only would a man be inclined to cook her breakfast, he'd do what he could to keep doing it. The addiction would happen so fast you'd never see it coming. It was best to steer clear from the start, which was what I was planning on doing.

"The whole situation is jacked. Sunny's got three older brothers. All cops. The eldest, Echo, is with the drug task force. He worked some cases with me when I was with the DEA."

"Echo?"

"Yeah. And advice—you meet the guy, do not give him stick about his name. He's a six-foot-five wall of muscle and is sensitive about his name."

Seeing as I had no plans to meet the guy I wouldn't have to worry about busting his chops about his name.

Jason's phone chimed with a text that made him wince.

"Everything okay?"

"Yeah, I forgot I had a meeting with Carter, Nick, and Quinn. You know, when we took over Triple Canopy I didn't think anything of it. My dad and The Uncles made it look easy. Now, I'm rethinking my commitment."

"Seriously?"

Jason Walker had left his job at the DEA to take over for his father, Jasper, and uncles. Nick Clark had also made the move from the FBI to Triple Canopy. His father, Nolan Clark was one of The Uncles Jason was referring to. Quinn Walker was Jason's sister. And Carter Lenox the son of Jason's other uncle, also named Carter, though thankfully everyone called the older Carter by his last name, Lenox. Being as TC kept employment mostly in the family there were a lot of Walkers, Lenoxes, and Clarks around. Brady Walker who was not a Walker by blood but by marriage had married Hadley Walker. When they tied the knot Brady had taken her last name, wanting his family's legacy to die. Something I didn't blame the guy for wanting. Brady's dad was a dick. The fourth uncle, Levi McCoy, only had a daughter but her man Drake worked at TC, and hopefully, when Liberty's Army contract was up she'd be joining our team, as well. Though by the time that happened Liberty would be a Hayes, seeing as her and Drake's wedding was imminent.

"No. I'm just bitching because I hate sitting through meetings when I'd rather be doing something else. Anything else."

Jason's eyes lit with a look that told me I wouldn't like whatever idea he'd hatched in his head, so before he could verbalize what his stare communicated I cut him off.

"The answer is no," I told him. "I took my med discharge because after the explosion I was facing a desk job in the Navy and not looking forward to three years staring at intel reports and sitting in on briefings."

"Worth a shot," Jason muttered. "And since you hate intel reports, I hate to be the bearer of bad news but Dylan was putting a file on your desk when I passed by your office."

"The case Ethan punted us," I offered. "I asked Dylan to run some of the names again."

Ethan was another Lenox. He was a detective and one of the last holdouts. He and Jackson Clark weren't ready to come aboard and work the family business. Though if I had to guess, Ethan would make the move before Jackson, who was living his childhood dream of being a fire fighter.

"The cold case?"

"Yeah. After reading the reports, I agree with Ethan. The original investigation was botched. The detectives were so focused on the family they didn't look at much else."

"The girl was taken from her bed—no signs of forced entry—and found buried in the backyard of a vacant rental property the parents owned," he told me something I knew.

And Jason knowing it meant he'd read through the files as well.

"Didn't say the family wasn't a good place to start, just that the investigation shouldn't have ended there."

Jason's phone chirped again and he sighed.

"I gotta go. But I wanna see what Dylan came up with."

"We'll talk later."

As soon as Jason left the gym, my thoughts wandered

back to Shiloh. Not the news her dad's a cop killer. Not that she has a six-foot-five brother named Echo and two other brothers besides. I didn't wonder about the four Kent siblings and how they all are in law enforcement.

Nope. My thoughts went to where they'd gone every time I'd thought about Shiloh in the last few days—to how my palms had itched to linger a little longer when I was straightening her hips. Her quick quip about buying her dinner first. How nicely her ass would fit in my hands when I cupped it as she rode me. Dirty thoughts that invaded and made my cock twitch. Fantasies that would go unfulfilled.

I shoved all thoughts of Shiloh back into the closet marked *Do Not Enter* and went back to my workout. An hour later I was in the shower when pretty blue eyes and gleaming blonde hair came to mind. The way the honey locks would look against my black sheets. How those pastel-colored eyes would darken with lust. My imagination was running wild with possibilities, my cock thick and ready. With no relief in my future, I slapped the spigot to cold and endured an icy hell until my dick was soft and my balls had crawled up to find warmth. Only then did I exit the shower, dress, and get to work.

Six hours later my desk was covered in background checks Dylan had run. I was reminded how much I hated intel reports. This was not my specialty. I was a door kicker, then I was a sniper. I had zero patience for reading reports. Send me out into the woods and I could lie motionless for hours. Silently stalk my prey for days if necessary. But sit me behind a desk for eight hours and I'd come out of my skin.

Luckily for me, it didn't happen very often. As in rarely.

But Ethan had been hung up on this case since another detective in his department had retired and the cold case hit his desk. Ethan seldomly reached out to Triple Canopy. That wasn't to say TC hadn't in the past contracted with local law enforcement from time to time but Ethan didn't like to use the family resource unless he truly needed to.

And after combing over everything he'd given us I could understand why he needed help. The case was ten years old. No suspects were identified other than the parents. It was Ethan's belief the parents were innocent. But the glaring question remained; how did the parents not hear an intruder? The mother's reason satisfied the detective. She was under the care of a sleep doctor, had been for years. Her medical records showed she'd had insomnia going back to childhood. Two years prior to her daughter's death she stopped driving after she was in a car accident that was her fault. She'd fallen asleep behind the wheel. The night the little girl was taken, the mother had taken a heavy dose of a sleeping aid that was prescribed by her doctor. But the husband? The master bedroom was twenty-three feet down the hall.

Why didn't he hear?

My wonderings were interrupted when the landline on my desk rang, the sound so foreign it startled me. I could count on one hand the number of times I'd heard it ring in the months I'd been at TC. Everyone called my cell.

"Hello?" I answered.

"Luke?"

"Yeah, who's this?"

"Sunny."

Shiloh. And she sounded out of breath.

"Everything okay?"

"Yeah. God, I must sound like a huffing bull. It's pouring

rain and I'm parked on the far end of the lot. I made a run for it but had my gear too...and...I'm rambling. To answer your question, yes, I'm fine."

Fuck, the girl was cute.

"Anyway, I was calling because the other day I left in a hurry and forgot to ask you if you wanted to meet for a drink sometime."

Grateful I was alone in my office and there was no one there to witness my body's reaction to her question. Stiff would be an understatement.

"Not dinner?" I returned.

Stiff turned into throbbing when her burst of laughter came through the phone.

"Luke, Luke, Luke, are you trying to get into my pants again?"

Damn, she was funny.

"I don't believe in trying."

"Then you won't take offense when I turn down your offer to dinner."

No, baby, I won't take offense. Dinner will be an unnecessary waste of time.

I wisely didn't share my thoughts.

"When would you like to meet for drinks?"

"Tonight?"

Was that hope I detected in her tone?

I glanced over my desk, happy to call it a day. I started to collect the papers.

"Works for me. When and where?"

"There's a bar called Balls on Havenhurst. An hour give you enough time?"

My lips twitched and I again bit back a wisecrack. Though I didn't stop myself from thinking I liked she was eager to see me and didn't bullshit and play games.

"I know the bar. I'll see you in an hour," I told her.

"Later."

Shiloh disconnected and I wasted no time cleaning up my desk and closing down for the night. With traffic, it would take thirty minutes to get to the bar—Balls. How apt since later I'd be going home alone with the same blue balls I'd had since I'd met her.

Drinks weren't a good idea.

Dinner was out of the question.

Getting into her pants was not something I was going to do.

Yet ten minutes later I was in my truck driving to a bar to have drinks with a woman who was a temptation. A woman I wouldn't allow myself to have.

When I walked in and spotted her at the bar I took a moment to take in her beauty and I did it wondering why the hell I was torturing myself. My second thought was why *wouldn't* I allow myself to have her?

I wasn't an asshole. I was upfront and honest. I only did casual and I made that clear. What if Shiloh was up for no-strings great sex? What if she wasn't looking for serious?

The woman forefront in my mind turned her head, and when she caught sight of me she smiled. I was reminded of all the reasons why casual wasn't an option.

Shiloh Kent was the woman I could fall in love with and I absolutely didn't want that.

I weaved through the after-work crowd and as I made my way to where she was sitting, her gaze never left mine. Oh, fuck yeah, I could fall in love with those eyes on me. The idea that now that she'd spotted me all the other patrons ceased to exist. It was just me and her.

"You're early," she greeted.

"So are you," I pointed out.

"Well, I was only ten minutes away and I didn't want to sound too desperate so I said an hour."

No games.

Damn, I liked that, too.

"I'd been staring at background checks and case notes for hours and courting more hours until you called."

"So breaking that down, you were happy for an excuse to leave work."

And there was that bright, teasing smile.

"Nope. Just happy to accept an invitation to drinks with a beautiful woman."

The beaming smile turned bright and it felt like a sucker punch to the gut.

Yeah, this was a shit idea.

"Case giving you a hard time?" she asked when I sat.

My gaze went to the drink in front of her and I grinned.

"Cold case. You know Ethan Lenox?"

"Yeah, you could say I know Detective Lenox."

Jealousy slammed into me—unwelcomed jealousy.

Shiloh's hand patted my forearm and she shook her head in amusement.

"We went through the academy together. I was with the four-seven but when I made SWAT I went to the six-ten where Ethan is."

I tamped down the jealousy, deciding not to further evaluate why I'd have that particular emotion, and swung back to the topic.

"I'm looking at a cold case he gave me."

"The Harper murder," she mumbled.

I was indeed looking into the Becca Harper murder.

"How'd you know?"

"Ethan's got a soft spot. Kids. And Becca's murder going unsolved has not set well with him for a long time. He's pissed he's not getting more resources from the department. So I'm not surprised he punted it to Triple Canopy. I'm just surprised he didn't do it a long time ago. It's been on his desk over a year."

Shiloh was correct; Ethan was pissed. He thought more man-hours should be allocated to the Harper case. The issue was fresh cases took precedent over a ten-year-old case. No one cared Ethan had a soft spot for kids.

"What about you?" I gestured to the tumbler of amber liquid. "Nothing says rough day like two fingers of whiskey."

"Bourbon," she corrected.

The bartender appeared in front of me and asked for my drink order.

"Rolling Rock in a bottle and a glass of what she's having."

With a nod and a smirk I didn't understand, the man behind the bar turned and pulled down a bottle I couldn't see and Shiloh chuckled.

"What?"

"Nothing." She smiled.

Before I could ask what was up with the shit-eating grin a tumbler appeared in front of me. I took a sip and nearly gagged.

"Jesus fuck, woman. What the hell is this?"

"Baby...baby...baby," she trailed off and sputtered a laugh.

"I'm not sure if you're breaking out into a Justin Bieber song or TLC. Either way, it's not helping me understand why'd you'd purposely drink this shit."

She was still carrying on when the bartender came back with my beer.

"I didn't know bourbon this horrible was available for consumption," I told the guy. "If you wouldn't mind dumping those and bring back Maker's Mark, I'd appreciate it."

"Hers, too?" he asked with a smile.

"Yeah. I fear if she drinks that her gut will rot."

"You ain't lying. I've worked here for years and no one's ever ordered Baby Hudson. I reckon most folks know to steer clear."

Ah, *Baby* Hudson. That explained a lot.

The guy left with the shittiest tasting bourbon I've ever had the displeasure of sipping. I took a long, refreshing swig of my beer hoping it would wash down the oak and fire still lingering on my tongue.

"Baby Hudson. What in God's name made you order that crap?"

"The bottle." She pointed at the wall in front of us lined with bottles. "I don't drink whiskey or bourbon. It was the first one I saw so I ordered it."

"Consider this an intervention, then."

"Intervention?"

"Yeah, babe, I'm intervening to save you a hangover from hell and your tastebuds from being permanently damaged. And I'm introducing you to good bourbon."

"Well, then, it's a good thing you came. I right like my tastebuds. But now I'm staging my own intervention. Justin Bieber?"

"You casting aspirations on The Biebs?"

"Um. Yeah." She drew out the last word like I was an idiot.

"The Biebs is my boy," I lied.

Shiloh's eyes narrowed and she asked, "Are you fucking with me?"

I wish I was fucking with her a whole different way that'd leave us both way more satisfied than a few laughs at a bar ever could.

"Yeah, babe, I'm fucking with you."

"Thank God. I was going to break up with you."

I blinked, then I blinked again against the beauty that was a smiling, teasing Shiloh.

"Can't have you breaking up with me before we've even had a game of balls."

"Um..."

Without thinking my hand came off the bar and brushed a heavy fall of hair off her shoulder before I leaned over and brought my mouth to her ear.

"I like the way you think, Shiloh. But I was talking about pool. The bar is named Balls for a reason. I'd offer you up a different kind of game but I wouldn't want you to break your rules."

"Rules?"

Breathy.

Fucking hell.

"Dinner before groping. And before you ask if I'm trying to get into your pants again, I'll remind you, I don't *try* to do anything. I assess what I want, plan, and execute. With trying comes a possibility of failure. And I never fail."

"Never?" she asked and dipped her chin, exposing more of the sexy column of her neck.

"Nope."

I leaned closer.

"So say you *wanted* to get into my pants, you're saying you'd get in there?"

I was being outplayed. Shiloh knew exactly what she was doing.

"Oh, yeah. So deep you wouldn't forget for days how in there I got."

Warning bells were already ringing but when Shiloh shivered they started blaring.

"But you don't want in my pants," she wrongly surmised.

"Truth?" I asked and she nodded. "I want in your pants. You naked in my bed is pretty much all I've thought about since I met you. And when I'm not thinking about you naked I'm thinking you just might be the funniest woman I've ever met. I think you're comfortable being you. You say what you say and do what you want and I like that, too. But that's not why I came tonight and that's not where I think we should go. So, as much as I know seeing your clothes on my bedroom floor tomorrow morning is something we'd both enjoy, it wouldn't be smart."

"And if I wanted my clothes on your bedroom floor —*smart* be damned—you'd turn me down?"

"I'll answer that after we have a few drinks and shoot a game of pool."

What the hell was wrong with me?

Just say no.

"Testing the waters?"

"Can you blame a guy for being cautious after the bourbon debacle?"

Shiloh snorted an unladylike huff and righted her head.

Why did I find that so goddamn sexy, too?

Because she was who she was and didn't give a single fuck what anyone thought.

"I really didn't ask you to join me because I wanted to seduce you."

"Didn't think you did. And just so you know, the fact you had a tumbler of bourbon in front of you when I sat down was my first indication of that."

"Maybe I was fortifying my courage to get you into bed?"

"Nope. You wouldn't need alcohol to find your courage. Tell me about your day."

"That obvious?"

"Quit stalling."

Before she could answer the bartender was back with our Maker's Mark. I reached into my back pocket and pulled out a few bills and handed them over. "Keep it."

"Thanks. Holla' you need anything."

With a lift of his chin, he was gone.

I turned to look at Shiloh, maybe make another inappropriate jab, but when I saw her staring at the drink I changed my mind and made a decision.

"Shoot it," I told her.

"Can't. I'm driving."

"I'll get you home."

She shook her head and said, "My gear's in my car. Can't—"

"I'll get you and your car home, Shiloh. Shoot it. Shoot as many as you need to. You have my word I'll get you home safe."

Those blue eyes were killing me. Contemplative and a little sad. Whatever was going on in her life was weighing heavy.

"Tonight we'll play pool, and have a few drinks. I'll listen if you wanna talk, and while we're doing that I swear you're totally safe to be you," I continued then quickly added, "your pants on my bedroom floor and everything that comes with that is off the table."

"Well, that sucks." She winked and picked up her glass.

In two swallows it was gone and she was sputtering incoherently.

When she finally regained command of the English

language—though her eyes were still wide—she licked her lips and said, "That wasn't much better."

A laugh burst from my chest. I threw my arm around her shoulder and pulled her close. This unfortunate lapse of judgment left me with an armful of sexy woman, one I'd declared off-limits, one that smelled like...

"Do you use Head and Shoulders?"

Her frame stiffened before it started to shake.

"Are you smelling me, creeper?"

"Hard not to when I've got your hair in my face."

With a mighty shove, Shiloh pushed me away and a smile raced across her lips.

"I forgot my shower bag in my locker. I had to use Riddle's soap and shampoo."

"Riddle?"

"Andy Riddle. He's on my team."

The smile died and a contemplative look came back in her eyes.

Something is definitely weighing heavy. "Come on, let's see how good you are at running a table."

"Fair warning, I'm good."

I bet she is, I thought.

I bet she's damn good at a lot of things.

4

"Babe?"

"Wha—" I barely got the mumbled word out of my dry-as-a-desert mouth before I closed it then groaned, "I'm dying."

"You're not dying."

Luke.

Awareness slowly crept in, intensifying the pounding in my head. I was in a bed. A soft, warm bed, but I didn't open my eyes for fear the swirling in my belly would turn into something unpleasant.

"Where am I?"

"You're in bed."

"And you're in my bedroom? I'm not dreaming?"

"Do you often dream of me in your room?"

Normally our flirty banter would make me smile but I was out of sorts and a little queasy.

I felt his hand on my shoulder—my t-shirt-covered shoulder—and I stayed still as it traveled up to my neck and around until he gathered my hair and held it loosely.

"You're home safe and sound just like I promised. I have

to get to work but I wanted to see if you needed anything before I took off."

"Work? It's morning?"

"Just after eight."

"You spent the night."

Duh. It was eight in the morning. Of course Luke spent the night. I was suddenly grateful I had a splitting headache and a hangover from hell. It gave me an excuse not to open my eyes. And when Luke went on, I was doubly happy I wasn't looking at him.

"How much do you remember about last night?"

I tried to think back but the bits and pieces and flashes of me drinking and us playing pool were mostly a blur and the harder I thought the queasier my stomach got.

"Not much after our second game. But enough to remember I kicked your ass the first round and barely lost the second."

Then I'd switched to tequila—and tequila and I were friends. I got chatty when I drank tequila. I was a happy drunk—that was, when I let myself get drunk which was normally saved for special occasions.

"Last night you said you didn't work today."

"Is it still Wednesday?"

"Yeah, babe, it's still Wednesday."

"Then no, I don't work today."

A full day off, which was awesome because I didn't think it was possible to get out of bed.

"Good. There's water, OJ, toast, and Tylenol on your nightstand. When you can open your eyes, drink the water, eat the toast, and wash the Tylenol down with the OJ. I'll be back around later and I'll bring dinner."

"Don't say dinner, or toast, or water. As a matter of fact, no more talking at all. My head is going to explode."

"Okay, babe. No more talking. See you later." And with that, the bed shifted and a moment later Luke's lips brushed my forehead. "Sleep."

Apparently, Luke had superpowers because my body obeyed and I didn't hear him leave.

Hours later I woke up no less hungover but I no longer felt like I was going to vomit.

But the room was still spinning.

Or maybe it was my life that was spinning out of control and now I was feeling the physical manifestation of months' worth of denial.

Maybe my life was in the toilet and instead of figuring out what was going on, I was behaving like a coward with my hand on the flusher ready and willing to push it and watch all my hard work spiral down the porcelain.

Weak.

One explanation that was unacceptable, yet it was true.

I tossed the covers off, caught sight of my jeans, and last night rushed back in an unfortunate stream of humiliation.

I was fully dressed, just like Luke had promised I'd be.

I had no doubt my car was in my garage.

And I had a sickening suspicion I knew why Luke had stayed the night. I hadn't been drunk. Drunk didn't cover what I'd been. More like blotto. Totally smashed.

Shit.

He probably thought I was going to puke in my sleep and die.

Shame washed over me.

I never lost control to that extent. Never, ever.

And since I never had, I was seriously worried I'd talked too much. Told Luke things I would never tell him sober.

That thought got me moving. In record time I was in the shower on a fool's errand. I washed and scrubbed but the shame clung to my skin. Not the morning-after-walk-of-shame kind. No, this was worse. I'd gladly take tromping out of a man's house in last night's clothes holding my high heels—not that I wore high heels but for the purpose of my misery I did—into an awaiting Uber. I'd be more than happy to see the driver's knowing smirk aimed my way as he drove me home with the knowledge I got myself a little something-something. I reckoned that would be uncomfortable but I could only guess because I'd never experienced it.

My shame came in the form of words—too many of them spoken.

Unguarded.

My shower hadn't helped.

Water, toast, OJ, and Tylenol didn't help.

Neither did doing laundry, washing dishes, vacuuming, dusting, nor did mopping. All my day-off chores succeeded in doing was cause my head to throb worse. By the time five-thirty rolled around I was sitting on my couch trying to come up with an excuse to call Luke and tell him not to come by. Of course, the truth would be too embarrassing.

I'd almost come up with a plausible lie when there was a knock at my front door. Then it swung open and my heart stopped.

River.

Not good.

Worse than Luke showing up thirty minutes early.

My brother did what he always did when he saw me. The big brother cursory top to toe check. He did this with narrowed eyes and I braced.

"You look like shit."

Awesome.

Insulted straight out of the gate.

"Thanks. Aren't you a peach?"

"Call out?"

Naturally, my brother would assume the obvious—work.

"Because I'm hungover."

"Hungover?" River jerked his chin and continued. "Surprised Gordy let you tie one on. He usually cuts you off."

"Yes, River, Gordy usually does. And why is that?"

My brother flashed me a megawatt smile—the one I knew got him laid and regularly. A fact no little sister ever wanted to know but unfortunately, this little sister knew everything about her older brothers.

"So you're not denying you told Gordy to babysit me?"

"I've never denied it. And not just Gordy—they all know to keep an eye on you."

This was the annoying part about having three overly dominant brothers. They butted into my business in a way that didn't feel loving and protective. It felt infuriating and bossy.

"How would you like it if I pulled Conley aside and had a word with him?"

River shrugged and said, "It depends on what you told him."

"That's bullshit and you know it. You'd be pissed if I went to *your* partner for any reason. But especially if I did it to tell him if he didn't watch your back I would kick his ass."

"That's different."

So freaking annoying.

"It's not different. And if you pull the 'you're a woman and I'm a man' card I'm gonna throw something at you."

"First, what the hell has crawled up your ass? I came

over here to see if you wanted to grab something to eat. I find you looking like shit and now you're pissed about something that's not gonna change. You're my sister, yes. But you're also my family. You, Echo, Phoenix are all I have. And I didn't threaten to kick Gordy's ass if he didn't look out for you. I told him I'd cut his balls off."

My heart had softened at the mention of family. Echo, River, Phoenix, and me. Just the four of us. We were the only family any of us had. No parents, no aunts and uncles, no grandparents. Echo being the eldest was more of a father to me than my father ever had been. And River being the second born stepped up when he could. Phoenix the same when he was old enough. My three big brothers had always taken care of me.

But he lost what little ground he'd gained when he admitted to threatening Gordy.

"Did you ever think that maybe, just maybe, I'd like to earn the respect and loyalty of my team without my big brother intervening?"

"Nope."

"Jesus, you're annoying as hell."

"So you've told me a million times."

We went into a brother-sister staredown. Me sitting on the couch, River standing with his tattooed arms crossed over his broad chest. I didn't need to look at his forearm to know my name was scrolled in bold ink from wrist to elbow. All my brothers had the same tattoo. It was weirdly sweet. They said it was their reminder of what was important. That it was because of me and for me the three of them had pulled together. That I was the glue that kept us close. The baby sister they'd sworn to protect.

But sometimes being the glue sucked.

That wasn't right. Being the glue was a lead chain around my neck.

I lost the staredown when I heard the knocking and I closed my eyes.

Seriously bad timing.

"Expecting someone?" River asked.

"Yes."

My brother being the second-born and my self-appointed keeper stalked to the door.

There was a beat of silence before my brother barked, "Who are you?"

"Don't be a dick, River!" I shouted from the couch. "Let Luke in."

"Luke?" River asked.

"Yes, his name is Luke and I swear on Gunner's grave you threaten Luke's balls or any other part of him I'm gonna cut you in your sleep."

Gunner was River's beloved Chow. He'd crossed the rainbow bridge three years ago and River was still devastated. It was a bitch thing to say and I almost felt bad but I also didn't because River was a menace and had chased away every guy that had ever looked at me.

"You suck," River said, coming back into the living room. "Not cool bringing up Gunner."

"The same way it's not cool the way you just answered my door?"

"You're my sister."

"I am. But that doesn't mean you get to be rude to my guests."

"It does when the guest is *male* and looks like him."

River pointed and my gaze followed the line of his arm until Luke came into focus and my heart flip-flopped in my chest.

So I could see how Luke would give my very protective brother a stroke. Tall, sexy, muscular—that was Luke. But more, there was an air of danger that surrounded him. River being cut from the same cloth as Luke wouldn't miss that.

"Bet you're happy you came back," I chirped. "Rethinking this morning's offer yet?"

Luke shook his head and smiled like he found me amusing.

"This morning?" River growled. "He the reason you're hungover?"

"Yep. I asked Luke to meet me at Balls for a drink. I got ridiculously drunk and this morning before he left for work he offered to take me to dinner."

"Shiloh." Luke's warning rumbled. "Cool it."

I felt my eyes get squinty and a twinge of my earlier headache started to throb.

"Cool it? He's being an ass."

"No, babe, he's being your brother and you're eggin' him on because you did get ridiculously drunk last night and you're likely still hungover." Luke stopped speaking to me and turned to my brother and offered his hand. "Luke Marcou."

"River Kent."

I watched as the two men shook hands. Luke was a tad taller than River but River was a tad broader. I didn't know Luke well but I knew River had an explosive temper and Luke had been right; I was poking the beast because I was tired and stressed and more than a little worried about what I'd said to Luke last night.

"I needed a night to let go," I admitted. "Luke was there to watch over me and bring me home. And he did spend the night, but not in my bed." I didn't know if that was the truth but I was going with it. "He was just looking out for me. So retract your claws, brother."

"You needed a night to let go?" River gently asked.

This was the side of my brother that made all the annoying shit he did worth it. The times when he didn't hide how deeply he loved me.

"Seven days on shift. Double, sometimes triple call-outs. Yeah, River, I needed a night to let go and not think about kicking doors in, serving warrants, and saving hostages."

Actually, it was only the hostages I needed to forget. One in particular who plagued my nights, turning my dreams into nightmares. The plus side of drinking myself stupid was I hadn't woken up in the middle of the night sweaty and screaming.

"The guys go with you?"

"No, I needed a break from them, too. It's all good. I'm good. Please don't make this a thing and just let it drop."

"Sunny—"

"I'm asking you to give me this, brother."

River unhappily jerked his chin in my direction and turned to Luke.

"Walk me out?"

"Absolutely."

"You know your way out," I snapped.

"*Babe.*"

That was all Luke said as he walked to the front door. Apparently, he thought I was fluent in badass macho speak. Luckily for him, I was. Unluckily for him, I didn't like what he said.

"Call you later, kid."

Gah. I hated when he called me kid. "Are you on call tonight?"

"Yep."

Damn. Then I couldn't tell him to screw off.

Instead, I said, "Love you. Be safe."

"Always."

River disappeared and I waited for Luke's return. This took a long time which meant when Luke's presence hit the room I wasn't dazzled by his good looks. I wasn't taken aback by the tingle that started in my toes and intensified as it rushed between my legs. What I was however was stupefied by the concern I saw.

"Are you feeling any better?" he asked and glanced around my living room.

"A little."

"I'd say a lot better considering you spent your day cleaning."

"Is that your way of nicely pointing out that I'm a slob, which incidentally isn't nice to point out at all."

"Shiloh, I had to search for your couch last night so I could find someplace to sleep."

Well, there you had it. Luke didn't sleep in my bed last night.

"It wasn't that bad."

Luke gave me a look that denoted my lie.

"I'm not a slob. Not normally," I defended myself with another semi-lie.

I was kind of a slob. But I eventually cleaned up my mess.

"Are you up for Thai?" he queried and I grimaced. "Right. Pizza?"

"That I can do," I told him.

Without asking what I wanted, Luke pulled out his phone and called in the order. Though he did get points for watching me as he ordered and before he hung up he asked if there was anything I wanted to add. So, he didn't ask, but kind of did. He'd ordered enough to feed five people and everything he'd gotten I liked. So I decided not to get my panties in a bunch over that. Besides, I had bigger issues to worry about.

"What'd my brother say to you when you walked him out?"

"He told me if I hurt you, he'd pull my heart out through my ass."

My mouth dropped open in shock. Not that River would threaten something so stupid but that Luke would openly share.

"I hope you told him to mind his own business."

"I told him I appreciated where he was coming from. Reassured him that you're safe with me. And explained I'm not a man who takes kindly to being threatened and he'd used his one free pass. I also told him he should pass that along to your other brothers."

I opened and closed my mouth several times, unsure what to say.

"Do me a favor, Shiloh. Don't use me to piss off your brothers, yeah?"

Damn. My heart sank and guilt started to build.

"Yeah," I quickly agreed. "That was super bitchy. I'm sorry."

"It wasn't bitchy and I get why you were doing it. But it puts me in a fucked-up situation that could lead to not good places with your brothers. I've heard about Echo. I've seen River. And I know all three are cops. Pitting me against them does no one any good. Most especially you."

"Again, I'm sorry."

"No need to apologize. I said what I had to say. You listened. Now it's done and we're moving on."

"That easy?"

"Why wouldn't it be?"

That was a very good question. But in my experience with my brothers, they didn't let shit go, they fought for hours about stupid stuff. Though not one of them ever admitted they were wrong. And they were brothers, not nonblood-related friends.

"I don't know," I admitted. "I guess it should be that easy. So thanks."

Luke's lips twitched. He moved across the room and sat on the couch. Not close but not in Siberia either.

"Does you not getting off the couch mean you're still not feeling well?"

"No. It means I'm tired. As you noted I had a lot to clean up today."

"Right."

Boy-oh-boy, Luke was hot when he smiled.

Tempting really.

However, as much as I flirted with him I really had sworn off relationships. Which led me down a new path of contemplation. One that made me feel funny.

"I'm not a tease," I blurted.

"Come again?"

"Last night," I started and winced. "I came on strong. I was flirting and teasing...shit...I mean...I don't know what I'm trying to say."

Heat crept up my neck and warmed my cheeks.

"Seems to me like you do."

"What does that mean?"

"You know what you want to say but for some reason, you're embarrassed to say it." He paused and held my eyes when he said, "You've had time so I'll ask again—how much of last night do you remember?"

"Not much," I admitted.

"Right. So to fill in some blanks I knew you weren't

coming on to me before you were drunk. You were being your normal playful self. It's cute; you work it, but I also know it was banter. After you were drunk you told me you hadn't had sex with a man in four years and you gave up masturbation three years ago when you couldn't get yourself off. Hence the nun comment I didn't get the other day. Which brings us to the part where you were thinking about masturbating instead of shooting which also explains why you were off your game."

"I did not," I breathed and prayed.

Prayed he was lying and making up tales.

"You didn't? Then how do I know you haven't had a man in four years? And it's been that long since you've had an orgasm."

"Why did I tell you that?"

"Fuck if I know." Luke shrugged.

"Just to say, I'm really embarrassed right now. Like more embarrassed than I've ever been in my whole life and that includes when I threw up on my high school boyfriend after he took me on a roller coaster that looped upside down three times. And if it wouldn't embarrass me more I'd get up and go hide under my comforter and pretend you weren't sitting on my couch."

It was safe to say that after tonight I would never be seeing Luke again. *No way, no how.* It was a miracle I hadn't yet burst into flames from the heat emanating from my face. I could never face him again.

He knew way too much.

"What else did I tell you?"

"Why are you embarrassed?" he asked instead of answering.

"Are you joking?"

"No. Last night, I told you I hadn't been with a woman

since I left the Navy." Luke shrugged like his admission was no big thing.

Like it wasn't personal.

Like we were lifelong friends who shared intimate details about our lives all the time.

"I appreciate you sharing that with me. And I suppose you knowing I haven't had sex in a while isn't the end of the world. It's the other part I wish I would've kept to myself."

"The masturbation."

"Was it necessary to clarify?"

"Absolutely."

"How long have you been out of the Navy?"

"A while," he evaded.

"That's not an answer."

"Then how's this? Less than four years but more than six months. And to clarify your unanswered question, I have no issue with masturbation. Though my hand is nowhere near satisfying, it works."

I forgot about my burning cheeks when a new very unwelcomed shiver happened.

"I wasn't going to ask."

Luke smirked disbelievingly.

"Seriously, I have no desire to know what you and your right hand get up to in the privacy of your bedroom."

"I'm left-handed," he returned.

"Huh?"

"I'm left-handed," he repeated. "What me and my *left* hand get up to. And I don't jerk off in bed. The shower always."

"This is the most bizarre conversation I've ever had," I muttered.

"Trust me, it's not. This is the second time we've been over this."

My eyes drifted closed and I prayed for the end of the world. An asteroid careening toward earth would've been much appreciated. A fireball of death and destruction to end my misery.

"I'm never drinking again," I muttered every drunk's famous last words.

"For the most part, you're a fun drunk."

"Awesome. I'm glad you think me sharing my secrets makes me fun."

"Darlin', we haven't gotten to the part where you were dancing on the pool table yet."

My eyes snapped open and horror washed over me.

"I didn't—"

"I'm joking. You didn't dance on the table. But you are a fun drunk and not because you spilled your secrets. Because you're fun sober. You're funny and open and hold nothing back. After a few drinks, you're the same you, just *more* of you. All of it good. All of it sweet and funny."

"Thanks for taking care of me."

All humor fled when Luke answered, "You're welcome, Shiloh. But I should be thanking you for trusting me. Means a lot to me you felt comfortable enough with me to give yourself something you needed."

The doorbell rang and I was saved from having to respond. Luke got up from the couch, handled the delivery, then dumped the pizza and salad on the coffee table and told me to stay put while he rooted around my kitchen. Luke came back with plates and utensils and we dug in.

It would be awhile—after I'd had three slices and finished my salad, after Luke had turned on the TV and perused the channels until he settled on a crime drama and the show had come to an end—before I drew up enough courage to ask the question that had plagued my mind since I'd woken up.

"Why'd you spend the night?"

I crossed my fingers in hopes his answer would be because I'd puked several times between the bar and home and he was afraid I'd do it more and choke and die.

Yes, that was how desperate I was—I would rather have puked in front of hot guy Luke than to have begged him to stay with me because I was now afraid to close my eyes and sleep.

When his gaze didn't leave the TV panic rose. I'd done or said something that caused him discomfort.

Shit. Goddamn.

"Luke?" I whispered.

His head slowly turned and when his eyes met mine there was pain staring back at me. So much pain it hurt just to see it.

A beat later he shattered my carefully contained world.

5

I'd had all day to contemplate this very conversation.

I'd spent a good amount of time rationalizing the difference between a lie and omitting information that had the potential to hurt someone. Twenty-four hours ago all I knew about Shiloh was she was beautiful, funny, and a danger to my wellbeing. But last night in her drunken state I got to know her well. She'd told me pretty much everything about her life with unfiltered detail.

I knew about her father. Her brothers. How guilty she felt that Echo had to step up and raise them even before her dad went down. How River and Phoenix had done the same. I knew her mother was a hippy and gave the Kent children what Shiloh called Hippy Names. Echo hated his name. River, too. Phoenix was glad his name wasn't Echo but didn't love the name Phoenix. But Shiloh secretly liked her name but she'd never told her brothers that.

She'd been resolute in her love for her brothers. They were all she had and she loved them more than anything but she felt the weight of their love. She lived under a cloud of worry she'd in some way disappoint them.

Shiloh had been completely open about her lack of a sex life and explained in great detail the reasons why she didn't want a man or a relationship. She was afraid of failure. Not a failed relationship but failing in a career she'd worked hard to have. I understood her worries and misgivings about distractions. When I was in the Navy, I had those same fears.

None of that was the issue. She'd been hilarious when she'd told me she'd given up "self-love" as she called it. Her forehead had been adorably crunched when she said she'd given it up because she was so bad at it she was more frustrated after she tried than she was to begin with.

Throughout the commentary of her misadventures in masturbation, I managed to keep my cock in control—more or less. That didn't mean as she told her stories I wasn't sporting an erection, but I'd done what I'd promised and kept it far, far away from her.

It wasn't until I was driving her home that the night took a sharp turn from fun to bad.

Five minutes after I put her in her car and she gave me her address she passed out. Ten minutes after that she jolted in her seat and scared the shit out of me when she started screaming. It got to the point where I had to pull over and get her out of the car to calm her. I got her settled back in the car and home. I carried her in and got her into bed without her waking up. While I was deciding what to do, she woke up again, this time crying *and* talking.

Nothing she said made sense. Someone had died and she felt it was her fault. That was all I knew. After the second nightmare, I couldn't leave her drunk and alone in case it happened again. I hadn't slept on her couch. I sat next to her in bed and watched over her.

I knew Shiloh Kent well enough to know she would not be happy I'd witnessed her nightmares.

And there was my dilemma.

Lie and tell her I stayed because I didn't want to leave her alone while she was drunk or tell her the truth?

Fuck.

I hated liars.

I made it a point to tell the truth.

I couldn't withhold what I knew even if in my gut I knew it was going to upset her and she'd likely tell me to leave.

"Last night you asked about the scars on my face. I know you don't remember asking nor do you remember my answer."

"Why aren't you—"

"I was in Lebanon on a mission. We were tracking a bomb maker. He had an S vest strapped on and detonated it. The senior officer had given me a move-out order and I didn't listen. I was caught in the explosion. That's what fucked up my vision. That's why I med boarded out of the Navy. Trey got it worse. I know you've seen him—he had a face full of scars. He blamed himself for not moving and taking me with him. And I blamed myself for the same. Trey almost lost his leg and according to Uncle Sam, I lost my ability to be behind a spotting scope. We were flown to Germany and for weeks I had nightmares—"

"Luke—"

I spoke over the panic in her voice. "At one point they were so bad my hands were strapped to the bed so I couldn't tear the bandages from my eye."

"Luke—"

Fucking hell, more panic.

"By the time I left Germany and got home they'd calmed but I still had them. Last night I didn't tell you why I hadn't had a woman in my bed since I left the Navy. Part of the reason is that I didn't want anyone to see me vulnerable.

The other part is because I was so fucking pissed I hated pretty much everything. Until I saw Trey drowning under an ocean of guilt that was not his to carry did I finally pull my head out of my ass and straighten myself out. I still have nightmares. Not frequently, but every once in a while I wake up in a cold sweat and it takes hours to shake the memory. It's so real I can taste the grit in my mouth. I can smell the rubber burning. I can hear Trey groaning. I remember every single second. Every detail, and I can play them back in slow motion and in hindsight see the exact moment I fucked up."

"You know," she whispered.

"I know, babe."

"I had one and you saw."

It would do no good telling her I'd seen two and the severity of the first.

"I did."

Shiloh turned her head away from me, brought her knees to her chest, and wrapped her arms around her shins. I didn't like what the protective ball conveyed. I didn't like she felt the need to hide from me. But I seriously fucking hated the look in her eyes before she'd diverted her gaze.

"Shiloh—"

"I think you should leave."

There it was. The brush-off I knew was coming. And even knowing she was going to do it I wasn't prepared for the piercing pain in my chest. This was the shit I wanted to avoid. This was why I'd kept to myself. There were many things I excelled at; feelings and drama were not on that list.

"Why?"

"Because I asked you to."

"I heard you, babe, but I wanna know why," I pushed.

Shiloh pivoted her head to look at me but didn't lift her chin off her knees, didn't come out of her protective ball, but at least her eyes no longer looked devastated. Those blue eyes were flashing anger.

"I'd like you to leave."

"Didn't take you as the type," I said as I stood, unsure why I felt I needed to make a point.

But I couldn't bring myself to leave quietly.

"Takes guts to face your shit head-on. To let people in who can help you sort your head. You think you're strong, sitting there suffering in silence, not opening up, not being truthful. That by doing it you're proving you're strong. Proving you're tough and got your shit wired tight. But you're wrong, Shiloh. It's weak. It's you being too afraid to open up—to share the pain.

"Thought you were a different kind of woman. Thought you had guts. Thought you were who you showed me at the range and at the bar. Then when I had you in my arms, shaking so goddamn bad I had to go to my ass on the side of the road so I didn't drop you, I thought there was something there. Something that could be deep and rich and lead to a friendship—"

"Is that what you want, Luke?" she cut me off and stood. "You wanna be friends? You wanna poke around in my head and help me? Poor Sunny, right? Can't handle *her* job. Too much of a pussy, *she* has nightmares."

I studied the woman in front of me. Night and day. Sunshine and beauty. Darkness and pain. Then something nasty hit me.

"Those men give you shit?"

"What?"

"You made a point to emphasize her and she. Called yourself a pussy for having nightmares. So, I'll repeat, any of the men you work with give you shit about being a woman? Your brothers give you grief about being a cop?"

Shiloh's torso jerked then her spine snapped straight.

"No."

"None of them? Your captain? Any members of your team give you pause, make comments, treat you differently? Your brothers ever make you feel like you can't do your job because you're a woman?"

"My brothers?"

"Answer me, Shiloh. Any of those fuckers you work with ever make a goddamn nasty comment to you because you're a woman on a SWAT team?"

"No!" she shouted.

Some of the tension ebbed. I'd spent enough years in the military to witness punk-ass bitches make snide comments to females. There was good-natured ribbing we all did to our teammates then there was flat-out wrong. Bullshit remarks that in my opinion earned a man a punch to the face, and since it was my opinion, I'd delivered a fair few beatdowns in my time. There was never a time or a place for that shit but when you rely on your battle buddy to have your back that shit is wrong on a whole new level.

Shiloh's answer saved me a trip to the station. One she would likely balk at. However, I was still of the opinion that if a man had an issue with a woman's job performance simply because she was a woman, that man needed to be taught a lesson. One he would never forget.

"So it's just you who has an issue with women."

"That makes no sense seeing as I'm a woman."

"Too much of a pussy *she* has nightmares," I repeated. "Or are you calling me a pussy because straight up, Shiloh, I told you I had nightmares after the explosion? Told you there are nights I still have them. So you think I'm a pussy?"

She threw her hands in the air and let out a frustrated growl.

"No. I'm saying...I don't wanna have this conversation."

"Right. Of course you don't because you're losing."

"How can I be losing when the whole conversation revolves around how I feel?"

"You're flat-out wrong about this."

I watched as Shiloh's aggravation grew and she started pacing. Then her hands went to her hair and she tugged. After that, her aggravation expanded until the room filled with it. She bent at her waist, let her head drop forward, and let out a feral wail that sliced straight through my soul.

"You don't know," she told the floor. "You have no fucking idea. What it's like. I can't stop seeing it."

"I'm telling you, I do know."

"No, you don't!" she shrieked and straightened. "I failed. I couldn't stop it. Every day I think about what I did wrong. Every day I wonder how I could've changed it. But I can't and someone is dead because of me. Seventeen. She was a kid. Smart. Good grades. Had her whole life in front of her. A dad that adored her. Friends, teachers, coaches. Everyone loved her and she's gone because... I...failed."

Fuck.

"So you see, no one treats me differently—not on a day-to-day basis. Not when we're out. Not when lives are on the line. I'm one of them and I know that to my bones. My team respects me. My brothers support me. But with this, the differences are blaring. I can't get over it. I can't stop dreaming about her father begging me to help. Her dad begging a cracked-out robber to let his daughter go. I can't unsee the look of horror when his seventeen-year-old daughter was shot in the fucking head in front of him. They can but I can't. My brothers can. But not me. I can't fucking unsee him falling to his knees and covering his eyes. He curled up into a ball in front of me. He screamed her name. I can't stop hearing him scream her name."

Fucking, *fucking*, hell.

"Shiloh, baby, please listen to me. You gotta let all this out. You can't keep it bottled up, it's just gonna keep eating at you until nothing's left. It gets worse—so bad, it fucks with your head until it consumes you."

"Thought I just did get it out, *friend*," she sneered. "You wanted it, now you can leave."

Leaving was probably the best thing to do, yet I still couldn't get myself to go. Which pissed me off. I didn't need to be there. Hell, I shouldn't have been there in the first place. I never should've come back. I never should've spent the night. Actually, I should never have accepted her invitation to the bar. I *fucking* knew better.

But I just couldn't stop myself.

And now she was throwing attitude and I was getting pissed in a new way.

"Hear this," I started and took a step in her direction. "You got shit twisted up so tight it's a wonder you can function." Shiloh's eyes flared and her posture went stiff but I ignored it and went on. "You think you can't sleep without seeing all that because you're a *woman*? That's jacked. Totally fucked-up. That has nothing to do with gender and everything to do with *people* handling shit differently. I've known some badass women in my day. Some can wall off what they see, what they do, and go on like it never happened. I've served next to men who were bigger than I am, stronger, tougher yet I've watched them crumble to their knees after witnessing something far less traumatic than what you've seen. You have enough to work through so don't take that on, too."

"I don't want to talk about this."

"Yeah, Shiloh, you've said that. But you need to."

Fear lit her eyes and if I was a better man I would've let her be. I would've turned and walked out the door and let her withdraw back to safety. But for some God-forsaken reason, I couldn't do it. I couldn't let her hide alone in her house. I couldn't leave knowing later she'd go to bed, then wake up in the middle of the night screaming.

Until she said, "You know, I have three older brothers who treat me like I'm some sort of helpless, defenseless child. I don't need more of it from some asshole who doesn't know one fucking thing about me."

"You're right. You don't. You need to pull your head out of your ass but you won't do that because you're too fucking stubborn, not to mention too goddamned worried what other people will think. Sweet dreams, Shiloh."

And with that, I left.

6

I sucked in a painful breath. Then I attempted to inhale again but my lungs burned and my stomach hurt.

I was still standing motionless in the same place I'd been when Luke delivered his highly effective parting shot.

Effective that is, if he meant to stab me in the heart and leave me breathless.

There was something seriously wrong with me and it had nothing to do with the nightmares I was having. I lashed out. Always had, as far back as I could remember. When someone got close I pushed them away. I knew I did it; I just couldn't *not* do it. The thing was, this normally took a while. I let people in as close as I could without forming any ties and if I felt like they were getting too close, too deep, I violently lashed out to make them leave.

I wasn't crazy, I knew this about myself. I just couldn't stop it. But as I said, this took a while—months, sometimes years of being acquaintances with someone before I felt the pressure build and did something to end the connection.

Lasting friendships weren't my thing. Never had been.

My brothers were the only exceptions. And that was mainly because no matter what I said or did, they wouldn't leave.

Sweet dreams, Shiloh.

I sank to my knees and rested my forehead on the floor and wondered what the fuck was wrong with me.

Luke had done nothing wrong but I was a raving bitch.

He'd tried to help me but I said nasty shit—on purpose to make him leave.

And he left.

Everyone always left.

And why was that? Because I was a basket case, a bitch who was mean to people on purpose when they dared to get close to me. Sweet as pie to strangers. I'd give the shirt off my back to anyone who needed it as long as they didn't try to strike up a friendship.

Why did everyone always leave me?

I pretended I didn't feel the wetness leaking out of my eyes. I pretended I didn't taste the salt as the tears rolled over my lips. I pretended I didn't hate myself for the things I'd said to Luke. I wasn't ashamed, I was mortified.

But I wouldn't fix it.

I never did. I never made things right because everyone always left me. Not one fucking person who was not one of my brothers ever held their ground, no one stayed. Same refrain every time.

It was getting old.

So old, I vowed to cut the few acquaintances I had out of my life before I did something mean. I'd stop going to the bar with my team. I'd stop going to the monthly golf games. It wasn't like I played golf, I just went to go. No, I went because I liked the guys I worked with, and I liked Gordy's wife, and liked having a good time. I just didn't like people asking questions about my life and that was what friends did. They shared. And since I couldn't share I had no friends.

That was better.

Alone.

Work I loved, my house, my brothers, and nothing else.

No more. Not after what I did to Luke.

The tears came faster and I wasn't sure if I was mourning the loss of a man I'd spent a handful of hours with or that I'd be missing the next golf game.

Totally messed up.

A golf game, *not* the company of my team.

I heard my front door open and slam shut. I was on my feet ready to bolt into my bedroom to get my service weapon when Luke appeared.

"I'm not fucking leaving," he growled. "You can be as pissed as you want. But hear this, Shiloh. You can throw that attitude of yours around and be a bitch just to be a bitch but I'm not fucking leaving."

I stared at a seriously mad Luke. I did this silently. I couldn't get my body to move, not even my lips to form words. His eyes narrowed and he took three steps and stopped.

"You got nothing to say? That's good because I think you've said enough."

Now my eyes narrowed. Unfortunately, he executed a staredown better than me. Actually, his squinted eyes coupled with his deep frown were better than any look my brothers had given me. That included Echo who had essentially taken on the role as my father when I was ten, thus Echo had perfected the art of a dirty look at a young age and I'd given him an impressive number of occasions for him to use it. But, still Luke did it better.

"You came back," I whispered.

"I don't want any—"

"No one ever comes back."

"What's that mean, baby?"

Soft, so soft. His voice drifted across the distance and wrapped around me and stemmed the flow of pain. I didn't know someone's voice could be so sweet. Could be the cure for a self-inflicted wound.

"No one ever stays and they never come back."

"Shiloh—"

"You came back."

"I get this means something to you, but I'm not tracking."

Yep, you guessed it—still soft and sweet but he'd added a dash of gentle, and for some reason that was my undoing.

"From as far back as I can remember, no one stayed. Not my mom, not my dad, no one. Everyone left us when we needed them. No one wanted anything to do with a cop killer's kids. But you came back."

"Christ." That was not soft and sweet and gentle.

It was angry and biting but in a way that felt good. And for reasons I couldn't begin to understand, I couldn't hold myself apart. I couldn't retreat. I couldn't find malicious words that normally came so easy. It was like they'd vanished from my vocabulary.

That was terrifying. I needed them to keep people away. I needed a sword and a shield and mean, spiteful words to make people dislike me.

But I couldn't find them when I needed them most.

He came back.

And I didn't know what to do with that except to reject it, shove it away.

I'm not fucking leaving.

A chill rushed up my spine.

"Why'd you come back?"

"Because leaving felt wrong."

I didn't know what to say to that. I didn't know *if* there was anything to say. But I knew there was something to feel because warmth flowed over me and for the first time in my life I wasn't chilled to the bone.

Then something dawned on me—he said he wanted to be friends. And weirdly that stung and not for all the normal reasons that it hurt when someone got close. Friend-zoned by Luke was a hit to a place I thought I'd locked away. I knew better than to want a man. I'd lied to myself for years —blaming my job, telling myself I had to stay focused—and it worked most of the time. But there were some nights when I was alone in my bed when I admitted the truth and let the painful knowledge that I was destined to live my life without a man, kids, a family, roll around in the dark. I didn't allow this often. It hurt, but I did it from time to time to help me stay on track. Keep the wound fresh so I didn't forget and let someone in.

"I don't have any friends," I admitted.

"No?"

I shook my head in confirmation and verbally continued so he'd have all the information he needed to keep himself safe from me.

"I don't have any because I cut out anyone who gets close to me. I do what I did to you, only worse. I do it in a way that makes it clear I don't want anyone in my life. And since everyone leaves and no one ever comes back, I'd say I'm damn good at it. The nightmares I'm having, those are new, those just started a few months back. But me being a queen bitch, that I've been doing since I was a kid. I don't know why your leaving felt wrong to you, but I'm telling you it was right. You should turn around and leave before I infect you with my bullshit. It's mean and nasty and when it takes over, I can't control it. It's like I'm not in the room and I'm not the one doing it. Trust me, you don't want any part of my ugly."

Luke was silent for a beat, his face carefully blank. With a lift of his chin, he said, "Noted."

That was all.

He did not make his way to the door, which I thought he should do with due haste.

Maybe he was waiting for an apology, and he absolutely should've gotten it so I didn't delay in offering one.

"I'm sorry I was a bitch to you. It was completely uncalled for. You were being cool with me, trying to help me and I repaid your kindness with malicious intent and you should know I did that on purpose and I'm sorry for that, too."

Luke jerked his chin again but still hadn't made a move to leave.

Weird.

"So, um, thanks for being cool. And maybe after a spell, we can go back to being what we were. You know, um, joke-around buddies."

Joke-around buddies? Did I just say that?

God. I was so lame.

What the hell was a joke-around buddy?

Someone who teases and jokes but never gets close. I answered myself in this reasonable little voice.

And I was now certifiably crazy.

"We're gonna be more than joke-around buddies, Shiloh."

Panic rose fast and furious.

"Uh..." I stumbled, unable to find the words I needed to put an end to this madness.

"We're gonna be friends."

Friends.

Oh, no, we weren't.

"Yeah, no, I'll pass on that."

Then Luke did something strange. Something bizarre and extraordinary.

His lips curved up into a smile.

"Funny, I don't recall asking."

Panic simmered until my old friend Queen Bitch made a reappearance as anger pulsed through my veins.

"Listen, Luke, I'm not taking applications, I don't need or want a friend. As you know it's been a long time for me. You wanna break the dry spell, we'll talk. Anything beyond that is a no-go."

When I was done Luke didn't smile.

He roared with laughter.

I watched him laugh for a long time. So long, I was lost in the way his eyes lit and danced with humor. So when he sobered I wasn't ready for his retort.

"Two things. One, I'm not applying for shit. Two, I have no intention of fucking you but if I was planning on taking you to my bed, I don't fuck women I don't like and respect— two things necessary to be friends. So breaking that down, I don't fuck women I'm not friends with. But fear not, your dry spell is safe to continue through eternity."

It sucked Luke could be funny when I was in a snit.

"Then I don't get why you'd want to stick around."

"No, baby, I don't think you would."

Back to soft and sweet and gentle.

What the hell was wrong with Luke Marcou? Maybe *he* was the crazy one. But at that moment it didn't matter which one of us was nuts. A funny feeling was creeping up my chest and I needed him to leave.

"I want you to—"

"Leave," he cut me off. "Yeah, I know, you keep saying it. But I've decided I'm ignoring all the fucked-up bullshit that comes out of your mouth and instead pay attention to what you're not saying with words."

"That makes no sense."

"I've never known anyone who can be open and honest and closed off and distant at the same time. Within minutes of meeting, you showed me three different Shilohs—blunt, funny, and open. Wary, nervous, and jumpy. Then flirty, teasing, and direct. The next time I see you I get fun, flirty, teasing, funny as hell, sweet, beautiful, and open. Now I get closed down, bitchy, and scared. But before that, I get funny and open. Wanna know why that is, why you gave me the real you before you turned?"

Was that a question? Because the answer was yes, I wanted to know why I had multiple personalities. Why I did exactly what he said I'd done. Why I did it to everyone and why I couldn't stop it.

"No, Luke, I don't want your opinion. But just to say, you wouldn't have to deal with me at all if you left."

"You'd like that. Me leaving like everyone else so you wouldn't have to face what's eating you. You'd like to pencil my name under the last person who you forced out of your life. Sucks for you, Shiloh, but my name will never be on your list. I know why I got open and sweet. I know you felt safe to give me that—because you never planned on letting me in. You said you weren't a tease but that's a goddamn lie. There are many ways to tease that have not one thing to do with fucking. You dangle yourself out there, let all your beauty and light shine, all the promise you hold, then you snatch it away. Only, the light doesn't dim. It's right there just out of reach but you make it so painful no one can get to it. Another thing that sucks for you, and fair warning—you better brace. I'm coming for you, Shiloh. You think your sharp tongue and bitchy comments are a deterrent. They are not. They're merely in the way. And I've told you before; when I want something I get it."

Too much.

Every word he said pierced my skin, sliced through muscle, and nicked my bones. It hurt like a mother, hurt more than anything had ever hurt me because I wanted him to come for me. I wanted him to find a way past the razor-wire I wrapped myself in. But I needed those razors to protect myself.

"I'm going home," he continued, and relief and anxiety simultaneously assaulted me. "But I want to make myself crystal clear—I'm going, but I am not *leaving*."

He wasn't leaving.

Right. That was what they all said, then they did.

"I'll call you tomorrow."

No, he wouldn't. He didn't have my phone number.

I must've given away something because once again Luke was smiling.

"I have your number, baby. It's on your paperwork and I left my number on your counter. Use it if you need me."

I wouldn't need anything from Luke—ever.

"Good night, *friend*. I'll talk to you tomorrow."

And with that, he left.

There I stood wondering which of his last statements were more effective: "sweet dreams" when he knew I'd wake up with nightmares or "good night, friend" knowing that would freak me out and cause me not to get a minute's rest.

Unfortunately, Luke calling me *friend* didn't cause a sleepless night. I woke up in a cold sweat, screaming. After that, I didn't go back to sleep. Every word Luke said replayed in my mind until the sun peeked over the horizon.

Pulse-pounding fear took root.

But something else tickled the back of my neck. It scared me, too, but only because deep down I knew Luke wouldn't fail.

7

Five fucking days Shiloh'd been ditching me.

And in those five days, I'd spent more time thinking about her than I should've. The woman was everything I thought she was and more. Dangerous. I'd known it wouldn't take much for me to get caught up in her, yet I hadn't done a damn thing to stop it.

I was in so deep with her I needed my head examined.

Shiloh wasn't a puzzle to figure out, or if she was, it was an easy one. There was no mystery as to why she didn't let people close. But she was an emotional minefield, and navigating through the obstacles she'd laid without blowing sky-high would be difficult.

I'd also given a lot of thought as to why I couldn't walk away. Why I'd sat in my truck after she'd called me an asshole and kicked me out. Why I hadn't driven away. Why I went back in. Shiloh Kent was everything I wasn't looking for. A complication that I didn't want.

So damn stubborn.

And scared out of her damn brain.

But that wasn't why I went back. I didn't have a hero

complex. I wasn't attracted to broken women with the hopes I could help them to feed my ego.

I went back because even when she was hiding behind her foul attitude she was still Shiloh. And I'd spent a lot of damn time thinking about that, too. Did she know that, as she tried to push me away she was pulling me closer? She couldn't conceal her surprise or relief when I came back and then she let it all hang out and told me, openly without prompting, that she didn't have friends and why. She even went as far as apologizing and admitting she'd been a bitch on purpose. That was not the hallmark of a broken, bitchy woman—it was the promise of what was under all those jagged pieces and sharp edges. It was her being honest when she was scared. And that kind of honesty was why I was willing to get cut to shreds to keep her.

And I lied. Something I didn't do, especially not to women. I lied with a straight face and felt no remorse. I was walking through thorns, had every intention of being her friend, showing her what that meant, doing that while she fought until we were both bleeding. But at the end of that journey, we'd be a different kind of friends. The type that ended up in bed together and dry spells were a thing of the past. But that was going to take time.

I'd give it a month.

On that thought, I picked up my cell off my desk and pulled up the one-sided text string. And tapped out a new message: *you have five minutes to text me back or I'm calling one of your brothers to make sure you're not dead.*

One minute later my phone beeped with a one-word message: *alive.*

Stubborn.

I smiled and went back to work.

It was nearing on lunch when Ethan Lenox walked into my office. If the scowl was anything to go by he was unhappy.

"What's up?"

"Just had a conversation with Jeb Dole. You were right."

I didn't reply to his comment because there was nothing to say. I'd had my own conversation with the former DA about Harper's case before I passed the information to Ethan. I wouldn't have done that if I didn't have confirmation my intel was good.

"He said he wouldn't prosecute the case against the parents because he felt it was unwinnable without concrete evidence," Ethan continued. "Detective Winshaw had only presented him with circumstantial evidence, no motive, and a weak theory. It was also an election year and the media was swarming the case looking for a conviction. Something Dole didn't think he'd get in absence of actual, solid, indisputable proof."

Again, I had no comment because that was indeed what Jeb Dole had relayed to me.

"Though, Dole was also candid and said there was another reason, not having to do with the oath of law but morality. He went on to tell me he'd deny it but he felt something was not right. His gut was telling him Detective Winshaw was feeling pressure from the chief, likely due to the media circus and the investigation was rushed."

At that I had something to add, "I agree with Dole. I looked into some of Winshaw's other cases. They were thorough, no stone unturned. The Harper case started and stopped with the parents. So unless he was getting lazy as he was coming up on retirement, I'd bet the chief was hellbent to nail the parents and advised Winshaw to do that. But that's not to say Winshaw wasn't systematic in his interviews. I ran the prints found in Becca's room, still no hit. But I did get a hit on the DNA from the hair sample found on her bed. Something Winshaw didn't have back then was the power of the at-home DNA test kits and people's curiosity to find long-lost relatives and their ethnic background. Liam McKay is a close match. I looked into McKay and found his cousin is Jeff Shepard."

"The contractor."

Not a question—Ethan knew exactly who Jeff Shepard was.

"The contractor Winshaw interviewed and nailed him down on record swearing he'd never been in Becca's room. I went over the interrogation. Winshaw asked three different ways if Shepard had been in her bedroom. All three times Shepard was adamant he'd never stepped foot in the room."

"Could be transfer," Ethan retorted. "Shepard was in and out of the house for weeks remodeling two bathrooms. The master, which is upstairs. Becca or her parents could've picked up that hair anywhere and brought it into the room."

"Agreed. But I bet one of the prints lifted from her nightstand will be his."

"I have no cause to compel Shepard to give a fingerprint sample and a department that's seeing an uptick in cases."

Shiloh had mentioned something about that, multiple call-outs for the SWAT team a day.

"Been a busy week?"

"Insane," Ethan replied. "I don't know if Mars or Mercury or whatever the hell people talk about—retrograde or some such shit has gone haywire or if humanity has gone to hell. But I've got cases landing on my desk ranging from petty to seriously jacked-up. I will get no help on a cold case right now."

I shoved the thoughts of Shiloh out dealing with seriously jacked-up shit out of my mind and focused on Ethan.

"Lucky for you I had time to take a drive and had the opportunity to watch Shepard. The asshole's a litterbug. Didn't even have to dig through his trash to nab a soda bottle he chucked at a jobsite. On the grass, out in the open, even got pictures for you. Since we don't have a backlog I sent the bottle to our lab. It'll take a week but we'll have something soon."

"No shit? Shepard moved to Alabama."

The Harpers' contractor had moved to Montgomery after he'd finished work on their home and I'd used the five-and-a-half-hour drive and overnight stay to stop myself from going to Shiloh's house or tracking her down. It was sad my self-control was so lacking I needed miles and a time zone between us. But there it was; I was in over my head.

"As I said, I had the time so I took a drive. Hopefully, it bears fruit and we get a match."

"Well, shit. Appreciate you takin' the time."

I gave Ethan a lift of my chin then glanced down at my ringing phone.

Shiloh.

I held a finger up to Ethan indicating I needed a moment and answered.

"Everything good?"

"No," she snapped in my ear. "Uncool threatening to call my brothers."

I couldn't help the smile that pulled at my lips.

"Seems it worked and I got a call."

"Un. Cool."

"Babe, maybe I didn't make myself clear. I've got no intention of being cool. You didn't want me doing what I had to do to get a response you should've picked up my calls or returned a text."

There was a pissed-off sigh on her end before she launched in, "I do not need this shit right now."

"Yeah, I heard things have been busy, something about planets in retrograde making the crazies come out. Wanna know who I didn't hear that from? You."

"Luke—"

"You set the board, Shiloh. I'm just playing your game. I gave you five days to come to terms with what's gonna happen. Your time's up. I'll be at your house after work. You're not there, I'll hunt your ass down."

"You show at my house, Luke, you'll find me armed and pissed off."

"Baby, now you're turning me on."

"I'm being serious."

She probably was.

"Friends don't shoot friends. But since you gave me the heads up I'll come kitted out ready for a showdown."

There was another loud huff.

"I don't want this."

"Baby, if I believed that I'd back off. But you're lying. You know it and I know it. I'll see you around six. Be safe."

I disconnected before she could levy any further threats and tossed my phone on my desk. When I looked up Ethan was staring at me with narrowed eyes. He had another few years before his grimace would be as effective as his father, Lenox's, but it was damn near close.

"Was that Shiloh Kent?"

"Yep."

Ethan let out a long low whistle and shook his head.

"Brother, do not go there."

"I've heard about her brothers and met River the other

day when I was at her place. I don't need another warning about them."

I wasn't worried about her brothers, her brothers were worried about her. River stated plain he knew something was up with her and asked if I was the reason she'd been withdrawn. I'd spent years answering to men and women who outranked me, years having my every decision questioned and scrutinized after a mission. Something I no longer had to do and vowed not to have to do again. Therefore, I wasn't pleased to have to explain myself to River, yet I'd done it out of respect for Shiloh. But I wouldn't be doing it two more times with Echo and Phoenix.

"That's good because I wasn't talking about her brothers, though just to say, Echo's more than a tad overprotective and takes the meaning of brother to an extreme. I was talking about *her*. The woman's got it all—funny, smart, tough, easy on the eyes. But under all that, she is made of stone. You know what her nickname is around the station?"

"Sunny?"

Ethan pinched his lips together and shook his head. "No. Killer Frost. No one gets close to Sunny Kent. Sweet and warm as long as you keep your distance. You get even a millimeter into her space and she'll ice you out and do it nastily."

Yep. That sounded about right.

"She already tried that shit with me. Turned up the bitch and attempted to freeze me out. Problem with that is, even as she was doing it she admitted she was doing it on purpose to keep me clear. Now you tell me; that sound like a bitch out to do damage or a woman who has yet to find a man who can withstand the blast and prove he's worth going through the pain she knows she'll endure before she can give the sweet and warm. Now, I suppose she's got more of Killer Frost bottled up and she can rachet that shit up if need be so I'm prepared for a cold chill when I show up at her place tonight."

Ethan did a slow blink. Then with a glare that clearly communicated he cared about Shiloh, he asked, "And you think you're the right man for the job?"

Christ. Now I was explaining myself to Ethan.

"What I know is, I've been in her presence three times. I knew after the first I should steer clear of her. Yet I didn't try too hard, considering my ass was on a barstool next to her less than an hour after she called me. The second time I knew I was in trouble. Yet when I had the chance to cut her out I didn't. And after the third, I knew I couldn't walk away."

"Doesn't sound like you," Ethan mumbled.

"No shit? I got no problems givin' the cold shoulder, especially when I'm doing something nice for someone and they throw that shit in my face and call me an asshole. But I cannot leave her."

"Leave her?"

Ethan eyed me and I ignored the leading question. Shiloh's business was hers and I wasn't going to tell anyone what she'd said to me.

"Leave her," I repeated.

"Shit, Luke, you're gonna have your hands full."

That was the God's honest truth. Shiloh Kent was going to give me a run for my money. The mere thought of the effort that I was going to have to expend to get past her front door should've woke my ass up and made me reconsider. But I'd done what I knew I was going to do and I fell head-first into Shiloh.

"Yep," I responded with an understatement.

"I don't know what to say except if you need something let me know."

"I'll take you up on that should the need arise."

After a quick goodbye, Ethan was out the door and Matt was walking in.

"Yo. Wanna go down to Savanah tonight?" my teammate asked as he plopped himself down in the chair in front of my desk.

"Can't. I have plans."

Matt's brow pulled together and he gave me a look.

"Plans? You never have plans."

He wasn't wrong. Since I'd gotten out of the Navy I rarely had plans with anyone other than my crew. Matt, Carter, Logan, Drake, Trey, and now Brady were safe. And after the explosion, my medical hearing, and discharge I wasn't in the best of places. I needed safe, I needed men around me who knew what I was going through without me having to talk about it. But that was then and after I'd watched Trey struggle thinking I was pissed at him, taking on a mountain of guilt that was not his to carry I realized I needed to get my shit together and stop being a dick with a chip on my shoulder.

I had people around me who would help; all I needed to do was let them. So I reached out first to Lenox, then to Jasper and Levi, and finally, I talked to Clark about my nightmares. The four men who had started Triple Canopy. But before they did, they'd all been in the Army, they'd all seen battle, they all had a heart for service. It was Levi who suggested I talk to his daughter Liberty, Drake's fiancée. Lieutenant Liberty McCoy was as badass as they came, a Special Forces soldier and part of a black ops team. She'd helped me overcome some serious self-worth issues. I needed to call her and ask if she'd talk to Shiloh.

If there was anyone who could relate to Shiloh it was Liberty.

"Earth to Luke," Matt called and I focused on my friend.

"Sorry. Yeah, I have plans."

"The way you spaced out, if I didn't know any better I'd say you had a head full of woman. But since I know you and you've developed a weird aversion to the fairer sex, which just sayin', friend, is A-okay in my book, more for me, but still a man's gotta get—"

"Enough." I put my hand up. "Ask Logan to go with you."

"Already did. He's onboard. I was just asking you to be nice."

I flipped Matt a rude gesture that he took no offense to. He also didn't let me off the hook. That was the problem with friends like Matt—friends you'd fought and bled next to. Men who knew your every move before you made it because at a time it was a matter of life and death. They knew you, straight to your soul, and gave zero fucks about calling you out.

"You met a woman," he rightly guessed.

"Shiloh Kent."

"The blonde? Blue eyes? Hot? Killer legs?"

Of course, Matt noticed her legs.

"That's her," I confirmed.

"You know she's highly trained in a variety of weapons, right?"

"Yep. Took her to the range. Know she's SWAT, has three brothers who will likely be up in my shit as this progresses. I also didn't miss her legs, but from here on out you're gonna refrain from staring at them."

"Damn." Matt chuckled.

Matt settled back in the chair and stared. The silence stretched until I finally broke it.

"Not sure there's anything left to say."

"You go months, lots of months working your shit through. We give you the space you need and only talk about what happened when you bring it up. We all get it. We all respect it. You get yourself straight and in the process, swear to God you get a personality transplant and go from a scowling, standoffish ass to...not friendly per se, but tolerant of other people. I see you smiling and sometimes I even hear you laugh. You become this well-adjusted civvy when I was worried you'd be the next Unabomber. Which brings me to the part about women. You don't say anything, no one asks, but you turned into Carter—a monk who turns down every hot chick who approaches. Suddenly that's changed and you have a woman."

Matt had a flare for drama. Though the part about Carter being a monk was true. When we were on the teams together Carter Lenox had never, not once, touched a woman in all the years we served together. No one got it until he brought Delaney to Virginia Beach and introduced us to her. He'd been in love with her since they were kids and had been in a committed-non-relationship that Carter had refused to commit to, yet secretly had. The situation would've been tragic and fucked-up if they hadn't ended up getting married and started popping out kids.

But me not having sex in months didn't constitute monk status. Though my dick was beginning to disagree with my newfound dislike of meaningless sex.

"Unabomber? Seriously?"

"That's what you're gonna focus on?"

"What else do you want me to focus on? You're right, I needed time to get my shit together. I didn't suddenly become anything, I adjusted. Adapted. And I did that because I had you and the team at my back. And I didn't take a vow of celibacy. I was sick to death of the nothing I felt. It was too fucking easy, I was tired of easy. I was tired of rolling out of some woman's place who I didn't know, was never gonna know, and had no desire to get to know. I didn't want a love match but fucking hell, I want to at least want the woman beyond fucking her."

"You *didn't* want love?"

"Not tracking."

"You said, *didn't*. Not that you *don't* want love. Does that mean—"

"I don't know what the hell it means," I cut him off. "Didn't. Don't. Fuck if I know."

Matt's face broke out into a full-fledged smile and I braced. It was a damn good thing I had.

"Holy shit. You're in love with Shiloh Kent."

There was nothing to say to that. Nowhere to go. If I denied it, Matt would call me out. If I confirmed, he'd hammer me with more questions I didn't want to answer.

So I said nothing.

Matt didn't have the same problem. "Company party's next weekend. You bringing her?"

That idea made me laugh. Short of cuffing Shiloh, physically carrying her to my truck, and committing felony kidnapping, there was very little chance I'd get her to a TC party.

But it was going to be fun trying.

Trying.

Fuck. I hated that word. But when it came to Shiloh, I had a feeling failure, regrouping, learning, trying again, and improvising were in my future. Failure wasn't so bad as long as in the end, I got what I wanted. I'd take my knocks.

8

I was pacing my kitchen. I was not armed. I'd decided against this—the temptation to shoot Luke in his ass was too great. I'd likely have to answer uncomfortable questions when I took Luke to the hospital with a GSW to his buttock. It would serve him right but I liked my job and might get fired for a bad firearm discharge. My captain was pretty cool, but not that cool and he was still watching me like a hawk, worried about my state of mind, and shooting a man in his ass because he'd pissed me off would only confirm my captain's suspicions.

I needed a break. That was what he thought. I was of a different mind and didn't want any downtime that would lead to me dwelling.

But surprisingly, I'd only had one nightmare in the last five days.

And I'd successfully avoided my brothers' phone calls. Unfortunately, that was due to my crazy schedule. I wasn't sure who'd told Luke that Mercury was in retrograde but maybe he was onto something.

It was on that thought my doorbell shrilled and I

wondered why the planets hadn't aligned in my favor to make Luke back off.

I wanted him to back off and go away, right?

Maybe.

Sorta.

Kinda.

But not really.

Can you say, *hello* straitjacket?

I tromped to the door preparing to kick Luke square in the gonads, rendering his sperm useless for the rest of his life. I opened the door and upon seeing him, I had second thoughts. But only because it would be a shame if he didn't pass his superior good looks to his offspring, populating Georgia with beauty.

Then he opened his mouth to say, "Shocking. I thought I'd have to break the door down."

Which caused me to have a third thought; I'd be doing the citizens of Georgia a favor by sterilizing him so he couldn't spread his pushy, macho arrogance. Something he had in abundance thus would pass from father to child without the mother's input.

"Shocking," I spat. "You didn't listen when I told you not to come over."

He smiled. Big and broad and so damn sexy I was momentarily stunned.

That was how he pushed into my house.

"Hey!"

I got that one word out, then Luke's hand came up, hooked me around the back of the neck, and he yanked me to his chest. And since I was still stunned by his smile I was catapulted straight to dazed when his arms wrapped around me. Dazed and confused and bewildered. My cheek was pressed against his hard pectoral muscle. Not knowing what to do with them, my arms dangled lamely at my sides. Luke didn't have this problem. One of his arms was low on my back, his hand resting on my hip. His other was diagonal across my back, his hand resting on my shoulder. He didn't allow an inch of space between us.

I should've protested but my mind was too busy soaking up the feel of him to tell my mouth to form words.

This was a problem.

A big, honking problem.

Not only did I like the feel of him, I liked the way he smelled. Man and Georgia sunshine. I liked how I fit perfectly in his arms. Like I was made to be right where I was. And I felt safe. Not safe like when my brothers hugged me. Safe like the man holding me would prop me up and never let me fall.

I never wanted him to let me go. But even scarier—*I* never wanted to let *him* go.

"Sorry you had a shit couple of days."

I heard his assertion but my fuzzy, stupefied brain was still on the fritz—more so now that I felt the rumble of his words on my cheek. So all I did was nod.

Luke, having all of his faculties and none of the current issues I was having, was in full command of his extremities. The arm that had been around my waist was now gone and I felt his hand grab my wrist, then he twisted his arm behind his back and placed my hand on his hip. He repeated his actions, only using his other hand to grab mine. Once he had my hands where he wanted them he kept me close.

This was nicer.

Having my hands on him, albeit loosely, was oh-so-much better. I wanted to dig my fingertips in—no, scratch that—I wanted to allow my hands to roam over his back. I wanted to turn my head and feel his chest under my lips.

Actually, I wanted to pull his tee off so my lips would be met with bare skin. After I explored all of his hard muscles with my mouth I wanted him to pull my clothes off and return the favor. I wanted this so badly I forgot he wanted to be friends. I forgot he scared me. I forgot he'd made it clear he didn't want me to kiss him or see him naked. I forgot a lot of things when my body started to tingle, so Luke didn't miss the full-on body quake.

This was unfortunate. His arms got super-tight around me and he dropped his mouth to my temple and brushed his lips there. They lingered a little too long and I trembled again. That broke the spell.

"Gonna feed you, then we'll watch a movie and relax. Are you on call?"

There was no way I'd be able to relax in front of a movie with Luke.

"I think you should go."

"Clue in, Shiloh, I'm not going. You had a shit week, mine hasn't been much better, I'm starving, my brain hurts from reading reports all day, yours likely hurts worse. We'll eat and veg out. Watch a mindless movie and relax."

My brain did hurt. Sitting on the couch staring at the TV not thinking sounded heavenly. And if I weren't so scared of Luke it would sound even better doing that next to him. But I *was* scared of him. He had the power to dismantle the carefully crafted fortress I'd built around myself. Hell, who was I kidding? He'd already ripped it apart, going straight to the foundation I'd laid and the rest crumbled down.

"Why was your week shit?" I asked.

"It started with a group of new three-gun shooters that were there for training but knew it all because they'd spent a shit ton of money on guns and gear. Collectively, they might've had a thousand rounds downrange. I had to listen to all the lingo until my ears were bleeding. This lasted nearly an hour. Then one of the guys explained to me how a reflex sight worked. Thank God, Brady's back from his honeymoon and he can take his classes back over. I don't know how he does it."

Three-gun was a competition shooting sport. I'd never competed but for training, we ran some of the same drills, alternating between handgun, rifle, and shotgun. When my team trained we didn't go for speed the way a competition shooter would; we trained for accuracy.

"Let me guess; the guy had a red dot on his shotgun."

"Yep. He swore up and down his target acquisition was faster and more accurate than my iron sights. Ten minutes later he learned differently."

I smiled against his shirt, picturing a disgruntled Luke with a shotgun.

"That doesn't sound like a fun day on the range," I noted.

"It wasn't, and the rest of the week sucked, too. Only good part about it was I drove to Montgomery and got prints to run on the Harpers' contractor."

"You went to Alabama?"

Why did the thought of Luke driving out of state and me not knowing he was gone give me a weird feeling?

"Yep. Jeff Shepard moved there. His prints aren't in the system and I needed something to run against the prints in Becca's room."

I didn't know much about the case. I wasn't a cop when the little girl was murdered, but being as it was still an ongoing investigation, I knew a little.

"You think the contractor did it?"

"I think Detective Winshaw was hamstrung by the chief who was too worried about the media. Winshaw did what he was told and hit the parents hard. I haven't cleared the dad, but Jeff Shepard had access to the houses—the abduction site and the vacant rental that served as the dumpsite. Keys to both places. Shepard's wife left him six months before and took their seven-year-old daughter with her down to Savannah. Stephanie was six. The girls were both small for their ages, with brown hair and brown eyes. I talked to a man who worked for Shepard back then. He said Jeff was undone when his wife left him. Wife was cheating on him with his business partner. Barely functioning."

"But prints and DNA would be expected in both houses. What's to gain confirming that?"

"Jeff Shepard swears he was never in Becca's room. There's a set of unknown prints on her nightstand, on the inside of her bedroom door, and a partial on the inside knob. If I can prove he was in that room, Ethan can get him back into interrogation. My guess is, Ethan won't take it as easy on Shepard as Winshaw did."

"Ethan doesn't take it easy on anyone in interrogation. I've never seen it but word is he's so good even the older detectives watch him."

"Might have something to do with who his dad is and some old Army techniques his uncles taught him."

"Unfair advantage." I laughed.

"What are we ordering for dinner?" Luke asked and tension sprang up fast. "Babe, I skipped lunch. I'm starved and I wanna sit and relax. What are we ordering?"

"What are my chances of talking you into going home and getting dinner on your own?"

"None."

Damn.

Okay. Maybe I can do this. I made it through talking about his week while in his arms and didn't spontaneously combust. Surely I could sit next to him and share a meal.

"I want Taco Bell," I told him.

"Sounds good. DoorDash or Uber Eats?"

"Neither. Taco Bell is around the corner."

"Babe, neither one of us is leaving. Pull up DoorDash. I want six crispy tacos and a meat and cheese burrito."

"Six tacos? You can't eat six tacos."

"I can when I skipped lunch and I'm fucking starving."

At that declaration, my hands moved. One slid around to the front of him and trailed up his stomach. The other glided up his back. No fat. Just dips and valleys of muscle.

"How's that possible?"

"How's what possible?"

My fingers on his back curled in and I tried to pinch the taut skin in an effort to find an ounce of body fat. I found none.

"Damn, woman, there a reason you're pinching me?" Luke complained.

"That just sucks." It was my turn to complain. "Why is it men can eat six tacos and a meat and cheese burrito and have not a pinch of fat? I'd maybe get two days of eating like that before my ass would balloon."

Luke's body started shaking and I stupidly nuzzled closer, enjoying the feel of his laughter. And when the shaking turned audible I enjoyed that, too.

Way, way, too much.

I was sitting on my couch with my knees bent, legs tucked under me, feet to the side resting between me and Luke. I also had a belly full of tacos and a meximelt. Taco Bell wrappers littered my coffee table next to where Luke had his socked feet resting. And for the record, Luke didn't eat six tacos—we'd ordered a twelve-pack—I ate two and Luke demolished ten and he rounded out his meal with his burrito.

We'd talked about nothing personal, nothing taxing. He asked about work, I told him what I could about the call-outs I'd been on. Luke listened and interjected. Sometimes he'd pull his brows together and his face would turn hard. But it wasn't until I told him about a particular takedown that I found amusing that Luke's scowl turned dark. We'd served a warrant and had to pull the guy out of bed. It was unfortunate he was naked as a jaybird and even worse that when he woke from his drug-induced sleep he fought like a mother. Which led to me grappling with a high-as-a-kite-full-nude meth dealer who obviously sampled his wares and used pharmaceuticals when he needed to come down. There was no other explanation for the scrawny dude's burst of strength. After that, I felt it prudent to end story time and turn on a movie.

That brought us to now. Me sitting close but not too close to Luke. I was surprisingly relaxed. Until Luke's hand found my ankle and pulled me out of my sideways tuck. I twisted at the last second so I wouldn't roll off the couch as he placed my feet in his lap.

"What are you doing?" I tried to sound irritated but I was worried it came out breathy.

This was because my feet were in Luke's lap and his hands were moving over my calves, his thumbs digging into the tight muscles.

It felt good.

Damn good.

Not his thumbs working the muscles, but his hands on me.

A tingle rushed up my calves, thighs, then straight between my legs.

His ministrations didn't stop when he said, "Giving you a leg rub."

I wanted him to rub more than my legs, and the mere thought of how his strong hands would feel in other places had my nipples tight and my panties wet.

Not good.

I tried to pull my legs back but Luke captured them and continued to knead the knots. I couldn't stop the groan that slipped out.

"So good," I whispered.

Luke's hands twitched and his thighs under my feet turned to stone.

Really not good.

"Watch the movie, Shiloh," he demanded.

I didn't turn to watch what was playing on the screen. I was too enthralled by the hard set of his jaw, the way his voice had deepened, his stiff shoulders.

He'd made it crystal clear all he wanted was to be friends. So why was he touching me? Why did he look like he was exhibiting a good amount of control not to touch me other places?

"Do friends give leg rubs?" I blurted out.

His neck craned and his eyes locked onto mine.

"This *friend* does."

Holy hell.

It was not what he said, or even the sexy rumble in his tone, it was the unchecked fire that danced in his eyes that took my breath. I'd noticed Luke's irises changed colors. It was a slight variance from brownish green to more green when he was in the sun to browner when he was pissed off.

But right then the green had taken over and there was no sunshine to be had. They were also holding me hostage.

Yikes.

With no choice other than to throw myself bodily at him and straddle his lap and beg him to rub other parts, I turned my gaze to the TV.

Relaxation was history.

9

"You weren't lying." Shiloh leaned back into the cushion and patted her stomach. "That was the best steak I ever ate."

I took a pull of my beer and kept my eyes averted. It was three days after Shiloh had stopped avoiding me. The third night in a row I'd been to her house after work. The third night we'd had dinner, engaged in playful banter, and watched a movie.

Tonight I got to her house before she did, this had been prearranged and she'd given me a key. There was only so much takeout I could handle. And since Shiloh had been forthcoming about her inability to cook, I took over that task. This meant I was there before her to get the potatoes in the oven and the steaks ready to grill.

This decision came easy. Last night before I left, Shiloh rummaged through a drawer in her kitchen, found her spare and gave it to me, then rattled off her alarm code, and that was it. I spent the rest of the night lying in my bed wondering if she understood what was going on between us. I'd kept both nights light—no deep conversations. Two friends hanging out. Both nights her legs ended up in my lap. The first night it had taken about twenty minutes for her to relax once my hands were on her. Last night when I pulled her feet out from under her and started rubbing it was instantaneous. No tension at all.

But right then, sitting on her couch, it was me who was tense. She'd gotten home later than she'd planned, rushed in still in uniform yelling her apologies. I hadn't fully recovered from how hot she looked in her gear when she came out in a pair of loose-fitting shorts and a tight tank top. I was grateful I'd been standing next to her kitchen island seasoning the steaks. Not only were the cabinets a welcomed barrier to prevent me from groping the hell out of her but they also hid my erection. Now with nothing to hide a hard-on, it was paramount I kept my gaze diverted.

As if she sensed my discomfort on her own accord she arranged herself in the corner of the couch and draped her legs over my lap.

Jesus fuck.

When my hands didn't go to her feet fast enough she shifted them and I looked down at her hot pink toenails.

Cute.

Something I learned last night—Tomboy Shiloh liked to get her "feet done" as she called it. Every two weeks she went and had a pedicure. Further, she explained her toenails were always painted a shade of pink. And when she offered that minuscule piece of information that seemed like no big deal but really was something oddly personal about her, my chest got tight. There was also something insanely sexy about her having pink toenails inside her combat boots.

"Luke?" Shiloh called when I didn't move.

Her voice was a little unsteady, a little nervous, a little unsure.

I preferred her breathy moans when I dug my fingers into her muscular calves.

I set my beer down on the side table and went to work on her legs.

Smooth, soft skin. She'd shaved between last night and today. A mental image of her in the shower wet and soapy assaulted my mind and I barely contained my growl of approval. Or was it arousal I was containing? I decided it was both—I approved of her naked in the shower—or did she take a bath and prop her foot up on the side of the tub while she shaved?

Christ.

Touching Shiloh was a slippery slope. My palms had a mind of their own and it was by sheer force of will I'd kept them below the knee. A respectable distance from where they wanted to roam. There were times I caught Shiloh staring at me and I could see desire. But there were other times when I saw apprehension. My hands were not venturing beyond her knee until that apprehension was gone.

"Luke?" she repeated.

"Yeah?"

"Everything okay?"

"Yeah," I lied. "Why?"

"You're acting funny."

She scooted her ass closer to me, this was something she'd done last night, too, so she could fully recline. Tonight, since I wasn't looking at her, two things happened simultaneously, and neither one was good. My hand, which had been just below her knee was now mid-thigh and her left leg shifted and was now resting on my hard dick. There was no hiding, no mistaking what it was.

I heard her suck in a breath. I did the same and slowly

turned my head to look at her. That was a mistake. I thought I'd see wide eyes and shock. Probably a whole lot of trepidation. But instead, I found soft features and eyelids half-mast. Her lips were parted and there was no wariness.

This was a problem.

"Shiloh?"

"Yeah," she breathed.

Good goddamn. Torture.

"Move your leg."

Her eyes shot open. They held mine for a beat, then they dropped to my dick, then came back to mine.

She didn't move her leg.

"Ignore it, baby, and watch the movie," I said.

"Ignore it?"

"Yep."

"Can *you* ignore it?" Her eyes went wide and I felt my lips tip up into a smile.

"Yeah, I can ignore it."

"How?"

"Um...what do you mean how?"

"Can friends talk about erections?" she queried.

My gut clenched in an effort to stop myself from busting a gut laughing.

"Depends," I told her through a chuckle. "The type we are—absolutely. The type you are with the guys on your team—absolutely not."

"So we're special friends?" she returned and smiled.

"Yeah, Shiloh, we're very special friends."

"Okay, so how can you ignore this?" To punctuate her question she moved her leg against my dick and I fought a wince.

"First way is by you not rubbing it," I explained and

watched her pinch her lips. "The second way is not to talk about it."

"So..." she started, drawing out the vowel, giving me a clear indication she had a smart retort and clearly she wanted to talk about it. "As long as I don't rub it you'll be fine?"

"Didn't say I'd be fine. I said I can ignore it. But just to say, we're talking about it so right at this moment I'm unable to ignore it."

"Is it uncomfortable?"

I blinked, then I blinked some more, and Shiloh being smart figured out my answer without my need to verbalize just how un-*fucking*-comfortable it was.

"Okay, stupid question. Of course, having something big and—"

"You're killing me," I groaned and let my head fall back onto the back of the couch.

"Sorry, sorry, you said special friends can talk about erections. I was curious. I don't have a dick, I wouldn't know what it feels like to have something hard in my pants. I'd assume it hurts but what do I know? Maybe it's like my boobs being squished in a sports bra—"

"Shiloh, baby, please for the love of all things holy do not talk to me about your boobs. Not in a bra of any kind. Or out of a bra. Your tits are off-limits while my cock is literally hard enough to pound nails and at this very moment trying to break free."

"Well, that's a shame," she mumbled.

"Dare I ask what's a shame?"

"Well, for starters that you don't want to hear about my boobs. I took you as a boob-man. But the real shame is that you're sitting way over there and I'm sitting way over here and you have a hard-on—"

I could take no more. I shifted, moving her leg off the erection she was hellbent on discussing, and whipped my head to the side and narrowed my eyes.

"In two seconds the special friends we are right now is gonna take on a whole new meaning of *special*. The kind that includes my hands and mouth on you. The kind that includes you getting intimately acquainted with my dick."

Shiloh wiggled and my gaze dropped to find her squeezing her thighs together. *Fucking hell.* I greedily took in her bare skin, the way she was clenching her legs together, and stopped to focus on where her shorts were bunched. She moved again and I swear to Christ she was trying to find friction. Seeing that, I remembered her drunkenly telling me she couldn't get herself off so she'd stopped trying.

She was not ready for me to take her where I wanted. We needed time for her to adjust and come to terms with a lot of shit that was going down in her life. I knew Shiloh well enough to know that if I fucked her now, she'd use it as a way to close off. In her mind, I'd be what she said she wanted—a fuck buddy—and I'd never move her past it. I intended to be more. I wanted all of her, so sex was off the table.

"Look at me, Shiloh."

Her eyes slowly came open and fuck me, she looked lust-drunk.

"Do you trust me?"

She hesitated and I was reminded yet again how painful it was going to be to break down her walls.

"Let me ask a different way. Do you know I would never hurt you?"

"Yeah."

"Good. Do you know I'd never do anything to embarrass you or make you uncomfortable?"

"Yes."

"Then tonight I want you to trust me."

Her eyes flared and her legs rubbed together.

"Luke—"

I cut her off by gently removing her legs from my lap and standing up. And since we were being open and she'd felt the evidence I didn't attempt to hide my hard-on. Not that I could but I made no move to turn away when I pulled her off of the couch. When she was on her feet I grabbed her hand, twined our fingers together, brought them to mouth level, and kissed the back of her hand.

"You can trust me. I swear it, Shiloh, just like the other night, you're safe with me."

She nodded and before I could change my mind I led us through her house, down the hall, into her bedroom, but didn't stop until we were in her bathroom. I let her hand go to turn the taps on, waited until the water was warm, then watched as the tub began to fill.

"Luke?"

I stepped behind her, fitted my front to her back, put my hands on her hips, and lowered my mouth to her ear.

"Trust me." She nodded and my hands slipped up and caught the hem of her shirt. I slowly pulled it up, gritting my teeth as my knuckles brushed the side of her breasts. Calling up all my willpower, I didn't linger. This was not about me, it was all about Shiloh. What I could give her without touching her. I tossed her tank aside and brushed my lips against her bare shoulder as I undid her bra. Shiloh tipped her shoulders forward and the bra slid to the floor.

I went to my knees behind her, hooked my fingers into her shorts and panties, and tugged them down her legs. They pooled around her ankles. I closed my eyes to ward off the surge of desire. But I didn't stop myself from inhaling.

"You smell so fucking good, Shiloh. One day I'm gonna be right here on my knees but you'll be bent over your bed and I'm gonna eat you just like this. My hands full of your ass and my tongue in your pussy."

Shiloh moaned and reached back. Her fingernails scraped my scalp and she tilted her ass back in a nonverbal plea to do what I promised right then.

That couldn't happen.

I kissed her thigh, her hip, the small of her back, and as I reluctantly stood I let my mouth run up her spine.

"Please touch me," she whispered.

"Trust me."

She groaned when I pressed close again. There was nowhere I could touch that was safe. Shiloh was fully nude standing in front of me trembling, needy, the smell of her arousal still fresh in my mind.

"Luke—"

"Trust me, baby, I'm gonna take care of you."

"I trust you. But I need you to touch me."

Christ, that felt good. So good, my chest burned and my cock twitched.

I pushed aside the emotions, my selfish need, and locked onto my control. One day I'd have her—all of her. But for now, I could do something with her she couldn't do by herself. I could offer her relief without jeopardizing my end game.

I stepped back and my gaze dropped to her ass. So goddamn perfect I wanted to sink my teeth into the flesh while I fucked her, and since that would be physically impossible I'd settle on two handfuls of fine ass holding her steady as I drilled into her from behind.

Do not touch.

Don't fucking touch.

Once I'd silently chanted the mantra a few more times I swiftly undressed. I hit the danger zone—both of us naked. Both of us turned on. Both of us in desperate need but only one of us was going to find what they needed.

I shuffled Shiloh forward, reached around her, turned off the taps, and ordered, "Step in."

On shaky legs, she did as I asked and craned her neck to look at me. I didn't miss the way her eyes freely roamed, the way her pastel irises had darkened, and when her eyes dropped to my hard-on I didn't miss the swift inhale followed by a mew. Without thought, I fisted my cock and gave it a long hard tug before I stepped into the tub behind her.

Seconds later I was in the seventh circle of hell.

Pure fucking torture.

My shoulders were resting on the back of the tub, legs spread, knees bent toward the ceiling, and Shiloh was settled with her back on my chest, my cock pressed against her ass, and her hands on my shins.

"Please."

One word conveyed a painful hunger, one I understood. One that was coursing through my body making my cock ache in a way I'd never felt before.

I dropped my chin, kissed the side of her jaw, and told her what I wanted.

"Put your hand between your legs."

Immediately she stiffened.

"Luke—"

"Trust me, Shiloh. Put your hand between your legs."

There was hesitation but her right arm moved and slowly she did as I asked.

"Are you touching yourself?"

She nodded and continued.

"Good, baby. Now I want you to close your eyes and gently circle your clit. Not hard, not fast, just tease it. Nice and slow."

I paused and allowed my mind to run wild. All the things I was going to do to her when the time was right. When I had her trust, her secrets, and her heart was so intertwined with mine there was no chance of them untangling.

"Do you have any idea how sexy you are? How good you feel against me? How badly I wish it was my tongue playing with your clit? Move your fingers lower, slowly glide them down, don't push inside, just feel how slick you are. Can you feel it? Are you wet, baby?"

"Yes."

Christ.

"I'm gonna lick you there, too."

Shiloh made a frustrated sound from the back of her throat and her nails dug into my calf muscle. Half moan, half grunt. The noise was so goddamn hot my cock throbbed.

"Tell me, baby, you need more?"

"I want you to touch me."

"I am touching you."

And I was; her warm, wet body was reclined against mine. My legs were cradling her hips. Her soft hair was brushing my face. The smell of her shampoo was all around me. Those were just the places I could think about. If I let my mind wander to my cock beyond how fucking hard I was, how easy it would be to lift her up over me and slide inside, I'd lose my mind. *So close.*

"I need more."

"More?"

"Yes," Shiloh hissed.

"Take your other hand, put it on your stomach." I waited for her left hand to come off my leg then I went on. "Slowly move it up. Just the tips of your fingers." I glanced down and watched Shiloh's hand come out of the water where it stopped below her breasts. Her fingers skimmed over the swell and circled her pebbled nipple.

I was wrong before. *Now* I was in hell.

"You have no idea how fucking hot it is knowing your fingers are teasing your pussy and watching you play with your nipple. So goddamn hot the only thing that would be better is if I had my mouth on you. Cup your tit, Shiloh, and let your thumb rub over your nipple."

Her hand shifted down and around and she did as I asked.

Seeing that, having her touch herself at my command, made my blood catch fire. I needed her to come and I'd get the fuck out of this tub.

I shoved my face into her neck, dropped a chaste kiss there. She shivered and moaned and that took the last of my sanity.

"I can see your hand between your legs, but I can't see what you're doing. Do you have your fingers inside your pussy?" Shiloh nodded and her hips jerked. "Tell me something; do you wish it was my cock inside you?"

"Yes," she groaned.

"So do I. I'd sink in deep. I wouldn't take you slow. I would just take you until I had you coming around my cock. Fuck your fingers, baby, show me how I'm gonna fuck you." Her hips jerked which added friction against my already weeping cock. "Just like that. Use your thumb on your clit. Hard, baby, I'm gonna fuck you hard and deep."

With a frustrated grunt, she moved her hand faster and panted, "I can't."

"You can. Take yourself there. I wanna watch you come around your fingers wishing it was my cock taking you there. Show me."

A few beats later she made another noise that was beyond frustrated.

One of my hands went between her legs. The other moved over her hand at her breast.

"Like this," I said and cupped her pussy as I guided her thumb to her clit.

"Oh, God," she moaned and I used her thumb to rub harder.

My fingers went over hers to roll her nipple.

"Luke."

There it was. Husky, breathy, close.

"Don't fight it, Shiloh. Move your hips and ride your fingers." I let the tips of my fingers brush her pussy lips and her hips surged. "Goddamn hot and so fucking slick."

It was my turn to groan into her neck. I was so damn close to coming if she didn't go soon I'd be joining her.

That was why I deviated from my plan. My hand on her tit knocked hers away and I took over. I watched myself toy with her nipple until she was squirming and the sounds she was making become louder.

"Does that feel good, Shiloh? Do you like my playing with your—"

"God, yes. Don't stop. More. So close."

I worked my hand between her legs faster, keeping her thumb under mine and moving on her clit while I rolled her nipple between my fingers.

"Fuck, that sounds so good. Let go, let me see it."

Her head dropped back on my shoulder, her back arched, and her legs tightened and tried to close.

"Keep 'em spread."

Shiloh's body locked and a long, sexy-as-fuck groan filled the room.

My jaw clenched and I closed my eyes, willing myself not to come.

"Luke."

Fucking hell.

I gritted my teeth and held on until the trembling stopped and she sagged against me. Then I held her longer until her breathing evened out. I moved my hand from between her legs and let go of her breast. I regretted that I needed to do both in an effort not to work her back up, culminating in a different outcome the second time around. One that would have us both crying out in pleasure.

Not yet.

Not until she was mine.

I brushed Shiloh's hair off her face and kissed her cheek.

"You feeling all right?"

The silence that ensued stretched into minutes. Worry crept in until she found my hand on the side of the tub and she laced our fingers together.

I closed my eyes and took in the moment. Shiloh fully relaxed, her soft skin against my chest, our thighs touching, her hand on mine. A moment that would forever be seared into my brain.

10

The water was cooling but I was so relaxed I didn't want to get up.

Either that or if I got up I'd have to face the reality of what happened.

"Thank you for sticking around and proving me wrong," I murmured, breaking the silence. Luke's fingers tightened before he slipped his hand out from under mine and maneuvered so our palms were now touching and our fingers threaded back together. "Or I guess you proved me right."

"How'd I prove you right?"

"You told me I was safe. I trusted you and you proved I was safe in doing so."

Behind me, his big body went solid and his grip on my hand got super tight.

"You'll always be safe with me. I'll remind you as many times as I need to but just to say, I'm looking forward to the day when you know down to your soul that's the case and you won't need the reminder."

There was a lot I had to say to that. How it made me feel,

how I was looking forward to that day and it was closer than he could imagine. But I was too overwhelmed to find the words I needed to explain how safe I felt with him. Not just being naked in a bathtub with him. I knew he wouldn't do *anything* to hurt me.

And that wasn't scary—it was downright terrifying.

I didn't regret what we did. I wasn't embarrassed. But I was a little shocked and not for the reasons I thought I would be. Luke obviously knew my situation, because in that drunken tell-all night I'd spilled my deepest secrets including not being able to get myself off.

I had no delusions that I was now cured of that issue.

The only reason I'd reached climax was because of Luke —talking me through it, feeling him behind me—but mostly because he'd helped in a big way by touching me.

None of that I found shocking, but the part where I trusted him surprised me. Twice he'd told me I was safe with him, twice he'd proven that to be true. I was naked, turned on, and vulnerable. He knew it would take no coaxing on his end and I would've had sex with him. But he didn't take us there even though I wanted him to.

Beyond that, I was stunned by how comfortable I was. *That* was the reality I was terrified of facing. We'd spent three nights hanging out. The first under protest, but the second I'd welcomed him in and already had takeout menus on the counter and his favorite beer stocked in my fridge. And tonight, I'd rushed home because I knew he was there waiting for me.

This was not me. And it scared the shit out of me how easily it had *become* me.

Which made no logical sense but it made perfect sense in my post-orgasm haze.

Before I could come up with something to say there was a high-pitched squawk followed by two long tones.

Luke moved lightning-fast and had both of us up and out of the tub.

"Pager," I sputtered as I attempted to get my bearings.

"Fucking hell."

"Sorry. I'm on call."

I'm always on call.

I turned and placed my hands on his chest and felt his heart thundering under my palms. The pager quieted and my phone's notification alert started.

"I'm really sorry, Luke, but I have to go."

His hands came up and landed on my shoulders. His choice of placement had me glancing up and smiling.

"We're naked," I noted.

"We are."

"Would it be weird after what we did if I asked you to turn around while I got dressed?"

He grinned back and shook his head like he found me amusing instead of stupid.

"Anything you need, baby."

After he said that he dropped a kiss on my forehead and turned toward the wall.

Anything I needed.

I believed that.

I rushed out of the bathroom suddenly feeling extremely exposed.

"Are you checking out my ass?" Luke called out.

I stopped to answer but didn't turn around. "I wasn't since I asked you not to look. It didn't seem fair if I ogled. But if you don't mind..." I let that hang.

Luke's deep rumbly laughter washed over me and I

smiled so big my cheeks hurt. This could've been uncomfortable but Luke slid us right back to playful, recalling our conversation the first time I met him. It wasn't that long ago, but strangely it felt like Luke had been in my life a long time.

"For the record, you can ogle whenever you want."

At that, I craned my neck and took in his naked backside. I stared for a while; there was a lot to appreciate—high and tight ass, thick tree trunk legs, narrow waist that flared out to broad muscular shoulders. But that wasn't all. He had a tattoo, a golden eagle, the wingtips spanning from shoulder blade to shoulder blade. There was a great deal of detail in that tattoo and when I had the time I planned on inspecting it further.

Which meant I'd have to get Luke naked again.

"You have a great ass," I told him. "Next time, I get the back."

I heard him chuckle and watched his shoulders shake.

"Doesn't work like that, woman."

"It will if you want a chance to do all that stuff you promised."

Luke groaned and his head dropped forward.

I added, "Don't worry, baby, I'll be gentle."

"You got two seconds to get dressed, Shiloh."

"Someone's testy about his ass."

"Someone's dick is hard again and all his self-control was expended holding you while you got off."

"Are you referring to yourself or your dick in third person?"

"I'm referring to my resolve being pushed to the limits. Help a guy out and put some clothes on."

Yikes.

"Fine. But just to note, you gave me permission to ogle

so it's not my fault your dick's hard because I'm expressing my—"

"Shiloh," he growled and I got a move on it.

I was dressed in record time and in my living room sending a text to my captain I was on my way when Luke joined me.

I looked up and smiled. He looked pained which made me smile bigger.

"If I didn't have to leave I promise I'd offer to—"

I didn't finish because Luke tagged me around the back of the neck and pulled me to his chest. I barely caught my breath when his mouth dropped to my temple and he kissed me there, stealing what little oxygen I'd been able to inhale.

"Be safe out there."

Maybe I'd been wrong and it wasn't pain I saw, it was worry. He certainly sounded worried.

I pulled back and tilted my head to look up at him. Oh, yeah, I'd been wrong. I studied the pinch of his brow, the creases around his eyes, which incidentally were more brown than green at the moment.

"I'm always safe," I returned.

He gave me a tight nod and pulled away.

We were both quiet as he carried my gear through the mudroom and into the garage. I popped the trunk and Luke hesitated a beat before he dropped my bag next to my tact helmet and vest—two things I didn't take out of the car. Guns, extra mags, cuffs, radio—those all came inside and were locked up safely but the vest and helmet stayed put.

The creases around his eyes turned into deep grooves. If I'd had more courage I would've asked what he was thinking about, but I didn't and I needed to get on the road.

Luke slammed the trunk closed and walked me to the

driver's side door. When he opened it for me I tried to break the tension.

"Were you checking out my ass in my cargos?"

The joke fell flat.

He didn't return my playful banter but instead gave me a tight smile.

"I'll see you tomorrow after work, yeah?"

"Yeah."

"If you're up for it, text me when you get home."

He wanted me to check in.

I didn't have time to process why that made my belly feel funny and my heart pound instead of pissing me off.

"Okay."

With another kiss to the top of my head, he walked out of the garage. Luke was in his truck with it idling at the curb when I pulled out. I waved goodbye and he flicked two fingers and gave me a chin lift.

I pushed all thoughts of Luke, the warm squishy feeling he gave me, the orgasm he helped me find, and seeing him again tomorrow out of my mind.

It was game time.

I pulled into the parking lot of First Central Bank that the team was using as a staging area. Two armored personnel carriers were parked next to a dozen vehicles and off to the side was the command post van the negotiator would use to do his work if necessary.

I parked, went to my trunk and pulled out my vest, and strapped it on. I was still shoving magazines in the front pockets when Echo stopped at my side.

I was surprised to see him. It happened from time to

time. He worked the drug unit and it wasn't unheard of for SWAT to get called in to serve a warrant.

"You've been dodging my calls," he accused.

"Personal lives don't cross into work," I reminded him.

This was a rule—a line drawn that we all agreed on. With four siblings in law enforcement, we needed it. Our paths crossed and when they did it was important that family ties didn't cloud our judgment. Our jobs intersected —Echo worked drugs, River worked gangs, and Phoenix worked guns. Between the four of us, we had all the special squads covered.

I loved that the Kent family worked hard to make a difference. Nothing would ever make what my dad did right, nothing would bring a dead man back to life, but the four of us could give something to the community, to the departments we serve. It wasn't enough but it was something.

My brothers felt the same way, only they wished I'd elected to be a traffic cop. It was too bad for them; growing up they taught me not to take shit from anyone and be who I was and who I wanted to be no matter who was standing in my way. I reckoned they never thought it would be them I'd go up against when it came to choosing my career. Obviously, I won. I became who I wanted to be and worked a job I loved and simply ignored them when they bitched and complained.

"You're not briefed, the job hasn't started."

I glanced down at my bulletproof vest then back up at my brother.

"Funny, I thought the second I put on body armor and holstered my weapon I was on the job."

"There's nothing funny about you not taking my calls," Echo continued. "River said he was at your house and some asshole showed up."

My temper flared and I'd learned a long time ago not to hold back when I was dealing with my overbearing ape of a brother.

"First, do not call Luke an asshole. Second, it wasn't River's business to tell you who was at *my* house. And third, it's not your business so back off."

Echo stood to his full six-foot-five inches, crossed his arms, and stared down at me. My brother was big, huge actually. He'd grown into his height by the time he was seventeen—that meant he'd towered over me my whole life. When I was a petulant teenager and he got this way, I'd stand on a chair so I was eye level with him. Once when I was in a tizzy because he was being particularly over-protective I climbed onto the kitchen table so I could look down at him for a change. He didn't find me amusing, never had, Echo was far too serious. He had to be when he was solely responsible for raising three younger siblings.

That thought should've quelled my anger but he'd called Luke an asshole and I wouldn't let that slide.

"Luke Marcou being at my baby sister's place is one hundred percent my business."

"How'd you know his last name?"

"River told me then I looked into him."

Fucking River.

Fucking Echo.

"Bet that was fascinating," I snapped. "Glad to know you have so much free time on your hands. Does that mean Georgia's streets are clean of drugs?"

My brother's eyes narrowed.

"Lose the attitude."

Gah. He was so annoying.

"No can do, big brother. Not when you're acting like a jerk. I'm at an age where I can invite who I want to my house and I don't need your permission. Or River's or Phoenix's. We're at work, I have a job to do, and since you're here I assume you have something to do, too. So this conversation is over. But to end it right I want to tell you that I love you, I appreciate you being the kind of brother that wants to look out for his sister, and the kind of man who loves his family. But you're out of line. Invading Luke's privacy was a shit thing to do. And *that* I don't appreciate."

I turned back to my trunk, reached into my bag, pulled out my thigh rig and strapped it on, loaded a second nine mil into the holster, grabbed my ear pro and helmet, and slammed the trunk closed. My rifle would be waiting for me in the APC.

Time to get to work.

"Do you know he was a SEAL?" Echo asked, not willing to give up.

"Sure do. I also know he was medically discharged and he works at Triple Canopy."

"He tell you about the explosion?"

"Not the details which, since the explosion happened while he was a SEAL, I doubt he can say much about it. Why?"

"Something like that can change a man."

I turned to fully face my brother. I tried to remember a time when he was a kid—carefree, no responsibility, free to be Echo, not a caregiver. But I came up empty.

Did my mother taking off leaving my criminal father with four kids change Echo? Of course, it did. It changed us all. Did my father being in and out of jail change him? Again yes. And when our father finally got locked up for good did it change Echo permanently, turning him into who he was? It sure did.

But Luke was not Echo. Luke was forthcoming. He smiled. He laughed. He teased.

My brother did none of those things.

"You're very right. But sometimes the change isn't bad. Sometimes it makes you look at your life in a new light. Sometimes it forces you to change in ways that make you a better person. I don't know Luke well enough to know if that's the case. But I can say this—I know Ethan Lenox. I know his father. And you know Jason Walker pretty damn well. If Luke wasn't a good man no way in hell he'd be working at Triple Canopy. No fucking way would any of those men trust him if they didn't believe in him. Again, brother, love you, but please stop talking before this turns into a fight before I have to kick in a door."

Another rule, no ugly words before work. The four of us were acutely aware of the dangers of our jobs. We didn't learn that from being cops, we learned when my father murdered one in cold blood.

"I'll let it go...for now," he conceded.

"Fantastic. Now tell me what's going on?"

"Todd English. Thirty-nine. I've been making buys from him for three months. This morning I finally got into the house. Three bedrooms upstairs—two used for packaging meth and fentanyl. The third is all pharmaceuticals. I didn't weigh it but I got a good look, I'd say he's got two kilos of meth ready for distribution and enough fentanyl to take out the town. He's got two women living with him. Bedroom's bottom floor, south side. Garage is north side. I couldn't miss the smell of ether when I was in the living room. Didn't get a look but I'm betting English has a lab in the garage."

That was a lot of meth, over four pounds of it.

"Why isn't the DEA involved in this?"

"They are. English is only a cog in this operation. We want him to flip—tell us who's running the heroin."

"Never fucking ends," I muttered.

"Nope. Never fucking does, little sister."

Echo threw a big, heavy arm around my shoulders and tucked me to his side.

"Easy there, big guy," I grunted and pulled my cheek off his vest. "You're gonna take out my eye with a corner of a mag."

"Wuss."

"Buffoon."

"Be safe in there. I clocked three shotguns in the living room, an AR in the weighing room, and English was strapped. And watch the women—"

"Not my first time kickin' in a door," I cut him off.

Echo sighed and squeezed my shoulder.

"My sister the badass. Where did I go wrong?"

"Do you want a list?"

"Brat."

I elbowed Echo the best I could through his vest.

"You love me."

"So much fucking much, Sunny, so fucking much."

Damn, my brother was a big ole softy when he wanted to be. Which luckily for me wasn't often because when he was, my heart filled to bursting and my eyelids got wet.

"Go, go, go," Valentine called.

McCarthy swung the battering ram and the door splintered. He tossed the Donker to the side and Soloman charged forward behind the riot shield with Reyes behind him. The rest of us followed.

Shots rang out.

Not from us—from English or one of his women.

More automatic gunfire and I was thinking my brother and the DEA was gonna be shit out of luck when the crack of a bullet whizzed by my head.

Be safe.

Luke's words flitted through my mind.

My go-to answer was "always".

But until that moment I wasn't sure I really meant it.

I didn't have a death wish.

I just never thought about my quick retort.

However, that night with drywall dust falling from the ceiling, glass shattering, the smell of gunpowder lingering in the air, the butt of my rifle pressed against my shoulder, I knew I was going to do everything I could to get home and text Luke.

I broke left, followed Gordy up the stairs, and cleared the rooms.

They were all empty of persons but Echo wasn't exaggerating. There was a shitload of drugs, stacks of currency, scales, baggies, latex gloves, masks, and everything else needed for packaging.

By the time we got back downstairs, all three occupants were facedown in the living room. Echo was in the house with a black mask covering his face, a long-sleeved black tee covering the tattoos on his arms, and gloves. He kept his distance when he looked over the man in custody. Without saying a word he jerked his chin at Valentine, then his gaze came to me. He did a sweep, tipped his head, and silently walked out of the house and he was gone.

Such was his life with the narcotics task force.

By the time I was done with all the after-action reports

the sun had come up. I waited until I was showered and in bed before I texted Luke.

Home safe.

I thought that said it all.

My eyes were drifting closed when my phone beeped.

Good, baby. See you tonight.

I dozed off immediately and I didn't have a single nightmare.

11

I felt his presence before I saw him.

Echo Kent.

I also ignored him and concentrated on the shooter in front of me who was looking to me for instruction.

"Your muzzle's high," I told Glen. "You're bowling down with no sights then leaving yourself a lot of clean-up. You're also going too fast. Half that speed and you'll have a smooth draw stroke which will leave you with less clean-up and faster target acquisition. Next fifty rounds practice slow."

"Got it."

When Glen turned back to the shooting platform to reload his magazines I took a long inhale and faced Shiloh's brother.

My first impression was he was a big motherfucker. My second was he looked like one pissed-off, mean, big motherfucker.

There was no mistaking he was Shiloh's brother. Same light blue eyes, same tanned skin tone, but unlike Shiloh, Echo had dark blond hair instead of Shiloh's honeyed.

Even if I hadn't expected him to show up I wouldn't've

missed the family resemblance. But I was expecting him. Truthfully, I was surprised it had taken him four days.

"Luke Marcou," he greeted.

"Echo Kent," I returned then continued. "Figured you'd be here sooner or later. I've got ten minutes left in the class. You can stay and wait or you can call the office and make an appointment with Lauren."

"I think I'll wait."

Right. Of course, he would.

"Great. Need you to wait behind the yellow line."

Echo glanced at the ground then back to me and jerked his chin. He moved beyond the range safety line without a word.

I clenched my jaw so fucking hard and remembered how Shiloh felt naked in my arms. Then I remembered the panic in her eyes when I told her we were going to be friends. And lastly, I remembered the relief I saw when I didn't leave. Relief so stark it pierced my heart and wounded my soul.

I fucking hated explaining myself.

Fifteen minutes later Glen was packed up and I was watching him walk back to the office.

I waited until he was a good distance away before I moved toward Echo.

"We need to talk about Sunny."

Not a great way for Echo to start but I held onto my patience and bit back a smartass retort. I didn't think Shiloh's brother was taking time out of his day to have a chat about the state of the world's economy.

"We do?"

"If you're fuc—"

"Respect, Echo, but if you finish that you and me are gonna have problems."

"Bigger ones than we have now?" he asked.

"Didn't know we had problems. But just to say, you showing up at my work, interrupting my class, staring me down like I'm a piece of shit, I was willing to overlook all that and give you time. You starting this conversation by disrespecting Shiloh, that I will not overlook. So, yeah, you trash-talk your sister we're gonna have bigger problems than we have now."

Echo narrowed his eyes and did his best to puff out his chest. I had to admit, the motherfucker was a Hulk. I wouldn't come out unscathed if we went to blows. But if he thought he could intimidate me like a pussy he was sadly mistaken.

"You got some fuckin' balls—"

"Seriously? You really wanna talk about the size of my balls? You wanna grab a ruler and measure my cock, too? Or do you wanna get down to what's on your mind? I'll help you out and start by repeating what I told River. I don't respond well to threats. You can make 'em and I'll respond by telling you to shove 'em up your ass. I know what I got in Shiloh. I don't need you or your brothers educating me. I'm seeing Shiloh and I'm taking it slow. Not only for her, but for me, too. What we have is new, it's good, and as time goes on it'll get better. You have a problem with that, I don't fuckin' care. You wanna bitch and complain about me, go find one of your brothers or your boys and talk all the shit you want. But do it knowing you're a fuckin' dick for doing it. Because you don't know me. You don't know what I feel for Shiloh. And you have no goddamn clue where I plan on taking this. The last thing I'm gonna give you is this; if I wanted a quick fuck, I'd find easy. She's your sister so you have to know Shiloh is the opposite of easy."

When I was done Echo was staring at me like he was

ready to brawl. Which was going to suck; I was wearing my favorite white Squash Daddy tee. It was old and worn and I'd had it since my first deployment and on every one after that. Getting blood stains out was going to be a bitch and a half.

"Sunny's not easy?"

Out of everything I said, that was the last thing I thought Echo would home in on.

"Do you *know* your sister?"

"Come again?"

Maybe he didn't know his sister as well as he thought he did, and as much as I wanted to call him out on it something inside of me knew Shiloh would be right mad if I told him what she'd said about everyone leaving her.

Shiloh played the part of Sunny well. She had the teasing, light disposition down pat. But the woman was full of darkness and holes.

"Shiloh's a great many things, easy isn't one of them. Now, why are you here?"

"Wanted to size you up," he said and shrugged.

At least he was honest.

"Right. And you thought it best to do that while I was at work and piss me off in the process?"

"Actually, I was here to talk to Jason about an old case he worked when he was with the DEA. You being here was a bonus. Two birds and all that."

"Great. You get what you need or do you have more to say?"

"You gonna tell Sunny I was here?"

Was this guy for real?

"You're worried I'm gonna run and tattle to my woman that her big brother stopped by for a chat?" I didn't miss the way Echo's eyes flared when I called Shiloh my woman. Best for him to get used to it now. "Brother, as you said, I got balls. Seeing as I do, I don't tattle. But I also won't lie to her if she asks me straight out if you've been here. And if you gotta problem with her knowing then you should've thought twice before looking for me."

"Twice a month, Sundays, we get together for dinner. Next one's this weekend. I expect you there."

Seriously, who the hell did he think he was?

"Two things, you want me at your table, you *ask* me and I'd be happy to share a meal. This Sunday's TC's company picnic—Shiloh and I have plans. You and your brothers want to stop by that'd be cool. Carter ordered two huge-ass pigs to roast and I heard Addy and Quinn talking about needing an extra table for all the food so there'll be plenty. The invitation comes with a warning; when the Lenoxes, Walkers, Clarks, and McCoys get together anything goes. It will be bedlam. You're up for that and don't mind kids, come hungry."

Echo studied me a minute and gave me a chin lift.

"I think I might like you."

"That'd be good seeing as I'm falling in love with your sister and it'd suck I'd have to explain to her why her brother's got a black eye and I got blood on my tee."

I startled—actually jerked back when Echo Kent let out a roaring laugh. It was loud, it sounded menacing, and I wondered how many men he'd scared away from his sister using that maniacal cackle.

I'd venture to say all of them.

"Yeah, I think I like you. Which is gonna suck if I have to break you if you hurt my sister."

"Just couldn't help yourself, could you?"

"Something you'll learn. I love my sister more than anything else. More than River. More than Phoenix. More than my own life. I will fight and die for her. That girl's had enough heartache and I'll make damn sure she never feels it again. If you can survive her Killer Frost freeze-out then you'll understand where I'm coming from. And if after *that* you learn what she's been through, if you think what I'm saying is a threat and for the promise it is, then you aren't very smart."

There it was. He knew his sister.

"She tried the freeze-out," I told him. "Landed a few good hits when she was throwing her barbs. Had me so fucking pissed I walked out. Sat in my truck and caught on to her play, walked back into her house. She was surprised I came back and told me everyone leaves. She learned fast how I am and I suspect you will, too, I'm not gonna be one more person in the long line of people who she's successfully pushed away. And she straight out told me she does that, too. So the threat isn't necessary."

"She told you that?"

"She's told me a variety of things I won't be sharing with you. When I told you I knew Shiloh wasn't easy, what I meant was, I know she's shit scared and I'm doing everything I can to move us forward in the least painful way possible. To clear something up, I'm not stupid. I know I haven't seen the last of Killer Frost. I'm just not gonna play her game. We're playing mine and doing it with the finish line in sight."

"And her nightmares?"

"I'm not breaking the trust I'm building and I hope you can appreciate why that is and leave it there."

"Fuck," Echo grunted and shook his head. "She got up in my shit last night before the takedown. When I asked her about you, thought she was gonna punch me or alternately shoot me. I should know better than to pick a fight with her when she's armed. Though FYI, she's got a mean right hook."

I doubted Echo asked about me. He likely gave her shit which led to her returning the favor.

"You gave her shit before she had to kick in a door?"

Fuck no. Hell to the no. Shiloh didn't need that shit when she needed her head straight.

Echo gave me a placating hand gesture that did not do a single thing to calm my anger.

"She'd been dodging me. It was the first chance I got to see her."

"I think you're beginning to get a read on who I am. But just in case I'll let you in more. I don't give the first fuck you're her brother, don't ever pull that bullshit with her again. Especially right now. She was almost asleep last night when she got that call out. She's fucking exhausted and needs to keep sharp, not you pissing her off and making it more difficult."

"Yeah, Luke, I'm reading you clear."

That was the best I was going to get and I wanted this over so I could get back to work.

"I got shit to do. Hope to see you Sunday."

"You will."

"Later."

I started back toward the office when Echo called my name. I turned, and gone was the pissed off, mean, big motherfucker, and in his place was a man who loved his sister.

"'Preciate you taking the time to talk to me."

"Any time. But it'd be best if you called next time. If you want, I'll get your number from Jason and send you mine so you have it."

"I want that."

Fucking Echo Kent.

He loved his sister, and like his sister, he was open when he wasn't being a dick.

I was at my desk shuffling papers and getting ready to leave when my cell beeped with a text.

How do you feel about fish? That was Shiloh to me.

I'm unclear how to answer that. Cooked fish, yes. Raw fish, hell no. Fish smell, that's a hard pass. Fish in a tank, as long as it's saltwater. Catching fish with a pole, yes as long as it's warm outside and I have a cold beer in hand. That was me back to Shiloh.

Apparently, my response required a call because it was now ringing in my hand with Shiloh's name on the screen.

"Shil—"

"You don't like sushi?"

"Before I answer that are you one of those people who think it's a challenge to get someone to eat something they say they don't like?"

"No."

"Thank fuck," I muttered and Shiloh giggled.

Not her husky laugh, not an amused chuckle, the woman giggled like she was happy.

My shoulders hunched and my head dropped forward while I soaked in every last second of the sound.

"I'm happy to finally meet someone else who doesn't like it. I feel like sushi is trending and I'm left out because the thought of raw fish makes me gag."

"Hates it," I corrected. "My dislike can be categorized as hate."

"Awesome. Then I can scratch that off my list of worries."

Shiloh made a "phew" sound and I could picture her wiping her brow in mock relief.

"Why are you asking about fish?"

"Some of the guys were talking about going to LuLu's after shift then hitting miniature golf. I was going to ask if you wanted to change our plans tonight and go out with them. But the only decent thing on the menu is fish. So if you hated fish I was gonna bag off and head home."

My neck tensed and my eyes closed. A one-two punch to my gut that winded me yet it felt far from bad. As a matter of fact, it felt so fucking good as the oxygen left my lungs it scared the shit out of me.

I vaguely wondered if she knew what she was doing. The invite was a nice surprise, her wanting me to meet her friends—though she'd deny they were friends—a welcomed surprise. But it was more than that; she was putting herself out there in front of the men she worked with.

"Sure. I'll meet you at your house and we'll go from there."

My response was met with silence.

"Shiloh?"

"Can we meet at your house?"

My gaze went to my key ring on my desk and I immediately spied the key to her front door. She hadn't asked for it back and I had offered. The last three nights we'd been at her place. I liked that it was me who left. The ball was in my court how late I stayed and the first two nights I'd pushed that until she was yawning and I knew she was ready to fall asleep. Last night I'd only left when I did because she was called out.

Shiloh at my place meant she could leave when she

wanted, as early as she wanted, and that didn't fit into my plan.

Yet I didn't deny her request.

"I'll text you my address."

"Great."

I heard someone call her name and she sighed.

"Sorry. I've gotta go. I'll see you later."

"Yeah, baby, you will."

Shiloh disconnected and I sat wondering what had brought on her sudden change. Then I sat there longer wondering if this was the warm feel-good breeze before the freeze-out.

Sunny Kent versus Killer Frost.

Polar opposites packed into one beautiful woman.

I'd be damn fortunate to come out on the other side unscathed.

12

I wiped my sweaty palms on my jeans and took a calming breath.

I was being ridiculous.

I lifted my now dry yet still clammy hand up and pressed Luke's doorbell.

And as I waited for him to answer the door I realized I'd need more than a breath to stop my heart from pounding in my chest.

I wasn't sure if my bout of nerves came from inviting Luke out with the guys or inviting myself over to his house.

For some reason, this seemed like a big step. I suppose him meeting my team was big—huge actually. I'd never brought a man around them—actually, I'd never brought anyone around them, male or female.

But going to his house felt bigger. Like I was stepping into his world instead of him being in mine. His personal space. And I'd invited myself over, which was kind of rude, and weird I'd even ask. But I was curious. I wanted to see where he lived. I wanted to see him move around in his space. I wanted to see his things.

My gaze took in his front yard and I was surprised to see neat, tidy shrubs lining his walk. Those shrubs continued into a mulched bed—no flowers just trimmed bushes—in front of his porch. Luke also had the greenest grass on his block. His house was the last one on the street in an established, older neighborhood. All of the houses were well-kept. Not huge two-story homes, but good-sized ranchers. Middle income, nice, kid-friendly, family homes.

I didn't know why this surprised me but it did.

All too soon Luke opened the door. The first thing I noticed was his hair was wet and that tingle started. Only this time was better since I had firsthand knowledge of how awesome he looked naked. My second thought was it sucked he hadn't waited and asked me to join him.

"Hey," Luke greeted.

That was all he needed to say for the dam to break and my verbal vomit to spew all over his front porch.

"I'm nervous about being here. I'm scared you're gonna meet the guys and I'm wondering if it's too soon but it's too late to back out without me catching shit at work since they know you're coming. And I'm really sorry if inviting myself to your pad was rude."

When I was done Luke did a slow blink then he smiled.

Yikes.

Luke was a good-looking man but when he smiled I felt the need to fan my face. Luckily I refrained from further embarrassing myself.

"Why don't you come in?" he asked and stepped aside.

"Are you sure? I was rude—"

"Babe. Come in."

I guessed he wasn't mad at me for inviting myself over.

Good to know.

I stepped in and while he was closing the door I took in

his house. One big open space—big living room, a dining room beyond that. To the back and left an open kitchen with a bar and kick-ass stools that separated the dining from the kitchen. A rectangle oak dinner table that sat six. A brown, slouchy leather sectional divided the dining and living rooms. A huge TV mounted on the wall, under it a handsome wood credenza devoid of clutter. And there was a hallway to the right.

It was not a pad, it was a home. Warm and inviting. Rich browns and taupes. No bold or bright accents.

Mellow. Like the man himself.

"Your place is nice," I told him.

"Thanks."

His lips twitched and I gave him squinty eyes.

"I'm giving you a compliment," I told him.

"I know you are."

"Then why do you look like you're trying not to laugh at me?"

"Because you looked shocked I don't live in a sty."

Well, he kind of had me there. I was shocked but not because I thought he'd live like a pig. I was surprised he lived in what looked like a family home.

Then it hit me—I didn't know him very well. Maybe he did have a family.

"Do you have kids?"

"Nope. No kids, never been married, never been engaged, never lived with a woman."

I was fairly certain it made me a bitch but I was happy he didn't have kids and he'd never been married, engaged, or lived with a woman.

"Do you have roommates?"

"Nope. But that's not to say that Matt and or Logan don't crash here if they've tied one on and can't drive home."

I'd met Matt and Logan in passing the times I'd been to Triple Canopy but I didn't know either of them.

"So just you," I lamely noted. "How many bedrooms?"

"Why? You wanna christen them?"

"No." I tried to sound irritated but I was pretty sure my lie came out breathy.

"Three," Luke answered through a wide smile. "But only two have beds, the third's junked up with gear."

Luke didn't strike me as a man who kept his gear in disarray and judging by how clean the rest of his house was I seriously doubted his idea of "junked" and mine were the same.

"You must think I'm a total slob."

"What?"

"Dude, your house is spic and span. It looks like it's been staged to sell. There's not even a pile of mail on the bar top. Nothing. Just clean."

"Dude?" He chuckled.

"Yes, *dude*," I returned. "I wasn't thinking much about you seeing the state of my house that first night because you're a *dude*. But now I'm thinking I should be embarrassed or maybe a little ashamed you saw my collection of dust bunnies."

"I don't clean this place, Cathy does. It looks like this because today's cleaning day. I leave for work, she shows, and like magic when I come home it's spic and span."

Huh. Maybe I needed to invest in a Cathy. My house magically clean when I got home sounded like heaven.

"If you want I'll give you her number," Luke said as if he was reading my mind.

"How'd you know that's what I was thinking?"

"You got this dreamy look about you. So either you were thinking about Cathy working her magic at your place or you were back to thinking about christening the bedrooms. For my peace of mind, I'm going with Cathy. Though I could swing the other way if you're feeling like taking a tour."

I was seriously thinking about taking a tour. A tour of his bedroom ending with us christening his room sounded better than coming home to a clean house.

Luke's shoulders started rocking with silent laughter and a beat later the silence went away and his jagged, rough laugh hit my ears.

God, I loved the way he laughed. Straight from the belly like he was sucking all the good stuff life had to offer right out of the air.

"Since you're not a woman you can't know this so I'll explain," I started. "It's a toss-up—a spotless house you didn't have to lift a finger to clean or an orgasm."

"You're wrong. It's not a toss-up. You gotta man who can give it to you good, the orgasms always win out."

"You're probably right," I muttered.

"I know I'm right."

My eyes squinted again and my hands went to my hips in the universal silent language of women all around the world who wanted to throw attitude but do it nonverbally.

"I'm not wrong," Luke continued.

"I know you're not."

"Then why do you look like you're getting ready to bust my balls for being right?"

"Because it sucks you're right. But it sucks more I don't know how right you are since I've never had a man who could give it good enough I wouldn't think it was a toss-up between a clean house and an orgasm."

"Fuck. You didn't tell me that," Luke accused.

He was matching my stare, narrowed eyes and all.

"What are you talking about?"

"The night you were drunk," he reminded me and I groaned.

For days I had successfully pushed that night out of my mind. I didn't want to give any headspace to the things I'd said. I was positive I'd told him too much. All of it would be embarrassing.

"I'm never drinking with you again."

"Yeah, you are."

"No, Luke, I'm on the wagon. I talk too much when I drink and apparently my tongue gets loose when I'm blotto. So no more drinking—ever."

"I'm looking forward to seeing what you can do with your tongue, baby, but you'll be sober when that happens. You don't talk too much when you're drunk, you just forget to electrify your walls. You're totally open. But that's not why I wanna see you drunk again. Normally you're funny, a few drinks in and you're gut-busting hilarious. Never laughed so hard in my entire life as I did listening to you that night."

Great, so now I was merely funny sober but gut-busting when I was making a fool out of myself.

Whatever.

Moving on.

"We should leave. Gordy's already waiting for us at LuLu's and the rest won't be far behind. But before we leave I need to warn you; the guys take miniature golf to a whole new level. And don't feel inclined to join in when the bets are placed. Actually, don't join in. It can get ugly. All of them are sore losers."

"Do I need to grab a wad of cash out of my safe?"

"Um, did you miss the part where I said not to join in when the bets are placed? And besides, they play with quarters. The most they lose is like three bucks. It's not about the money, it's a pride thing. The first time I won I learned the hard way that it wasn't worth the bitching and moaning for days after. Now I throw the game on purpose."

"You throw the game?"

"Hell yeah. Their fragile little egos can't take that I'm better than they are."

Luke stared at me a beat then stepped close and I realized we were still mostly standing in his entryway. This wasn't a faux pas on his part; I'd simply started blathering before we'd made it into the house then continued before he could invite me in farther.

"Do you really think that?"

"Yeah. And you'll see later how competitive they are and how the winner gets razzed the rest of the night."

Something strange came over Luke, something I didn't get, and his next inquiry confused me more.

"You strapped?"

"Come again?"

"You packin'?"

"Of course."

I almost always carried; on and off duty I rarely went without my sidearm.

"Let me lock it up."

"Why?"

"Because tonight you're gonna throw a few back and I don't want your weapon to be your excuse."

"Luke—"

"Listen to me, Shiloh," he interrupted. "Tonight you're gonna relax, have a few beers, enjoy the company of the men you work with, and you're gonna learn something."

I wasn't a fan of being told what to do. Echo called it oppositional defiance. River called it being hardheaded. Phoenix called it a pain in his ass. And my captain called it disobedience. Luckily, I mostly listened to my captain so he didn't get in my face often. I'd never disobeyed a direct order. I just played fast and loose with the definition of 'direct.'

What could I say? I was raised by three alpha men who thought their sole mission in life was to boss me around when I hit adulthood. I was basically feral.

"How about we learn something right now? That being, my least favorite thing is being told what I'm gonna do."

Luke's lips curved into a cocky smile and he didn't miss a beat when he said, "Given the right time and circumstances, I think you'd very much enjoy being told what to do."

"Well, playboy, I can safely tell you right now is not one of those times."

"Right, then how about this?" Luke paused and the cocky left his smile and he gave me a sad smile. "You've had a rough week, have a few drinks and relax."

"I don't need to drink to relax."

"You're absolutely right you don't. I know of far better ways to relax you. Unfortunately, those aren't on the table and you're wound up tight. You don't wanna have a drink, fine, but do me a favor? Tonight don't throw the game, kick their asses. And tomorrow when they're giving you shit about it? Pay attention—they're not giving you shit because of ego. They're not complaining. They're pulling you in. That's what a team does. That's friendship. That's camaraderie. Having something to talk about."

I was stuck back on the better ways he could relax me and why those were off the table. Luke had stated plain we were special friends. I'd kind of hoped the special part of that meant more of what had happened in the bathtub.

"Shiloh," he growled and I blinked.

"Huh?"

Luke blew out a frustrated breath.

"You're *killing* me."

I did another slow blink. His groan indeed sounded like I was killing him. When my lids fluttered open Luke was in my space. His hands went to my face and I couldn't remember a time I'd been touched so gently.

"Pay attention to this part, yeah?"

His question was strange but I couldn't focus on that when his face was getting closer...and closer...then his lips were on mine.

Feather soft.

Chaste, yet the sexiest kiss I'd ever had.

Luke's tongue came out and grazed my bottom lip. Mine came out and trailed behind his. There was something so weirdly intimate about the whole thing and it turned into something more when the tip of his tongue touched mine.

Then he pulled away and it was over.

Just a touch of tongues.

So slight that I could convince myself it never happened.

But it did.

What was that?

Luke's hands dropped from my face and he murmured, "We better get on the road."

His quiet words pulled me from my haze.

"Yeah."

"I'll drive," he told me and tagged my hand.

Next thing I knew we were in his truck and he was backing out of his driveway.

What just happened?

13

Shiloh hadn't lied; she was oddly good at miniature golf. She was also hilariously sexy every time her ass wiggled when she sank a ball under par. It was becoming increasingly difficult to remember four members of her team were with us, especially when she smiled brightly and looked totally carefree. I, of course, now knew that was a façade. But she was goddamn stunning in her charade.

Dinner at LuLu's had gone as I'd expected. The inquisition had started as soon as my ass sat down. A man called Gordy took the lead and immediately started grilling me. It wasn't aggressive but it was assessing. Much like I'd done when I had my run-in with River and Echo, I reminded myself that these men cared about Shiloh and I set aside my anger. They were simply looking out for her.

Shiloh might've told me she didn't have friends but that was untrue. Not that she lied—it was like she had a mental block when it came to the word *friend*. The men she worked with respected her, treated her like she was one of them without reservation. They joked and teased her the same way they did each other. The same I did with my team. It was Shiloh who held herself apart. Yet she did it in a friendly way. It was the oddest shit I'd ever seen and before I'd witnessed it firsthand I would've said it was impossible to be friendly and distant at the same time, but Shiloh pulled it off.

So there I was standing at the seventeenth hole of the game, one Shiloh was going to win by a long shot. She was dancing around smiling, the guys around us were giving her shit, and she was completely fucking oblivious to what she meant to them when she should've known down to her bones these men cared for her. They didn't hide it.

Shiloh's ball slowly rolled into the cup, her second putt on a par four hole. Her head came up, her gaze slid through the men watching and stopped when it reached mine and she smiled.

Fuck, she was gorgeous.

"I don't know how you're doing it but you're cheating," Chip boomed.

Earlier I'd learned that Chip's name was Allen. But he'd earned the nickname Chip after he took an elbow to the mouth during a takedown, chipping his front tooth. He'd refused to get it fixed. As the story went the suspect was nearly seven feet tall and three hundred pounds. Chip was five-nine and maybe one-eighty. Further, the story went Chip had taken the guy down by himself, thus keeping the chipped tooth was a reminder he was a badass. The story sounded like a fish-tale if I ever heard one but I said nothing at the exaggeration.

"I'm not a cheat," Shiloh retorted, with mock affront.

"It's his fault." Andy pointed to me. "She's showing off for her man."

I'd put two and two together and figured out Andy was Andy Riddle, the Head and Shoulders shampoo guy.

"Why does it have to be someone's fault? Admit it, I'm better than you," she went on.

"Stop bitching and take your shot so we can move on," Valentine called from the green. "I got shit to do."

"Is that what you're calling your dating life now, shit?" Gordy put it. "I keep telling you those apps don't work, brother. It's best to meet a woman the old-fashioned way."

"Listen, old man, I know this is a hard concept for you seeing as you got married in the Dark Ages before the internet was invented but I'm not interested in trading sheep for a bride. I don't want a bride, I want a..." Valentine paused, looked at Shiloh, then went on. "Fun. I'm just looking for fun."

Something I'd noticed, all of the guys teased and joked amongst themselves and with Shiloh and she returned the jabs. But she didn't tease with them the way she did with me. There were no flirty undertones, no innuendo, and the men went to great lengths to keep their comments clean. There was plenty of shit-talk—they cursed in front of her— but the topic of sex or anything that could make her or them uncomfortable was clearly avoided.

Gordy flipped Valentine off then swung his putter, taking his shot. Once his ball circled the hole and dropped in he addressed the crowd.

"That's your problem. You think keeping your sheep is the fun part."

"Someone, anyone, please take their turn before we get the twenty years of marriage sermon again," Chip groaned.

"Right," Gordy drawled. "Yet I'm the only one going home to a woman tonight. The rest of you are gonna be sliding into cold sheets thinking about how Sunny kicked your asses and I'm sliding into...beauty."

I had no idea what Gordy's wife looked like but I figured he was telling the truth.

My gaze went to Shiloh and she was staring at Gordy with a soft look. It wasn't lost on me she was closest to Gordy. He was the oldest of the bunch and it was obvious he had a soft spot for her.

"Well, since I'm winning I'm moving on to the next hole."

That comment earned her groans but not a single one made an inappropriate comeback.

I had to say I was impressed; I'd barely bitten mine back. Though I'd have the opportunity later when she slid between my sheets to whisper all the pent-up inappropriate thoughts I'd bottled up.

By the time Shiloh and I were in my truck heading back to my place, it was late. The mood was mellow but my thoughts were heavy. The night had gone great. Shiloh kicked ass and had fun rubbing it in at the end of the game. But she still didn't get it. Which made no fucking sense. She dished it out, she had three older brothers who undoubtedly ribbed her, but when the guys reciprocated it was like she wasn't sure if they were being mean or joking.

I couldn't understand this.

It was bizarre the way she watched them.

"Thanks for coming with me tonight." Shiloh broke the silence as I pulled into my driveway.

"It was a good time. Thanks for asking," I told her.

I cut the engine and before I could ask her to come in she finally addressed what happened before we left my house.

"Earlier you kissed me."

"That wasn't a kiss, baby."

"Um." She pinched her lips and arched her brow. "Your mouth touched mine, you licked my lip, and our tongues touched. I think that's the definition of a kiss."

Fuck, she was cute.

"Nope. Not even close."

"Okay, then what was it?"

"That was my way of ending a conversation."

"I don't remember what we were talking about," she admitted.

"Exactly."

"You're a very weird man, Luke."

"I'm not. What I am is a man who knows his limits. And you standing in my house looking at me like you wanted me to take you to my bed and show you how much you'd enjoy me bossing you around was pushing me to the brink."

All of that was the truth. The part I left out was I'd been dying to get my mouth on hers. The problem was as soon as that happened, I knew I couldn't kiss her the way I wanted or we would miss dinner and mini-golf. So I ended it before it began.

"So you kissed me?"

"Again, that wasn't a kiss."

"And again, it sure felt like one."

I had nothing to say to that so I remained silent and so did Shiloh. And there we sat in my truck in the dark staring at each other—eyes locked, both of us willing the other to look away. She felt it the same as I did. I knew it by the way her lips parted. With each second that ticked by the air was growing thicker, the tension growing stronger. The safe thing would've been to get my ass out of the truck and walk her to her car. Yet I couldn't find it in me to move and I was pleased as fuck she was right where I was—caught deep in a moment that felt so fucking right.

My eyes dropped to her mouth as the tip of Shiloh's tongue wet her bottom lip.

That was when my self-control splintered.

But when she whispered, "What's happening?" That was when it cracked.

"You know what's happening."

Our eyes met again and I wasn't sure who moved first. Our mouths collided, my tongue surged in, hers met mine in a slow glide, and she moaned. My hands slid into her hair, gathering it as I went until I had two handfuls of sleek, shiny softness wrapped around my fists. Her hands went to my chest and they roamed.

Fuck. Yes.

I took the kiss deeper and groaned again. I did this until her hands turned frantic and started yanking at my shirt. I was not fucking her in my truck in my driveway.

With unholy effort, I broke the kiss. Her eyes slowly came open and she smiled.

"That's a kiss," she whispered against my lips.

"Yeah, baby, that's a kiss."

And it tasted like heaven. But I was keeping that part to myself.

"Are you gonna invite me inside?"

"No."

"You're not?"

"Nope. I'm gonna put you in your car and send you home."

Shiloh stiffened and jerked her head back. I loosened my hands in her hair and moved them to her shoulders, not ready to stop touching her but needing someplace safe to put my hands. Not that there was really a safe place anywhere on her body but her shoulders would have to do.

"Why?"

"Because if you come inside I'll be tempted to fuck you. Or I'll be *more* tempted to fuck you."

"I want—"

I leaned forward and pressed my lips to hers. I could not hear Shiloh tell me she wanted to fuck me. Not when my dick was hard and aching. Not after that kiss.

"Not yet," I told her.

"I thought...never mind."

She quickly righted herself in the seat, leaned forward, grabbed her purse from between her feet, and went for the door. She was out of the truck before I could stop her. I hopped out and met her at the hood of her car.

"Hey." I tagged her hand and she twirled to face me.

"Listen, Luke, I get it. We're...um...friends."

Baby, you don't know the meaning of friends.

"Yeah, Shiloh, we're friends. But we're also something else. And so all of this doesn't get twisted and fucked we're gonna take it slow."

"Slow? You call us naked in my bathtub with your hand between my legs slow?"

She has no clue how damn slow that was.

"When what I really wanted was to have you naked, not in your tub but on your bed, yeah that's slow. And when what I really wanted was my fingers in your pussy, not guiding yours but *inside* you, hell yeah that's slow. But really what I wanted most was my face between your legs knowing when you came it was my tongue that got you there, not my words. Now, you coming into my house when both of us are feeling the way we're feeling right now would not be smart.

No lie, Shiloh, I'd have you stripped naked in two seconds and I'd be tasting more than your mouth."

There wasn't much light coming from the streetlamps, but there was still enough illumination I could see her blue irises had darkened.

"You didn't like what we did?" she whispered.

"Fucking hell," I growled.

I gave her hand a yank until we were chest to chest. Shiloh's head tipped back and mine tipped down. When I had her attention I continued, "Baby, you were naked in my arms fingering yourself. Your ass was rubbing on my dick while you were working yourself up. I had your tit in my hand and I was toying with your nipple. If I liked it anymore I'd be dead. Just so you know, we're doing that again, but next time we're doing it where I can watch and I'll be joining you."

I felt Shiloh shiver and saw her eyes widen. Then I realized my mistake. I shouldn't have pressed my luck. Stubborn mixed in with desire and she smiled.

"Then let's do that now."

"Shiloh—"

"I'm not on birth control," she announced. "I don't have a condom with me. We'll take all of yours and throw them away or poke holes in them. That way even if we want to we can't go further."

She smiled and shrugged like she'd just solved all of our problems.

And maybe she had.

"I don't have condoms."

"Then what are you waiting for?"

Good fucking question.

14

"Luke," I whimpered and my back arched off the bed but my eyes stayed on him.

I was watching Luke and he was watching me.

This was after he'd stripped me naked two seconds after he'd locked his front door. After he'd tossed me onto the bed, told me to spread my legs, and made me watch him as he undressed. Once his chest came into view and without him having to tell me I started touching myself, this happened before his pants had hit the floor.

The good stuff started when he crawled into bed.

Unlike last night, he touched me while I touched myself. He instructed me to play with my nipples while he kissed the curve of my breast. He told me to play with my clit while he kissed my stomach and glided his fingertips along my inner thigh. Feeling Luke's tongue and hands on me while avoiding the places I really wanted them was a form of torture.

This went on a long time.

I squirmed.

I writhed.

I moaned.

And Luke watched and told me all of the things he was going to do to me.

Now he was sitting—ass to his calves between my legs, my thighs draped over his spread wide, and he was stroking his dick.

It was my turn to watch and I was getting distracted. My eyes were riveted, taking in his long, hard tugs. The way his stomach muscles tightened when his hand slid to the root. The bead of pre-come leaking from the head, the way he swiped the moisture away with his thumb. The sight before me was so incredible I could no longer concentrate on what I was supposed to be doing.

"Keep at your clit," he told me. I rolled my thumb harder and my hips jerked. "Fuck yeah, ride your fingers, baby, let me see you fuck yourself."

I did what I was told with my gaze glued on his hand stroking his cock. Like Luke had told me to do I was imagining what it would feel like with his thick cock inside of me. How good it would feel to be stretched. How hard and deep he was going to fuck me.

Luke shifted his hips, his right hand went to my thigh, and his fingertips grazed along the juncture of my leg, right where my panties would be if I'd been wearing some. Throughout this, he didn't stop stroking.

"I'm gonna fuck you just like this, Shiloh, back on my knees so I can watch my dick dip into your pussy and watch it come out wet."

I moaned.

Luke grunted.

"Whatever you want, honey," I panted.

"Right now, I wanna hear you make yourself come. Right

now I wanna watch you play with *my* pussy. Because I'm claiming it."

I was so close to giving him what he wanted, but just like last time, I needed more.

"I need you to touch me."

Luke shifted again, this time lowering his hand until the head of his dick was brushing the back of my hand between my legs.

"Oh, God."

My legs were trembling and I was closer.

"You like feeling my dick while I'm stroking it?"

"Yes," I hissed.

"You like knowing I'm gonna blow all over your belly?"

Holy shit.

I could take no more, I was so damn close, my orgasm right there. Right. There. Just out of reach. I needed it so bad. So damn bad my hips were thrusting up reaching for it.

"Please," I groaned. "I need—"

I didn't finish because suddenly Luke curved forward and dropped his mouth on my nipple and his tongue was swirling.

God, yes. That was what I needed.

Then his lips tightened and I felt his teeth scrape the sensitive bud. I felt his hand working his dick, the tip bumping my hand and I was gone.

Gone.

Washed away in complete bliss. My back arched and my pussy spasmed around my fingers.

"You want my come?" he growled and I shivered.

"Yes, I want your come. Now, Luke. I want it now."

"Fuck, baby, fuck," he groaned.

Then I felt a splash of warmth on my belly. He jerked back to his knees. My eyes opened and I watched as he finished himself off. Ropes of come shot onto my stomach and chest. With each one he grunted and with each one, I felt twinges of my climax persist.

When he was finished he dropped down and kissed me.

It was safe to say, I now understood what it meant to be kissed by Luke. It was fantastic. Deep and wet and commanding. By the time he ended the kiss my legs were wrapped around his hips and I was mewing.

I was ready to get up and drive to the store and buy condoms. Hell, I'd run there naked if I had to.

"Shower," he muttered.

"More," I returned.

His face dropped to my neck and he kissed me there.

God, I loved his mouth on me. Loved his hands, his body, his tongue. I just plain loved the feel of him.

"I see I've created a monster."

"Are you really complaining I wanna suck you off?"

"You didn't mention that part." I felt him smile against my throat. "You should've led with that."

"Alright, honey, how about this? After watching you stroke your dick, feeling it on my hand, I wanna feel it in my mouth. Does that work for you?"

"Only if you sit on my face while you're doing it."

"You're gonna give me more?"

This was surprising. A welcomed surprise, but I figured it would take some begging on my part for him to allow me to touch him.

"I'm gonna give you everything, Shiloh. Every-*fucking*-thing."

My body tingled and fear filled my lungs.

"But tonight I'm gonna eat your pussy until you beg me to stop. You wanna do that with my dick in your mouth, I'll give you that, too. You just wanna ride my face and enjoy it

I'll finish myself off when I'm done with you. But first, we're gonna take a shower so I'm not licking my come off your tits when I taste those, too."

The fear slid out and tingles took over, making my skin feel like it was electrified.

"I want you to finish in my mouth," I told him.

"Fuck," he groaned. "My dick's not even soft yet and you're getting me hard."

"Then we better hurry and shower so we can get down to it."

Luke was up and out of bed. I squealed when he yanked me up and dragged me to the bathroom. He had me in the shower before the water was warm and I squealed again when the icy water hit my back. He turned us so he was under the spray. Then he looked down at me, all the playfulness gone.

"You okay?"

"Were you not in the same bed as I was?"

"I know you got off on what we did. But are you okay?"

I wasn't sure what he was asking but I knew it was important to him so I stopped screwing around and started paying attention.

"With?"

"With us going out with your team, for starters."

"Yeah. Didn't you have a good time?"

"Already told you I had a good time, baby. What I'm asking is, are you okay with how tonight went?"

I was so confused and that confusion must've shown because finally, Luke got to the heart of his question and he did this with his arms around my waist and my hands resting on his chest.

"I like the way they are with you," Luke started. "Total respect. They have a mind to you being female but they don't treat you like an outsider. You're one of them—totally —but they curb some of the shit-talk. They're careful to keep the topic of sex off the table."

I scrunched my nose at that.

Gross.

The same way I didn't want to know what my brothers did with women, I didn't want to hear about the guys I worked with.

"Exactly." Luke smiled, catching my grimace. "With that being said, they don't hold back giving you shit. I liked that, too. I liked the way they didn't get carried away with it and when you gave it back, they took it and smiled. All of that is good. What isn't is you not understanding why they do it."

I was feeling the stiffness creep in, the unwanted fear, the itch on the back of my neck. Unfortunately, Luke kept going.

"You told me you didn't have friends, and, baby, that's just not true. Those men consider you a friend—"

"We work together." I cut him off, not liking where this was going. "They're acquaintances."

"No, Shiloh. They're your friends. If you called any of those men right now needing help they'd drop what they were doing and come help you. Well, maybe not Valentine, he seemed eager to get to his date, so right about now I'd say he was—"

"Gross. Please stop."

"Point is, that's what friends do. They stop what they're doing when a friend needs them. An acquaintance is someone you shoot the shit with when you happen to see them in passing. A teammate is someone who has your back when the vests are out and the guns are drawn. You seeing the difference?"

I was getting pissed. I wasn't stupid. I knew *what* a friend was. I just didn't have any.

"I'm not dumb."

"Didn't say you were. What I'm saying is you lied when you told me you didn't have friends. And I'm seeing you didn't lie on purpose but it doesn't make it any less untrue. Those men are your friends. They're reaching out to you, trying to grab hold, and you're holding yourself back. And that shit's not right. And it's really not right because I know you'd take a bullet for any one of those men but you wouldn't invite them to your house for dinner or call them if you had a flat."

Fear was turning into anger, and as hard as I wanted to stop it I couldn't. I felt it coming on—ugly and mean—choking me as it slid up my throat preparing to strike.

"I can change my own damn tire, Luke. I'm not a fucking—"

"Shiloh, look at me."

"I am," I snapped. "I'm looking right at you, unclear why we're talking about this shit."

Luke's face lowered and my breath caught.

"Hear this—you can dim your light and turn up the frost, but, baby, I'm still not going anywhere. You wanna lash out and get pissed, you're gonna do it naked in my arms knowing when you burn yourself out you're crawling back into my bed. You wanna throw up your defenses and dial up the bitch thinking it's gonna make me push you away—do your worst. I've got your number, Shiloh. Make your plays, hide behind whatever bullshit you can dream up. I'll wait you out. I'll tunnel in. I'll climb over. I'll bulldoze through. Don't matter to me because at the end of the day I'm gonna outplay you and win."

None of that sounded good. None of it sounded fun.

What it sounded like was agony. No, worse than agony. It sounded like determination.

One of Luke's hands slid up my spine to the back of my neck then around to the front and up again until he cupped my cheek in his big palm.

"What you have to trust is while you're making your plays and I'm making mine you're safe. Totally safe."

"I won't be safe if you push me on this. I like the way my life is."

"I didn't say it wasn't gonna be uncomfortable, but you'll be safe."

"I don't want this."

Luke's face gentled and his thumb stroked my cheek.

"I'd believe that, Shiloh, if it wasn't such a goddamn lie. And I know it's a lie because the night I came back into your house, the relief I saw in your pretty eyes, gutted me. I'd believe you if you hadn't invited me to meet the guys tonight. I've decided I'm not listening to the things you say but the things you do. And everything you're doing is pulling me closer."

I had nothing to say to that because he was right. What the hell was wrong with me?

"Now, I'm gonna clean you up so we can get back into bed and get dirty again."

"I'm no longer in the mood."

Luke's kissable lips tipped up into a smug grin. The seriousness slid out of his eyes and the playfulness returned.

"Right. You will be when you're sitting on my face and I'm tongue-fucking your pussy."

I squinted my eyes and his smile widened.

After that Luke cleaned us up and took us to bed. I didn't sit on his face, not right away. First, he took his time working me up, his mouth on mine while his hands explored. When he had me begging and whining *then* he sat me on his face. I held onto the headboard and shouted my orgasm. Throughout this, Luke didn't let me touch him.

It was the best orgasm of my life, even if fear was licking up my spine, chasing away the pleasure.

Five minutes later, I fell asleep lying half on top of Luke.

I didn't dream of hostages being shot and fathers breaking down.

I dreamed of tremendous pain and loss.

Mine.

When Luke walked away.

15

"Shake a leg!" I yelled once I heard the blow dryer go off.

"I would if you'd tell me where we're going."

This was a huge gamble. One that could backfire on me big time. But after our conversation in the shower after mini-golf, I decided to play it cool for a few days and avoid all heavy topics. I'd also added orgasms. Lots of fucking orgasms—minus the fucking. I hadn't lifted the ban on sex or blowjobs but Shiloh'd jerked me off brilliantly several times. Mostly while I had her tits in my hands and a nipple in my mouth, though sometimes I switched it up and fingered her while she stroked. She'd spent two nights at my house and I'd spent last night at hers. This was strategic. I wanted her to wake up this morning in her bed so I could get her up and dressed for the picnic she didn't know she was attending.

Tonight if she didn't pitch a holy shit-fit we'd be back at mine. If she did I'd follow her back to her place, we'd have it out, then I'd sleep in her bed. Either way, we'd be sleeping together.

Three nights I'd slept next to her and just like I knew it

would happen, I was addicted. Tangled tight and I was taking her along with me.

"It's a surprise," I told her.

"I don't like surprises."

"Too bad."

The bathroom door swung open and out she came in nothing but a bra and panties. Her hand went to her hip and my gaze dropped, took in the cherry red lace, and I bit back a groan. Something new I learned about Shiloh—under her work cargos and tactical vest she wore unbelievably sexy bras and panties. I couldn't say I'd paid attention the first night I got her naked for the bath. I was more interested in her soft skin and the way she smelled. The second time I got her naked I was in a rush and discarded her clothes at record speed. But the next two times, I'd taken my time and discovered her girly, lacy underthings. And just like her hot pink toenails, knowing she was hiding a sexy secret under her uniform did crazy things to my dick.

Another new development—Shiloh was completely comfortable walking around naked in front of me. Not since that very first time had she shown any uneasiness. This fucking thrilled me.

"Are you sure you don't want to just run out, grab some lunch, and stop by the store to pick up a box of condoms?"

I had condoms in my truck. I'd bought some yesterday, which was kind of like tempting Satan with your soul, but I hadn't brought them into the house. So luckily, last night I'd managed to occupy my time dispensing orgasms until Shiloh passed out.

"That's the plan."

Shiloh eyed me suspiciously then asked, "Why do I feel like you're not telling me something?"

Fuck.

"Because there's a lot I'm not telling you. Which, just to say, if you'd move your sweet ass and get dressed I wouldn't have to tell you anything—I could show you."

"You think I have a sweet ass?"

The smirk accompanying her question told me she knew I did but I answered anyway.

"Your ass is definitely sweet but your pussy's sweeter. And tonight I'd like to get better acquainted with it. So please, baby, I'm begging you to get dressed so we can get the hell out of your house before I forget we have plans today and I go out to my truck, get the box of condoms, and we start now seeing how many we can blow through before you gotta be at work tomorrow."

"What? You bought condoms and didn't tell me?"

"Yep."

Shiloh's eyes narrowed.

"Not cool, *friend*, not cool."

Fuck, she was cute when she pouted.

"You gonna get dressed?"

"Are you planning on bringing in your condoms when we get back?"

"Yes." I chuckled.

"Fine. I'll get dressed."

Shiloh stomped to her closet and once I lost sight of her sweet ass I busted out laughing.

"You mad?" I unnecessarily asked.

Anger had been rolling off Shiloh from the second she got out of my truck and realized what was going on.

"Furious."

"Right, then since you're already pissed—"

"Furious," she corrected.

"Since you're furious I should tell you now I invited your brothers."

"You did what?"

Shiloh rocked to a halt and I stopped next to her, pleased as fuck she'd locked her sidearm in her safe before we'd left her house. She didn't look furious. She looked like she was ready to cause bodily damage.

"Echo invited me to Sunday dinner at his place. I told him we couldn't make it to dinner because of the picnic and invited him and the others to join us here."

"Echo invited you to dinner?"

"Yep."

"Yep?" she parroted.

"Are you planning on repeating everything I say?"

Wrong thing to say.

"I don't know, Luke, are you gonna tell me when you had the occasion to speak to my brother? Or better yet tell me why the fuck you didn't tell me you talked to him? No, wait, before you do that, explain to me why the hell you didn't ask me if I wanted to come to your company picnic."

"Echo was here to talk to Jason. When he was done he felt like having words with me. We had them, then he asked me to dinner. I didn't tell you about the conversation because as much as it might piss you off—or infuriate you more—straight-up it's not your business. Your brother had something to say and what he said is between him and me and will stay that way. And I didn't ask you if you wanted to come to the picnic because I wasn't going to risk you saying no."

"You...you...you..." she sputtered and stopped. "I don't know what to say."

"Nothing to say. We're here. There're tables full of food.

Good company all around. Most of the people here you already know. Your brothers will be here soon. We'll hang with them awhile then go home."

"I can't believe you did this," she whispered.

I stood and watched emotions chasing each other across her face. One after another. I'd seen them on her before. Uncertainty, hesitation, insecurity. None of them I'd seen since that first argument so I'd forgotten.

Fuck.

I hauled her close and wrapped one arm around her lower back and placed my other hand on her cheek. It took two beats for her to do what she always did when I cupped her cheek. When I felt her nuzzle my palm, I explained.

"I want you to have this, baby, and I was afraid you wouldn't allow yourself to come. I also didn't want you thinking on it and stressing out. If it's too much for you we'll leave and you can text Echo and tell him we're not gonna be here though your brothers are still welcome."

"You lied."

"I didn't lie. I just didn't tell you we were coming to TC for lunch."

Stubborn shifted into her features and her forehead wrinkled.

"Fine. Though for future reference you not telling me something is the same as lying. I don't like shit hidden from me."

Future.

At that, I let out a breath.

"Noted."

"But we're still talking about my brothers."

"No, we're not. I said all I'm gonna say about that."

"They're my family—all I have." My body froze and my chest began to ache. "So they're my business."

Fuck me.

"Shiloh, baby, please trust me on this. Echo was doing what he needed to do. It's all good."

"I want to know."

She didn't want to know that her brother had come at me like a dick. Her head would likely pop off and spin around in a circle.

I dropped my forehead to hers and held her tighter.

"All you need to know is it ended well enough that he invited me to his house for dinner."

"Likely to poison you. Which is what I'm gonna do tonight if you don't tell me."

It was then I realized she was being cute. She wasn't pitching a shit-fit which she had every right to pitch. I had tricked her into coming to a picnic I knew she'd try to get out of. Further, she was right that her family was her business. It was just that I wasn't going to snitch on her overprotective brother.

She was also being funny, cracking jokes.

It was all good even if she was going to hold on to her stubbornness.

"Are you smiling?"

I hadn't realized I had been but since she asked I guess I was.

"Yep."

"I'm not smiling," she snapped.

"No, Shiloh, you're not smiling."

"Then why are you?"

I couldn't stop it, though I tried really hard.

"Are you laughing?" she growled.

Fucking shit, she was cute.

"Yep."

"Why are you laughing?"

Another growl.

Fuck, I couldn't hold it back. I tilted my head back, crushed her to my chest, and burst out laughing until I felt her arms slide around me and squeeze.

"You owe me huge," she mumbled against my chest. "Tonight we're going three-to-one odds."

"Three-to-one odds?" I asked.

"You owe me three orgasms for every one of yours."

I burst out laughing again and this time Shiloh joined me.

Oh, yeah, everything was just fucking fine.

16

"Am I interrupting?" Phoenix asked.

No, actually he didn't ask; he simply interrupted and did it snidely.

"You are," I told him without lifting my cheek from Luke's chest.

"Babe," Luke rumbled.

"For fuck's sake, you mind taking your hands off my sister?" That was Phoenix again.

Luke's body went still.

Shit.

We were off to the side, not yet in the middle of the festivities, but the tables and people milling about weren't far. And when Luke and I had walked around Triple Canopy's main building I'd noticed kids were running around.

Not the time or the place for me to get into a smackdown with my brother. It also wouldn't be good if Luke kicked his ass. Though Phoenix was being a jerk so I figured I'd let Luke get in two good hits before I pulled them apart.

"There're kids here. I'd appreciate you watching your mouth," Luke rumbled.

At that point, I felt it prudent to intervene. I pushed off Luke's chest but only far enough to slip one arm behind his back and place the other around his abs.

I was making a statement—one Phoenix didn't miss.

"I'd appreciate—"

"Knock it off," I seethed. "And you're lucky there are kids around or I'd step away and let Luke handle you."

"Babe," Luke rumbled again. "Thought we talked about this."

"No, you asked me not to use you to egg my brothers on. This is not that. This is me telling Phoenix he's so far out of line it's not funny. You caught it from River, which I kinda understand because we took him off-guard. Echo heard about it and sought you out. That was way uncool. But Phoenix, he knows River and Echo already went at you, yet here he is acting a fool for no reason. He didn't walk up and introduce himself like a normal human being. He didn't say hello to his sister and offer brotherly love. Nope, he walked up, interrupted us, then proceeded to be a *jerk*. And that's fucked."

I lowered the *fucked* part to a whisper but Phoenix still heard.

"Not five minutes ago you read me the riot act about your brothers. Told me they were all you had, they were family, and family is always your business. You were right. So you gotta know, baby, that goes both ways. You're their family. You're their business. You are all they have."

"It's not the same and you know it. This is him being an ass."

"No, it's him being your brother. It's him being protective. I gotta suck it up and you do, too. So cool it, yeah?"

Throughout this exchange, Phoenix's eyes were dancing back and forth between me and Luke. He'd lost some of his dickheadedness but not all of it.

"Fine," I huffed and Luke smiled. "Phoenix, this is Luke. Luke, this is my youngest brother Phoenix."

Neither man said anything and I almost felt relief when I saw Echo and River walking toward us. I had a few angry words I wanted to say to Echo but I knew he'd handle Phoenix. There was one thing about my eldest brother that had not changed in all the years since he'd started raising us; a Kent never misbehaved in public—that was what he told us when we were teenagers. When we got older he drilled into us that a Kent never acted a fool and embarrassed themselves in public. And when we all got to the age where we were making our way as adults and starting our careers he set in stone that a Kent went above and beyond to do good work, to be a good person, to be honest, to be our best. Not *the* best—our *personal* best.

I knew it was because of who our father was—a criminal, a felon, a cop killer—that had led Echo to push us to be these things. Not that any of them were bad. But my brother took these things to such an extent sometimes I thought they were unhealthy or at least the reasons behind them were.

So I knew, there was no way in hell Echo would be happy if Phoenix caused a scene.

"What's going on?" Echo boomed when he stopped at our huddle.

"Nothing," Phoenix lied.

Echo took one look at my narrowed eyes and Luke's posture and he sighed.

"Told you, brother, it's all good," Echo told Phoenix.

"Yeah, you said that. But is it?"

"What's that mean?" I asked nastily.

Echo glanced between Phoenix and me, then his gaze settled on Luke.

"Everything all right?"

Interesting. Echo asked Luke that question and not Phoenix.

"All good," Luke returned then greeted my other brother. "River, good to see you."

"Yeah, you, too."

Well, two out of three wasn't bad.

At least that was what I was telling myself.

Then I took a good, long look at Phoenix and noticed the dark circles under his eyes and his unshaven face. He looked like shit which was not my brother's style. Out of the four of us, Phoenix was the one who primped. He always had designer gear and a fresh haircut.

"What's going on, brother?" I asked, all the hostility gone.

I didn't miss his flinch and neither did Echo.

"Got a letter from Dad. He's sick, says he wants to see us all. You know, like a family reunion in the big house. Says he doesn't have long and wants to see his kids so he can say goodbye."

I sucked in a breath then froze solid.

"Fuck," Luke grunted and tucked me close.

"Not good, brother," Echo seethed. "You think maybe you coulda cushioned that?"

"Right. Like it was cushioned for me when I got his letter outta the blue. Not that I give one fuck the bastard's dying. The faster the better as far as I'm concerned. You all can do what you have to do, but I'm not going to see the asshole."

Phoenix cared. He cared a lot and it pissed him off he

did. Out of all of us, I think it hurt Phoenix the most what Dad did. For some reason, Lester Kent loved Phoenix more than the rest of us. When we were kids before we understood who our dad was, Phoenix was closest to him. To me, Lester was just a man who lived with us while Echo was my dad. But Lester was Phoenix's dad.

"River, head on to the party with Sunny and Luke. Me and Phoenix are gonna take a walk."

River dipped his chin to Echo and moved my way. Echo patted Phoenix on the shoulder and shoved him back toward the parking lot. As soon as my brothers were out of earshot I turned to River.

"You okay?"

River glanced at Luke, then the two men's gazes locked in some sort of manly silent communication that would've pissed me off if Phoenix hadn't just dropped a bomb.

Whatever my brother needed to work out was done when he broke the stare and looked back at me.

"Yeah, sis, I'm good. But this is gonna rock Phoenix."

"I know."

"He had a different dad than we had."

"He did," I confirmed.

River nodded then turned to Luke and shocked the shit out of me.

"There are a lot of reasons to hate Lester Kent. For the most part, he ignored me, Echo, and Sunny. But he took Phoenix everywhere with him. He taught Phoenix how to work on cars. He even bought this beat-up junker of a dirt bike so he and Phoenix could fix it up. They spent a lotta time together, so it hit Phoenix especially hard the first time the cops came knocking. The second time the cops came with a warrant, we were minors but we were still cuffed and set on the porch while the house was searched. Something inside my brother died that day. There was no more denying who our dad was. I'm telling you this because something was obviously going on when Echo and I walked up. My guess is Phoenix was being a dick. I'm not excusing whatever he said, but I hope you can understand what getting a letter from our dad would do to him."

Holy wow.

River was being cool. That meant Echo had talked to him. And the only reason Echo would tell River to stand down was if Echo respected Luke. There was no other explanation.

"It's all good," Luke answered magnanimously.

I felt Luke's arm squeeze around my middle and my eyes went to his.

"You need to go home, baby, you say the word."

That was sweet.

"No. I'm good."

Luke's hand came up to cup my cheek, something he did when he wanted my attention but also when he was getting ready to lay it out. He'd do it gently but he wouldn't hold back.

"Straight up, Shiloh, you can't bury shit like this. I don't care what the man's done, he's still your dad. You need to leave, we'll leave. You want your brothers with you we'll all go back to your place. But you cannot lock this away and carry the burden."

You need to go home.

We'll leave.

We'll all go back to your place.

Luke had gone behind my back to get me to this picnic. I couldn't say I was happy about that but I understood why he'd done it. He knew I'd try to get out of it. He knew I'd be nervous about being around his friends. He'd also made it clear when he wanted something he didn't "try" he simply "did" and I would never admit this to him but I was almost glad he'd maneuvered all of this. So knowing all that he'd done, Luke offering to take me home if I needed to go said something. And what it said was he was putting me first.

I liked that.

"This is the honest truth and River can confirm. I laid my feelings about my dad to rest a long time ago. I did this with my brothers after he was sentenced to life in prison. I didn't have a lot of love for the man before he killed Officer Smith but any I had died when he took that man's life. I will not be visiting my dad. That is not because I hate him, it's simply because he doesn't exist for me. Lester reached out to Phoenix and not me, Echo, or River because he knew it would fuck with Phoenix. Which in turn means he fucks with all of us. Lester is a sonofabitch but that doesn't mean he's stupid. Phoenix is tweaked, we'll circle around him, but it will be Echo who will do what he always does.

"So, Dad will win, because he just earned himself face time with his eldest son. My dad won't care Echo's there to ream his ass. He'll just be happy knowing he's hurt Phoenix and pissed off Echo."

I tilted my chin toward the tables full of food. "Now, we're here, my brothers are here and you promised me lunch. I suggest you feed me, and while you're at it you should eat, too. You owe me huge and I reckon you're gonna need lots of energy for payback."

Luke silently stared at me a moment before he smiled. After that, he dropped a kiss on my forehead.

My brother made a hurling sound that made me look at him and grin.

"Don't start, River. Not with all the face I've seen you suck over the years."

"I don't suck face," my brother returned.

"Well, when I was ten and I caught you with Amy in your room on your bed it sure looked like you were sucking her face to me."

"Give me a break, I was like thirteen." River smiled wide and looked at Luke. "Amy was sixteen, took a liking to me, came over to teach me a few—"

"Stop. I'm sorry I brought it up."

"You done talking about your man needing energy for payback?"

Everything stopped. Well, for me it did. My breath caught and my muscles tensed but Luke didn't have the same problem. His body was shaking. He was laughing again.

My brother had called him my man and Luke didn't care.

He was laughing at my brother like he *was* my man.

"Come on, let me introduce you around."

Luke slid his arm from around me but grabbed my hand. River said nothing.

Drama over, time to eat.

And mingle.

As awkward as that sounded, I had a feeling it would be easy with Luke by my side.

Three hours later I was sitting on a blanket spread out on the grass. Next to me either on their own blankets or towels were Lauren Saunders, Liberty McCoy, Addy, Hadley, and Quinn Walker.

Addy, Hadley, and Quinn were sisters. Their other sister Delaney was a few feet away standing next to her husband Carter Lenox, but their daughter Emma was sitting on her Aunt Addy's lap sucking on a popsicle that was melting faster than she could slurp up the sugary goodness.

The women were talking about weddings and babies and I was sitting quietly. I was all talked out. I would bet I'd said more words in the last four hours than I'd said in the last two weeks. These women could gab. They were family, they were close, they knew everything about each other, so they'd asked me a million questions—and before them the guys had.

Something to note, not a single man Luke worked with was surprised to see me there with Luke. They also didn't bat an eye that my brothers were there. Of course, most of the guys knew my brothers and the ones who didn't were totally cool with them being there.

My gaze went from Delaney and Carter to my brothers and Luke. Jason and Ethan, along with three new guys I'd met, and Logan and Matt, were all standing in a huddle. Beers in hand and smiling. I focused on Phoenix and my heart clenched. He was faking it. Whatever Echo had said to Phoenix had settled him enough to join the party, but I knew my brother—he was hurting bad. And that meant I was hurting.

Lester Kent was a motherfucking asshole.

"Your brother's hot," Lauren said, pulling me from my thoughts.

This was not new. I'd heard my whole life how good-looking my brothers were and in a detached, they're-not-my-brothers kind of way, I could see how women fell all over them.

"Which one?" I asked.

"Well, all of them. But River's super-hot."

Before I could tell her River was the dawg out of the bunch and to steer clear unless she wanted a little fun and nothing more, Hadley piped up, "You better not let Logan hear you say that."

Lauren rolled her eyes and shook her head. "Trust me, Logan wouldn't care."

"Trust *me*, he would," Hadley returned.

"Okay, then trust me, I no longer care."

"Bullsh...rubbish." Hadley caught the curse at the last second. "The two of you have been circling each other for months."

Interesting. Lauren seemed the shy and quiet type. A little skittish. I wouldn't have guessed she'd have the hots for Logan.

"Well, I'm done with that. He made it clear he's not interested. I want a husband and kids one day and he straight out told me that he doesn't believe love is real."

Lauren shrugged like it didn't matter to her when clearly it did.

Liberty sighed and sadness washed over her face. "Logan is..." she trailed off then started again. "Logan needs time and there's a reason he does. I'm not saying you should wait around for him, though in my opinion, he'd be worth the wait, but that wait might be long."

Two pagers went off simultaneously and my heart immediately jumped in disappointment until I caught the tones. Not mine. Thank the Lord.

Quinn stood and the commotion started. Her fiancé, Brice, was coming our way and my eyes caught Echo doing the same.

"Gotta run, sis, call out," Echo told me when he got close.

Damn.

"Be safe."

"Always." My brother pulled me into a bear hug and kissed the top of my head. Before he let go he whispered, "I like him. Don't fuck this up."

"Don't piss me off when you're leaving to answer a call."

"Only time I can say this when I know I won't catch attitude. I'm being serious. Luke's solid. He's all-in. Drop the walls, sister."

My body went solid in my brother's embrace.

"Did he tell you that?"

"Yup. Now, be a good girl and listen to your big brother."

Ugh.

So annoying.

I shoved away from Echo and gave him my best scowl. This was wholly ineffective.

"Love you, Sunny." He smiled.

"Love you, too, big jerk."

Echo said his goodbyes to the women, and he was off.

Brice was jogging toward the parking lot and Quinn was watching him go.

"Three-alarm fire," Quinn announced. "They need more trucks."

Brice was a firefighter. Echo was a narco. My best guess was a lab had exploded.

Addy stood with a sticky Emma in her arms and said, "I'm taking her back to her parents."

I couldn't blame Addy. Emma was covered in popsicle juice and so was Addy's shirt.

"I'll be back." Hadley followed her sister.

"I'm getting another beer, want one?" Quinn asked.

"I'll go with you," Lauren chirped and stood.

"No thanks, I'll have a water," I answered.

"Are you on call?" Liberty inquired when the rest of the ladies walked away.

"No. But these days that doesn't mean much."

Liberty nodded as if she understood, which she probably did, considering most of her family had been in law enforcement or the military. And she herself, was still active duty.

"I heard Drake say you weren't reenlisting."

"No. I'm ready to start a family and I don't want to deploy after I have kids."

That made sense but there was something in her tone that didn't sound happy.

"But you're not ready to leave the military," I surmised.

Liberty was silent a beat while she studied me closely.

Crap. Maybe I'd overstepped. That was a personal question. I didn't know this woman and had no business asking her something private.

"Sorry, that was rude. Forget I asked."

"It wasn't rude. I'm just trying to figure out how to answer. My whole life I knew I wanted to be in the Army. I went to college, joined, trained hard, and worked my ass off to prove I had a place in Special Forces. It wasn't easy. But the harder it got the more I wanted it. And I earned it. I earned my tab. I earned a place on my team. I proved to myself I was good enough. Then I had to prove to my family I was strong enough to go back out after I was captured. I did that, too. I've served honorably. And now I'm ready to get out. Drake's never said and he never would, but I know he's ready for me to be done. And honestly, the way he stood by me after everything that happened, I owe it to him to be done. No more deployments. No more getting called out with five hours' notice, unable to tell him where I'm going and how long I'm gonna be gone. I know he gets it; he was a team guy. But still, it sucks, having that between us. And I want kids."

I wanted to ask her about being captured. I wanted to ask if she was okay even though she was sitting across from me. I wanted to ask what she meant by "everything that happened". But I didn't because that would be crossing a line, with the potential of her asking personal questions of her own.

I also wanted to tell her I understood what it was like to have to prove you're good enough to be on a team comprised of men. I understood the fire that ignites in your belly when someone tells you you're not strong enough or tough enough—which translates to *you're not a man, so you don't belong*. But I didn't tell Liberty any of that because I was too afraid to open myself up.

"Who are you if not a soldier," I finished for her.

Liberty smiled and dipped her chin.

"I figured you'd get it. You're pretty much in the same boat I am. Surrounded by men, having to work three times as hard to earn their respect. I feel like I've been doing that so long I don't know how not to do it."

Yep. I was in the same boat.

"There's a rush that comes with it. Not adrenaline. Not the same rush you get kicking in a door, but a rush all the same. Accomplishment is addictive. It becomes necessary. It pushes you to be better, do better, prove to yourself you're the best you can be."

Liberty was staring at me with her crazy-cool cat-like eyes and I suddenly felt exposed.

Vulnerable.

"You have a purpose," Liberty said. "A personal mission."

God, we were the same.

That was exactly what I felt.

"I lost that purpose once," she continued. "After I was taken and Drake, Logan, Matt, and Luke found me. After the explosion. Trey almost lost his leg. And Luke, he lost everything that day. I was drowning in guilt and couldn't see myself through it. I'd failed. Everything I'd worked so hard for seemed like a mistake. Drake held me through my nightmares. My family propped me up when I fell. And once again I had to work my ass off to get back to me and I did. I made it through. So, what happens when I get out and that personal mission is gone? Who am I? What am I working toward?"

I swallowed, then I swallowed again but the lump in my throat was stuck. The warmth of the day was now stifling. The sun felt like it was blistering my flesh. Panic rose and I wanted to flee.

"Shiloh?"

I was weak. So fucking weak.

I'd been wrong.

"I'm not like you. I thought I was. But I'm not."

"What?"

"As you were talking, I was thinking we were the same. Because of our jobs. How we feel about them. But I'm not like you. I'm weak. I don't deserve my place on my team."

As soon as the words left my mouth, I realized they were the truth. That was what I was struggling with. Acknowledging I was not strong enough, I wasn't tough enough, I wasn't as good as my teammates, as my brothers.

"Why would you say that?"

"Because I am weak. Because I can't stop the nightmares. I messed up and a girl is dead. Her father is broken, and that's on me. I did that."

God, I was gonna throw up.

"She didn't scream," I blurted out. "She was so scared she didn't make a peep."

"Who's she?"

"Penelope. All she did was go to work and died. Her dad watched. He begged me to save her. I didn't. And he saw his daughter's head explode. He has to live with that for the rest of his life."

Compassion shone on Liberty's face and my insides turned to ice. I didn't deserve that emotion.

"I need to go."

"No." Liberty reached out quick as lightning and grabbed my hand. The instinct to fight rushed to the surface. "Don't, Shiloh. You know I mean you no harm."

The last thing that needed to happen was Liberty and me getting into a brawl, and she was right; I knew she meant me no harm but I still didn't like her touching me.

I felt Luke's presence before I saw him.

"What's going on?" he asked.

I didn't answer because overwhelming embarrassment had taken over.

"It's all good, Luke. Just give us a minute," Liberty told him.

"Shiloh?"

"I'm good," I gritted out.

"Nuh-uh, you're not good. What the hell is going on?"

"You're right, Shiloh's not good. But if you give us a minute, I'll see that she gets that way."

"Really, I'm good. I shouldn't've said—"

"I'm gonna tell you something, Shiloh, something that was told to me at a time when I didn't want to hear it, which means it was the time I needed to hear it most," Liberty started, and I braced. "It was said at a time when I was overcome with guilt. A time when my power had been taken from me and I was lashing out at everyone who dared to speak to me. A time when all I felt was weakness.

"Right now, that guilt that's eating you up, it feels good under there, it feels safe. It feels right to wrap yourself in it because you think you deserve it. You feel weak? Change it. And the first step is never to say that word again, not ever, Shiloh. What comes out of your mouth, your ears hear, what your ears hear you start to believe. The more you say you're weak, the more you believe it. Once you get rid of that word, reach out and talk about it. The nightmares will never go away unless you do."

She scooted closer. "You find it too hard to talk to your brothers, you call me. If it's too hard for you to open up to Luke, you call me. Whatever you say stays between us and that's a promise. You asked me, if I'm not a soldier then who am I. Well, Shiloh, you just solved that mystery. I don't need to wear that uniform to be me. I don't have anything to prove to anyone. Not anymore."

Everything Liberty had said sliced me to the bone. She didn't know me, yet she seemed to know me better than I knew myself. I was doing exactly what she said—wrapping my guilt around me and holding on to it so tightly I was now afraid to let it go.

"Who are you if not a soldier?" I asked again.

"When you're ready to talk about Penelope and what happened, you come find me and I'll tell you who I am." Then Liberty leaned closer and with a face full of fury she said, "There's one thing I'll tell you right now. And pay close attention, Shiloh—you are not the uniform you wear. You are not your job. You are human and as such you're not perfect. You never will be. So cut yourself some slack. I. Am. Here. Day or night. Don't hesitate to reach out, sister. If you do hesitate I'll be seriously pissed off."

With that, Liberty did the unthinkable.

She wrapped her arms around me and hugged me.

I was a total stranger.

I was no one to her.

Fuck.

What was I supposed to do with that?

17

Shiloh's living room was not big enough for all the bodies currently taking up the space. We should've gone back to my house after the picnic. But after her talk with Liberty, I sensed she'd want to be in her own bed at the end of the day. I also knew that while her brothers had given me space to take care of Shiloh they weren't going to be put off and they'd be following us home. Which they did.

Now River, Phoenix, Matt, Logan, Dylan, and Ethan—sans his wife and kids—were lounging on her furniture and I was in the kitchen where Shiloh was pulling chicken out of the fridge so I could man the grill and feed our company.

I didn't want food.

I didn't want company.

Shiloh did because it would delay the conversation she knew we'd be having. Or maybe she thought I'd forget about it altogether. Either way, she was sadly mistaken. I'd given her time after Liberty laid out the truth. We'd spent another hour at the picnic, which was how long it had taken for us to say our goodbyes before we left.

I still didn't know what had brought on the intense

conversation. I'd stayed away, giving the women time to talk —that was, until Shiloh looked like she was ready to bolt. I'd watched as her face got paler and paler trusting Liberty to guide Shiloh. But when Liberty had grabbed Shiloh's hand, I was afraid Shiloh would lash out, so I'd interrupted.

Much to my shock, River and Phoenix had done as I'd asked and didn't rush to Shiloh. They trusted me to handle their sister. I would've taken a moment to appreciate how good that felt if I wasn't so worried about Shiloh.

"Babe?" I called.

"Huh?"

"Please look at me."

"We have a house full of people. I need to get this done."

She was correct but it was an excuse.

"Please, Shiloh."

She dropped the package of chicken on the counter then grabbed the edge and dropped her head forward. What she didn't do was look at me.

"I don't want to talk about it."

"Okay," I agreed.

Her head came up and her beautiful eyes met mine. So full of anguish.

"You've had a shit day," I noted the understatement of the year. "I need to know what you need from me."

"What?" she whispered.

"You want everyone gone? I'll get them out. You want just your brothers here? I'll tell the rest to leave. You want to go lie down? I'll sort dinner. You need me to go with you? I'll get River to take over in here. Whatever you need I'll give it to you, but you have to tell me."

"I feel like..." Shiloh started to say.

"Feel like what?"

"Like I'm losing control."

Shit. That wasn't good. Shiloh feeling that meant she'd do whatever she felt she had to do to wrestle that control back. Killer Frost would come out and she'd freeze out everyone around her and I'd be the first to feel that chill.

"Maybe that's what you need. You're holding on so tight you can't let go of the things you need to. The things weighing you down."

"She's coming, Luke. I know it and I'm doing everything I can to stop it, but I told you what happens when someone gets close—I turn nasty. I don't want to do that to you but I'm losing control and all I want to do is make you go away so I don't have to face my life."

Well, fuck me.

"Baby, that's probably the most self-aware thing I've ever heard. Maybe you're not losing control, maybe you're finally finding it. You know what's happening, you're brave enough to be honest about it, and strong enough to admit why you're doing it."

"I don't think I'm strong enough to stop her."

Fuck. She knew.

"Killer Frost?" I asked and she nodded.

"I know that's what they call me, and it fits. Anyone who has ever tried to get close gets blasted."

"Do you want them to stay?" I asked and tipped my head toward the living room.

"Yeah."

"Okay. Do you need help?"

"No. You go sit with them. That way you can reassure my brothers I'm good."

Right. Nothing was going to convince Phoenix and River their sister was okay. But I wasn't going to argue.

"Need you to promise me something before I go."

"What's that?" she asked warily.

"That you understand no matter what you say to me, how hard you try to push me away, I'm not leaving. Not physically but especially not emotionally. I will not abandon you. I will not allow you to close down and keep yourself from me."

"I'm counting on that," she whispered.

I stood motionless as the burn worked its way through my body. A burn that cauterized old wounds I hadn't realized weren't healed. Leftover abrasions on my soul that had yet to be treated. Some were minor—the residual pain of losing my career. Some were bigger, marks that would never fully go away but hadn't yet scarred over. Things I'd done and seen and failed to do. But one thing I knew for certain, Shiloh Kent, a woman who did not trust, did not allow herself to connect, held herself remote, would not believe in me unless I'd earned it. So, yeah, fuck yeah, the old wounds sealed over.

"If we didn't have company including two of your brothers sitting in your living room, I'd drag your ass into your bedroom and show you what your trust means to me."

"They have to leave sometime," she returned with a smile.

"I'm being very serious, Shiloh. Means the world to me, baby."

Her face softened—no, everything softened as she silently stared at me.

"The world," I repeated.

"Means the world to me, too, Luke, knowing you won't leave me."

Fucking hell. She knew that, too.

Thank Christ.

"I'm walking out of the kitchen now before I stop having a care your brothers are here and would likely be displeased, they saw me hauling you through your living room."

"That's a good idea. I'm not sure if Phoenix or River could live through that kind of trauma."

"Right."

I tagged my beer off the counter and hightailed my ass out of Shiloh's kitchen. Not because I was worried my control would slip and her brothers would witness something that would likely turn them off sex for a very long time. Something bigger was at play, something that needed to be contained. Because while Shiloh was holding on, acknowledging what she was feeling, telling her I loved her might push her too far. And I needed her as close as I could get her right now.

~

"Please tell me you made brownies," River said from across the table.

It was after dinner; dirty plates, empty serving plates, beer bottles, and balled-up napkins littered the table. No one was getting up to clear or clean. Not because the men around the table were being rude, it was because no one could move. Even though everyone had eaten at the picnic they'd still decimated the meal Shiloh had made.

"Sadly, I did not," Shiloh returned.

"Ice cream?" River tried.

"Nope."

"Cookies?"

"Jesus, Riv, you ate half a pig earlier," Phoenix said. "And just now, two pieces of chicken and a plate full of broccoli salad."

"I didn't eat half a pig. I only had one sandwich. Though

I did have three plates of potato salad. Which reminds me, I'm gonna need the name and address of whoever made it, so I can get down on my knees and ask her to marry me."

"Actually." Ethan chuckled. "My dad made the potato salad."

"Well, damn," River muttered.

"You need a wife," Shiloh told River.

River shot her a filthy look even though he'd just said he was down to propose marriage to the potato salad maker.

"Bite your tongue, woman. I need no such thing. Though that shy redhead at the picnic was damn cute."

Oh, shit. The only redhead at the picnic was Lauren. My eyes slid to Logan and just as expected his jaw was clenched. He would never make a move on our pretty receptionist, but it seemed he didn't want anyone else to.

Silence ensued.

Then it stretched to uncomfortable.

"What?" River asked. "I thought she was single."

"Oh, she's single," Matt put in. "But good luck getting in there. She's on the shy side."

Logan growled.

Matt smiled.

"It's the shy ones who are always wild," River continued.

The guy had no idea he was digging the knife into Logan's chest, and with Matt egging him on River was likely going to twist it.

"She's not a natural redhead," Matt noted. "But I bet she could be fiery with the right...persuasion."

Logan growled again.

"Well, hook a brother up."

Yep, there was the knife being twisted.

"Yeah, no," Shiloh cut in. "I know Lauren. She is shy. She's also sweet. And you, big brother, are a dawg. You'd

chew her up and spit her out. Go find someone else to play
with who understands what one night, no repeats, means
because that is not Lauren. Just today she told me she's
looking to settle down. She wants a husband and kids and
she's serious about finding a man."

Fuck.

I was wrong; it wasn't River who twisted the knife, it was
Shiloh.

Logan wanted Lauren something fierce. But he didn't
want a relationship. Didn't believe love was real. And he
really, really, didn't want kids.

"Hell, yeah," Dylan barked, and all eyes went to him.

His head was bowed and he was looking at his phone.

"What?" Ethan asked.

"Got the prints back," Dylan announced. "Jeff Shepard
was in Becca Harper's bedroom. Prints on the door handle,
nightstand, and also on the shovel at the rental property he
swore he never touched."

Ethan looked shell-shocked and Dylan looked like he
was ready to pump his fist in triumph.

"Is that enough to haul his ass back to Georgia?" I
queried.

"You talking about the Harper cold case?" Phoenix was
looking between me and Ethan.

"Yeah," I answered.

"Righteous."

"Fucking finally," Ethan muttered. "Thanks for dinner,
Shiloh, but I gotta run."

"Hey," Shiloh called softly and waited for Ethan's attention to come to her. "Good work."

"Not me who drove to Montgomery. That was your man
who broke the case."

With that, Ethan jogged through Shiloh's living room.

"Be good that little girl can finally get justice."

River wasn't lying.

A high-pitched squawk followed by a long tone filled the room and Shiloh's eyes drifted closed.

"Shit," Shiloh muttered.

"Thought you weren't on call," Phoenix protested.

"I'm not, but two warrants came yesterday, we only got to serve one. Bravo was going to serve the other one tonight. If they're caught up in that." Shiloh shrugged and sighed. "You know the drill."

"Go get ready, I'll start cleaning up," I told her.

"Will you be here when I get home?"

"If you want that, yeah. If not, I want you hitting my place when you're done."

"Stay here. All of you. Make yourselves at home."

"Go get ready," I urged.

Her gaze went around the table then settled on me.

Then she leaned over and brushed her lips across mine.

Christ, that felt sweet.

Shiloh was out of the room when Phoenix cleared his throat.

"Haven't had time to apologize. I was in a bad mood and took that out on you. It was a dick thing to do. My apologies."

"No worries."

"Not lost on any of us you're moving in and doing it fast."

I clenched my teeth and remained silent.

"That's the right play," Phoenix continued. "You gotta do this fast. Get in there and dig in before she sees you coming. We talked about it, and before today I wasn't all that sure I was on board with my brothers. But after watching the two of you, I'm all-in."

"All-in for what?"

"We got your back. Sunny pulls a cut-and-run we're dragging her ass back to you."

Jesus, that felt good.

"Appreciate that. But right now the way you can take my back, take your sister's back, is by being honest about what's going on with your dad and not cut Shiloh out of that. She's feeling vulnerable. I've heard her call herself weak too many times and I'm putting an end to that shit. Show her how strong she is and lean on her. Lay everything you got about your dad on her and know when you're done, I got her. She's safe with me and I'll get her through. You pull back and keep this between the three of you and cut her out you're proving her right thinking she's the weak one."

Phoenix looked less than pleased.

I knew he would.

"Echo was right. You got some big fucking balls, brother."

I shrugged and asked him the same thing I asked Echo, "Want me to find a ruler and you can measure my dick, too?"

"Leave it to Sunny to find the one fucking guy on the planet with a dick big enough to swing it in your face and slap you with it," River retorted.

"Yeah, he pulls his dick out and measures that shit anywhere near me, and my sister will be looking for a new man."

"Um...what?" Shiloh choked.

Neither of her brothers said a word. Neither did Dylan, Logan, or Matt. They were all too busy laughing their asses off.

"Nothing, baby."

My eyes swept her body—black cargos, black tee with SWAT written in white across her chest, nine mil already holstered at her hip, black combat boots on her feet, and her shiny blonde hair pulled into a ponytail.

"Damn, you're hot," I blurted.

A playful smirk tugged at her lips.

"Play your cards right, honey, and when I get home I'll show you what I can do with a pair of cuffs."

"Fuck, Sunny, my ears are bleeding. Like, painfully bleeding in a way that I know I will never use a pair of cuffs again in my life," River stated.

"Oh, shut up. We all know you prefer rope over cuffs. And besides, y'all were talking about my man's dick when I came in so don't act like a prude."

And there was Sunny Kent. The teasing, bright, open, playful woman I'd first met. I wasn't stupid, I knew her hurt lay just below the surface, but she still gave her brothers what they needed before she headed out the door.

"She's not wrong, Riv, you do like rope."

"*One* time. One damn time I was feeling like switching it up. Not my fault the two of you didn't knock before you came in. Hell, as far I'm concerned you deserve what you saw."

Right. As amusing as story time was, I didn't want to hear about River tying his woman up. And further, I didn't want Shiloh to have the visual in case in the future I felt like switching things up and tying her to my bed.

She also had to get out the door and I was absolutely going to kiss my woman before she left.

"I'll walk you out," I rejoined.

Shiloh winked at her brother and took my outstretched hand.

"Night, guys," she called.

Both her brothers told her to be safe, she returned an "always" and I walked her to the garage.

Then I made out with my woman, with her sidearm pressing into my hip reminding me she was getting ready to put on a bulletproof vest and put herself in danger.

And suddenly I understood real fear.

The kind that ate you up inside because you had to let the person you loved be who they were and there was nothing you could do but hope to God they came home.

"Be safe out there and come home to me."

Shiloh's hand came up and her fingers grazed the side of my face, stopping at one of the scars on my temple.

"I promise I will always do my best to come home to you."

I love you.

It was right there waiting to be said.

Soon.

18

"You're in a hurry."

I slammed my trunk and looked over my shoulder at Gordy.

"It's six-thirty. I'd like to get home in time to say goodbye to Luke."

I'd been so focused on Gordy's wide smile I missed the way he was staring at me. If I hadn't, I would've known it was assessing and calculating and I would've been prepared. But I was too busy thinking about how much I liked his smile. I'd pay for that.

"Are you happy?"

"Huh?"

"Happy, Sunny. Are you happy?"

That was an odd question. No one I worked with had ever asked if I was happy.

That's because they know better.

"Um. I guess."

"You guess?" Gordy's head jerked. "What do you mean, you guess? Are you happy or not?"

At that, it was my turn to lurch in retreat. I didn't like where this conversation was headed.

"Just what I said. I'm happy when I'm with Luke. I'm happy when I'm with my brothers when they're not pissing me off and I'm not plotting how to kill them and get away with it. I'm happy at work when we're not called in on our day off. Though I'm not happy my dad's reached out to Phoenix to spread his douchebag cheer and the news he's dying. I'm not happy we just pulled a twelve-hour shift on our day off. I'm not happy two of my brothers were total assholes to Luke and the third was a mild asshole. I'm not happy I'm standing here having this conversation instead of headed home to Luke. So with all of that, yeah, I guess I'm happy."

Gordy being Gordy was unperturbed.

He also ignored both comments about me wanting to get home.

"Lester's dying?"

Shit. Why'd I tell him that?

"That's what he told Phoenix in the letter he sent requesting all of us visit him. However, I wouldn't put it past him to lie about being on his deathbed to get a rise out of Phoenix and face time with Echo. It's not like he hasn't tried to get us all to visit him before. Though I will admit, he's never gone as far as telling us he was dying."

"That motherfucker has tried to get you kids to come see him?"

Kids.

That was kind of amusing and I would've reminded Gordy that he was only ten years older than me, which meant it was asinine him calling Echo, River, Phoenix, and me *kids*.

"Yep. The last time he did it was a few years ago. Wrote

to Phoenix and said he was sorry and wanted to finally explain why our mom bailed. Echo visited and Dad told him the bitch left because she was a bitch."

Sadness suffused Gordy's face. The only look I hated more than sadness when discussing Lester Kent was pity. I didn't want or need anyone feeling sorry for me. Life was what it was and there were plenty of people in the world who had it far worse than I did. I was not some victim of childhood trauma. I wasn't a survivor. I was me. Just me.

"Don't feel sorry for me," I seethed. "I don't need that shit. Lester's a cop-killing asshole. He's been dead to me for years. Whether or not his body will soon be under dirt doesn't matter to me. Good riddance."

Gordy didn't respond verbally for a long time. Though I didn't need words for him to communicate his anger—his hardened eyes and scowl were loud and clear.

"Stow your claws, kitten."

"Gordy—"

"You got your say, now you're gonna listen to me," Gordy cut me off. "I can't feel sorry for a woman who against the odds has succeeded. I can't feel sorry for a woman who, despite being taught wrong has done nothing but good in her life. I can't feel sorry for a woman who works her ass off, is great at her job, and has earned the respect of every person she works with. But I can and do feel compassion. I can also feel loyalty and friendship. So that brings us to what I do feel sorry about—you not opening yourself up to receive that loyalty and friendship. You're the first person to give Valentine a pep talk when one of his dates screws him over. You're the first one to boost morale after a shitty, twelve-hour shift. And you're the first one to turn your back on all of us when we reach out. You're so goddamn selfish, Shiloh, it's unbelievable."

Shiloh?

I didn't think Gordy had ever called me Shiloh.

"I'm selfish?"

Yes, that was what I chose to comment on. Examining and questioning any other part of his soliloquy would lead to me having to reflect. And at six-thirty in the morning after spending ten hours outside a house with an active shooter and five hostages I was in no mood for self-reflection of any kind.

"What else would you call someone who gives everything but refuses those she gives to the opportunity to show gratitude? It's goddamn selfish, Sunny. You give, but then throw our friendship in our faces and slice and dice anyone who attempts to get close."

Oh, shit.

"What do you want me to say, huh? That I don't want friends because I know they'll leave and it will hurt? I don't want anyone caring about me because that will lead to fucked-up conversations like this and make me feel like shit because I'm incapable of a normal relationship? Admit that I've hidden behind my brothers my whole damn life and used them as a buffer to keep people away? Confess my deep, dark secrets and tell you there are times when I cannot breathe, when I think of all the ways I've disappointed myself. Jesus, Gordy, just tell me what you want so I can go the fuck home."

"Yeah, sweetheart, all of that. That's what I wanted to hear," Gordy whispered, and I went stone cold.

What had I done?

This was all Luke's fault.

He was pushing this friendship shit on me, doing it nice and slow. Sneaking shit in and giving it in small doses until he'd done it—he ruined me. Now I was blurting shit out not realizing what I was saying until it was too late.

I was done with this.

All of it.

I turned to leave but Gordy was faster and blocked my car door.

Bastard.

"Move."

"You know if your fucktard of a father wasn't locked up, I'd kill him with my bare hands. And I've thought myself a man who couldn't harm a woman, but I'd slap the shit outta that mother of yours and not feel a moment of regret. What those two fucking idiots taught you was a lesson. But instead of you learning the real meaning, you've twisted it in your head. Yes, people leave. But, Shiloh, those who are worth your time do not. Those who truly love you never leave.

"I'm sorry to say this because it's the worst thing a person can know but your father is fucked. He is incapable of loving anyone. And that mother of yours didn't love you. If she had, sweetheart, she would've held on to you and your brothers and got you clear of your father. She didn't and that's on her. *Her*, Shiloh. She's the one with the problem, not you. You need to open your damn eyes and learn a new lesson—you are not them."

My eyes drifted closed. I couldn't bear to look at Gordy. I couldn't bear the fury, the anger, the sadness, the grief. He was feeling all of that for me.

He wasn't supposed to feel anything for me.

I wasn't supposed to feel anything for anyone.

Fucking Luke. He did something to me. He cursed me. He made me feel things I swore I'd never allowed myself to feel. Even how standing here hollowed me out and I wanted to run home to him so he could fill me up. He'd take this pain away; I knew he would. But at what cost? He'd make me open up more. He'd make me talk about why I was upset. He'd break down more walls and steal the last of my strength.

Panic was nearing the red zone. I itched to crawl out of my skin.

"What's wrong with me?" I wheezed. "Why didn't they love me?"

"There's nothing wrong with you, Sunny. And you're asking the wrong question, sweetheart. What you should be asking is: why didn't they love themselves? What was broken in them? Darlin', hear this; you cannot love *anyone,* not even your children, if you don't first love yourself. They had nothing to give you or your brothers because they were empty."

"He loved Phoenix. He took him everywhere."

"No, Sunny, he used Phoenix as a weapon to hurt you, Echo, and River. That piece of shit used his boy and is still using him."

God, that was the truth. The disgusting truth.

When I was little, I used to be jealous that my dad loved my brother but not me. Then I was angry because Phoenix would defend Dad. The cops would show up to question Lester and Phoenix would get mad and say the cops were out to get Lester. Phoenix never believed that our dad was filth until he killed Officer Smith. Then Phoenix was crushed.

You did not do that to someone you loved. You didn't lie and use them. I didn't know a lot about love, but I knew that much.

I knew you didn't steal, cheat, abuse, and kill people.

What the hell was wrong with my father?

"When my mom left it hurt. She wasn't much but she

was a body in the house. She was there when we got home from school. Then she wasn't and as useless as she was it sucked. And Lester's scum, total filth, so it wasn't much of a loss when he went to prison, but Echo felt it. We all did but Echo especially. He had to step up and be our parent. They both left us."

"Yep, they did," Gordy said evenly. "They both left and in doing so they inadvertently gave you and your brothers something special. They gave the four of you an unbreakable bond. It goes beyond biology and is rooted in unwavering loyalty. Think about that. The four of you took loss and pain and turned it into beauty. The four of you built an indestructible foundation. Echo gave you that, Sunny. Now you need to learn how to build on it."

Gordy was correct about one thing for certain—Echo had given me a lot. He'd given his whole life to supporting me, River, and Phoenix. He was our rock, our shield, our shoulder. And I was no longer going to allow him to stand in front of us. It was time for me to step up and stand beside him.

A chill swept over me and it was terrifying.

Completely.

I desperately wanted to fire my barbs. I wanted to call up nasty words that would wound Gordy and make him leave. I wanted to aim all the pent-up hostility inside of me and lash out.

But I couldn't.

I. Could. Not.

Fucking hell.

Why couldn't I?

"I dream about Penelope and her dad," I rushed out. "Not every night. But a lot. I dream about Clive Hutchinson begging me to save his daughter. Then I see him on his knees screaming with blood spattered on his face. He's covered in her blood."

"God, Sunny."

Tortured.

Gordy sounded utterly tortured.

Did friends gut their friends because they couldn't keep their issues to themselves?

Then J.D. "Gordy" Gordon did something he had never done before. He wrapped his arms around me and crushed me to his chest. His chin tucked and he rested his cheek on the top of my head.

"Jesus Christ. Why didn't you say anything?"

Shit, now he sounded mad.

"Scratch that, I know why you didn't say anything. I hope what's happening here is sinking in, woman. We waited, all of us, for you to give us some indication you were ready for us to push you to open up. You bringing Luke to dinner the other night was the sign we needed. You've opened yourself up to him, and while he's keeping you busy dodging his bullets, we're gonna sneak in. No more shutting us out. No more bullshit. You've gotta trust us with more than your life. And I know that sounds all sort of screwed up but we know you'd catch a bullet for us but you wouldn't dream of leaning on us for help. That changes now. You can be as bitchy as you want and we're not backing off this time."

"Okay."

Okay? What the hell? Am I crazy?

"Okay, Sunny. I feel it's important that right now we talk about these dreams. Give Luke a call and tell him I'm taking you out for breakfast."

"Gordy—"

"No. This isn't important, it's im-port-ant. As in, you're

not outta my sight until we go over this. It's been fuckin' with your head for months. We're talking this out."

Hard. Impassable.

Damn.

"Okay. I'll follow you and call Luke on the way."

Gordy gave me a squeeze and let me go.

"Mable's?"

"As if I'd participate in a heart-to-heart under extreme duress without a stack of chocolate buttermilk pancakes and scrapple."

Gordy wrinkled his nose.

"You know the rules. No mystery meat at the table."

"You're breaking your rule. If you want me to spill my guts, I need high in cholesterol meat products."

"Whatever," Gordy grumbled, then ambled to his SUV.

I watched him walk away.

His shoulders were slumped, his head hung, and his gait quick.

Damn.

19

"Yo, Luke," Drake called my name.

I stopped and took a step backward to the doorway of the conference room.

Jason, Nick, Carter, Drake, Brady, and Hadley were all sitting around the table.

An executive meeting. Or was it a shareholders' meeting? Whatever it was called the five of them were essentially my bosses. Though Brady was my direct superior since he handled all of the training and that was my main job. There were times I was pulled in for other things like helping Ethan but thankfully that was rare. Sitting in an office wasn't my favorite thing to do.

"What's going on?" I asked.

"Good work on the Harper case," Nick said.

"Wasn't much to do on my part. Dylan got the intel."

Nick shook his head and smiled. "Y'all are the same. None of you like to take credit."

I didn't need to ask who "y'all" was. Nick was referring to Matt, Logan, Trey, Drake, Carter, and myself. Once upon a time, we were a team of another kind. Brothers who relied on the competence and skills of the man standing at his back. We didn't take individual credit. Everything we did was a team effort.

"Jeff Shepard will be picked up today for questioning," Nick continued.

"Good news."

"Yeah, good news," Nick finished.

"I'll let you get back to it."

I started to step out of the room, but Drake stopped me.

"Everything okay with Sunny?"

This was dangerous territory. I didn't want to spread Shiloh's personal business but everyone in the room had been at the picnic. Everyone had witnessed Liberty and Shiloh's exchange. I still didn't know what exactly was said and I figured Drake actually knew more than I did seeing as he shared a bed with Liberty.

"I'm not sure." I gave Drake the truth. "Phoenix landed a blow announcing her father's dying—not in the sense she's torn up the guy's gonna die but it opens up bad shit for all of them. And I didn't get to talk to her last night before she was called out. Did Liberty tell you what they were talking about?"

Shiloh called this morning after I got out of the shower to tell me she was going to breakfast with Gordy then home to crash. There was something in her voice—a hitch, a wobble, sadness, wariness—something I couldn't quite put my finger on. I wasn't sure if she was just tired or if something had happened. Though she did report no one was hurt and they'd apprehended the suspect and all the hostages—the man's family—were unharmed.

"All Liberty told me was, Sunny reminded her of herself when she got home after we rescued her. She said she recognized the anger. I hope you know Liberty's not gonna let this slide. She's gonna reach out even if Sunny doesn't."

Fuck.

"That's not a good idea. Shiloh's got issues with people getting close. It would not be good if Liberty tried to get friendly. Shiloh will push back, and it'll be ugly."

Drake stared at me a moment. Anguish flashed in his eyes before he masked it and jerked his chin.

"She hasn't forgotten, brother. Not any of it. But you know what makes it easier for her when her mind goes there? Her knowing that you, Logan, Matt, Trey, and I were there. That when she was vulnerable we took care of her. She will never forget that for those hours the only thing between her and death was us. She also remembers what it's like to not want anyone close, to lash out, to be mean, to push everyone away. There's a reason why she recognizes the anger—she's lived with it. This is two-fold for Liberty. She feels a kinship with Sunny. A sisterhood that not many women belong to and she wants that connection with her. The other part is, Sunny's yours and Liberty knows it. You know Liberty; you know she can endure whatever Sunny throws her way."

I was not worried about that. Liberty was tough as hell. Shiloh could turn up her Killer Frost routine and Liberty would laugh at her.

"And what about you? And the others? If Shiloh lashes out and says nasty shit in anger are you gonna be able to look past it? Because Liberty's right. Shiloh is mine. I don't want there to be hard feelings. And until I help her through what's eating her up inside that anger is swimming close to the surface, and when it comes out Shiloh goes for the kill and she slices deep. What's that gonna do to you?"

"Don't be dumb," Drake clipped.

"I'm being real."

"Liberty lashed out at you. At me. At her mom and dad, uncles, cousins, all of us felt her terror. Are you pissed at Liberty?"

"Hell no."

"Right. No one's pissed because we all understood. I'm not asking. If one day Sunny wants it out in the open where it should be, she'll tell us what's going on. But I do know whatever it is that's fucking with her head is bad. And you know I know what it means to have to dig that out. You know I know how heavy it gets when all the hurt and anger is dumped on you. Don't go at this alone. Use all the tools available to you, including Liberty. Include me and your brothers."

Drake absolutely understood the weight of carrying his woman's pain. When Liberty finally unloaded it wasn't pretty. Then being waterboarded and beaten nearly to death wasn't pretty. But Liberty survived and she healed.

Shiloh would, too.

"Appreciate it."

"Don't give me your gratitude, give me your word you won't go at this alone."

Fucking hell.

In the beginning, there were days when I wondered if I'd made the right decision getting out of the Navy. If I'd taken the coward's way out because my ego was bruised, I was no longer fit for deployment. I could train SEALs but I couldn't be one. I'd be a man with a trident pinned on my uniform, but everyone would know I was a has-been. A washed-up, team guy reduced to the compound.

But now I knew differently. There was no other place for me. I needed my brothers more than I needed the uniform.

"You got my word."

Drake jerked his chin. After that, I said my goodbyes and got back to work.

I sat on the edge of Shiloh's bed and brushed her hair off her shoulder. I knew she was awake even though her eyes remained closed. There was no way my girl would miss me unlocking her front door. But if she had she certainly wouldn't have missed me entering her bedroom.

"Did you bring in the condoms?" she muttered sleepily.

I was smiling when I told her, "No."

I smiled bigger when she grumpily told me, "Go get them."

"Babe, I just got off work and I haven't talked to you since lunchtime when you told me you were crawling into bed for a nap. Maybe we can talk some before we get down to business."

Shiloh pried open one eye and crinkled her forehead.

"You look like an angry pirate." I chuckled.

My woman didn't look amused when her other eye snapped open and she scowled.

"No, I look like a woman who was promised something last night and didn't get to cash in. Condoms, handsome. Now."

"Really? And what were you promised?"

"Orgasms. Lots and lots of orgasms. And you better hurry; if my pager goes off before I receive them, I might do something regrettable."

I wasn't sure if she was dodging us talking or if she was in need. We'd spent the better part of the week teasing each other. Not that our foreplay hadn't ended spectacularly but there were more pleasurable ways to end the festivities. Ways that would turn spectacular into fucking fantastic.

"This morning—"

"Luke," Shiloh groaned. "Please. I promise. Cross my heart, hope to die, stick a needle in my eye, I will tell you all about my morning and my talk with Gordy if you please go out to your truck and get the condoms."

So, she was in need.

"Don't need condoms to take the edge off, baby."

And I didn't. I'd spent a fair amount of time with my mouth between Shiloh's legs. I could get her off and soaring in under five minutes.

"You've got two minutes, Luke. After that, I'm tackling you and we're using the old pull and pray method."

"Bossy," I muttered.

"Luke," she moaned again, and I smiled.

"All right, baby, I'll go get the condoms." I bent forward and kissed her neck. "Get naked for me. I wanna see you spread out for me when I come back."

"Now who's bossy?"

Shiloh shivered when my tongue traced the shell of her ear.

"You gonna be naked with your legs spread for me?" Shiloh nodded. "Good."

I got up, went out to my truck, grabbed the condoms from the glovebox where I'd stored them, and retraced my steps back to her room.

Shiloh was naked, sheets thrown off, knees bent with the soles of her feet on the mattress, spread open for me.

"Christ, you're sexy," I told her from the doorway.

She lifted her head off the pillow and our gazes locked.

Those pretty pastel eyes darkened with desire.

"I could stand here all day just staring at you," I told her and tossed the box of condoms on her dresser. "Spread wider for me, Shiloh."

She did as I asked and I toed off my shoes.

"Last night I lay all alone in your bed thinking about you," I continued and pulled my shirt off. "The sheets smell like you." I ditched my shirt, picked up the box of condoms, walked to the edge of the bed, and dropped the box by Shiloh's hip. "It was torture lying there thinking about you. Open the box, baby, get one out."

I unbuttoned my jeans and Shiloh's gaze lowered to my hands. "I couldn't stop thinking about the sounds you make when you touch yourself. How hot you are when you grind your pussy in my face when you're close." I heard the box rip open as I pushed my pants and boxers down. "How good your hand feels wrapped around my cock. How your eyes get wide when you make me come. How fuckin' wet you get when I fuck you with my fingers."

I put my knee on the bed but paused to kiss the inside of Shiloh's thigh before I knelt between her legs, fisted my hard cock with my left hand, and dropped my right and teased her clit.

"Thought about jerking off," I continued. "Lying in your bed, thinking about this right here." I dipped my finger into her pussy and found her soaked. "Thinking about how sweet your mouth is, how hard your nipples get, how you never hold back when we're together, but when I play with your tits you detonate."

"Did you?" Shiloh rasped.

"Nope. Started to, had my cock in my hand, started to stroke, but stopped."

"Why'd you stop?"

"Because you weren't here."

I slid my finger out and pushed back in two.

Tight, hot, and wet.

I let go of my cock, grabbed the string of condoms Shiloh had unearthed, and tore one free. I had my cock sheathed in record speed.

I could swear I heard Shiloh sigh in relief, or maybe it was a groan of impatience.

I fell forward, catching myself on my palms, and slowly gave her some of my weight.

Shiloh's legs wrapped around my hips. Her hands went to my chest then glided up until they rested on either side of my neck.

"Reach down and guide me in, baby."

One of Shiloh's hands left my neck. I shifted to my elbow to give her room.

Throughout this, her eyes didn't leave mine.

She didn't blink.

She didn't hide.

She didn't conceal.

Totally open.

I felt her hand on my hip, then it moved around and down until her fingers brushed my cock and I sucked in a breath.

"In case I forget to tell you later I need you to know now," Shiloh whispered and fisted my cock.

"Tell me what, baby?" I asked through gritted teeth.

I locked down my control when Shiloh guided the tip to her wet opening then dragged the head to her clit and rubbed.

Sweet Christ.

"Tell me what?" I repeated.

"That you're everything," she softly murmured and guided me back down. "That you've changed my life."

My eyes drifted closed and my chest burned.

I felt her hand slide away but I couldn't move.

"Everything, honey. Changed me in all the best ways."

Jesus.

"Come inside," she whispered.

Something was happening. Something that went beyond sex, beyond an orgasm, beyond us connecting physically.

I felt it.

The very second it happened.

My soul fused to hers.

I let that settle over me, I let it linger, then I locked the memory away.

After that, I drove down and in one thrust, I sank my dick in my woman.

And I did it knowing she was fucking mine. Not because I'd claimed her, but she'd claimed me.

20

I brought my knees high.

Tipped my hips.

And took Luke deeper.

"Ohmigod," I whimpered.

"Fuck, you feel beautiful."

I loved he thought that. But he was doing all the work, making the tingles of excitement I always felt when he looked at me turn into blazing shafts of beauty.

It was all Luke.

His hand went to my thigh to hitch it higher. His face dropped to my neck. And he started driving me into the bed with his powerful thrusts.

"Beauty," he groaned.

I felt the vibration at my throat right before I felt his mouth on my skin. He licked and grazed his teeth and kissed and nibbled and sucked. I started to tremble. The feel of him everywhere. I dug my nails into the tight muscles of his ass and groaned when he rolled his hips.

Nothing else existed. Just me and Luke and the pleasure he was creating.

Luke's hand slipped up into my hair. He pulled his face from my neck which made me whine in protest, but when he righted my head and tipped his down giving me his eyes, that protest died.

"Baby," I gasped, and his lids drifted closed in a slow blink.

When his eyes opened and locked onto mine my world narrowed further, not just to us but this single moment in time. This moment of magnificence with Luke staring down at me with something that looked a lot like adoration—like he loved me. But that was coupled with hunger, want, need, and more desire than I'd ever seen.

Then I lost sight of that glorious look because his lips dropped to mine. Wild, rough, and demanding. Wet and deep and hot. He took my mouth and I struggled to keep up. I couldn't give fast enough, and I wanted to give it all. I wanted him to have everything he was building in me.

Luke rocked harder. I tightened my thighs to hold on. He kissed me deeper. I held on tighter. I kissed him until I couldn't breathe then I kissed him some more—totally breathless. I was there—right there. I could feel it deep in my sex. My muscles tensed. My skin felt funny—hot chased by cold then back to hot. My heart pounded. Luke's grip on my thigh turned to steel.

I was being consumed.

I was falling.

So close.

Luke wrenched his mouth off of mine and growled, "Let go."

But I couldn't. I wanted to but this feeling was so huge it would destroy me.

Luke drove in harder and groaned. Then he did it again,

adding a roll at the end that had my inner muscles spasming.

Oh. My. God.

"Baby, I can do this all night." To punctuate his statement, he ground his pelvis against my clit, and I was soaring. "Give in to it, Shiloh. Let me have it."

My back arched and I let go.

The waves of pleasure rolled through me, lasting an eternity. So long, I didn't think it'd ever stop. My sex was still pulsing when Luke pulled out and I squeaked in surprise when he flipped me over. Then I was up on my knees and Luke drove in. No, that wasn't right, he slammed in and I pitched forward.

Luke hauled me back, clamped an arm around my middle, and held tight while he rode me. I bucked back into his driving thrusts and panted. His lips went to my shoulder where he rumbled a groan that instantly seared through me.

"Hand between your legs, Shiloh."

I went down on my forearms. Luke followed me down, not missing a single punishing thrust. My hand went where it was instructed and I fumbled until I found my clit.

Oh. My. Lord.

"Yeah, baby, that's it. Fuck, you feel so *fucking* good. Knew you'd feel like heaven. But I had no idea how sweet your pussy would be wrapped around my dick. So goddamn sweet."

Luke forged deeper and my second climax built fast. So fast that when it broke it took me by surprise and I screamed through it.

"Christ, your pussy's sweet."

With one last thrust, he planted himself to the root and groaned. Long and loud and rough.

Amazing.

Now that was beauty, hearing Luke's pleasure. Feeling it rumble against my skin. Feeling his big body pressed close. Feeling him shudder.

Yes. Amazing.

Sheer beauty.

He began to slowly glide in and out, giving me time to come down. This lasted a while. And I knew he was done when he gently kissed my jaw, then my neck, then my shoulder. After that, he pulled out and tapped my hip.

"Stretch out, baby."

"Can't. I'm stuck here forever."

He chuckled. "You won't hear me complain about the view, honey. And I certainly want you on your knees, ass tipped high so I can eat you. But I need to toss this condom."

I lowered my cheek to the bed and sighed.

"I can't feel my legs. Just push me over and I'll roll."

I might've been exaggerating a skosh, but my thighs were still quivering, and I was oddly comfortable.

Luke didn't give me a push but when he was on his feet next to the bed he did help me roll to my side. One could say the view from my new position was magnificent. I'd seen Luke naked. I'd spent time exploring his chest and abs with my mouth. I'd trailed my fingers over the ridges and valleys of his muscles. But the sight never ceased to amaze me.

"Be back."

Yes, indeed, the view was magnificent. Going or coming Luke was a sight to behold. The front of him spectacular. But the back of him held a good amount of merit as well. He had a great ass. Who was I kidding? Luke had a great everything.

Every. Thing.

I was laying there sated, feeling good—so good I knew I'd never felt *this* good before. I was sore in all the right places and wondering if Luke was telling the truth when he told me he could 'do this all night long.' I'd like to test that even though I was pretty sure he could. I smiled at the thought and that was how Luke caught me when he came back into the room.

He walked across my bedroom and crawled right into my bed like he'd been doing it forever. I liked that, how comfortable he was in my house, in my bed. How he was with me.

Luke shifted, rolled, tugged my arm, adjusted my leg, and finally settled me where he wanted me. Then we lay there in silence. Instead of it being awkward or weird it was peaceful and comforting. His hand was resting on my hip, mine was resting on his chest, both of us relaxed.

And after spending most of my day in bed snoozing then waking up and receiving two outstanding orgasms, I should've been relaxed. But it was more.

It was us just *being*.

Just being together.

Just being quiet.

This lasted a long time.

Then I took a heaving breath. I promised Luke I'd tell him about my morning, and I didn't want him to have to prompt the conversation.

"Gordy ambushed me in the parking lot," I started.

Luke's hand on my hip twitched and I knew I was doing the right thing.

"It wasn't pretty," I admitted on a sigh. "It started off with me being defensive and pushing him away. He called me selfish then laid out the rest. He's done with me holding myself separate, the rest of the guys are done with that, too, and they were all waiting for me to give them an opening so they could set me straight. Gordy said me bringing you around was what they'd been waiting for. I was pissed, I was freaked out, I felt like I was backed into a corner, and I wanted to draw up my armor and be a bitch, but I couldn't find it. And that made me madder. Not at Gordy but at you. Before I met you, I was quick to pull away. As much as I felt guilty after, it was easy to be nasty. To say mean things and make people leave. But I couldn't do it. Then I stopped being pissed and started listening to what Gordy was saying and started feeling bad. Like, horrible how I'd held myself apart. Then I told him about my nightmares."

I stopped to take a breath and that was when I noticed Luke had gone solid.

"I wasn't *really* mad at you," I rushed out. "It was just in the moment, when I couldn't make myself tell my friend to fuck off, I had to blame someone. Then I just started willy-nilly blurting personal shit out and I'd never, ever done that before. Not before you. Then it was almost like a relief when I told him about the dreams. Unfortunately, my relief was short-lived when we sat down at breakfast and Gordy was so mad at me for not talking to the team about what I was going through that I thought his head was going to pop off."

I stopped talking again and waited for Luke to say something and when he didn't, I rambled on.

"He's had dreams before, too. So have the others. And they talk about it. I didn't know that and it's my fault I didn't because I'm a shitty teammate. They've all been there for each other and I've never been there for a single one of them. You were right, they are my friends. I've just been too stupid to see it. And before I forget I wanted to tell you that the last three nights we've shared a bed I haven't dreamed about Penelope. And I need to get in contact with Liberty and apologize. I was a bitch to her when she was trying to be nice to me."

I quieted and waited but Luke lay there still as could be and didn't utter a word. My nerves were already frazzled, and his silence was scaring me.

"I mean, I won't call her if you don't want me to. But she offered if I needed someone to talk to I could reach out. That was really cool of her, especially after I was such a bitch. I don't think I need to talk about my dreams with her. I have Gordy and the guys, they were there. They saw it so they know. And if I need someone else, I know I can talk to you about it."

I got no more out.

Luke rolled us until he was on top of me, his hands on my cheeks holding my head still and holding my eyes hostage.

God, he was beautiful.

Fierce.

Strong.

Ferocious.

"You got me," he confirmed. "But Liberty already made it clear to Drake she was gonna make contact. My guess is she'll do that soon. And you need to know when she comes to you, she'll be bringing reinforcements. Liberty's tight with her family like you're tight with your brothers. Where one goes, the others follow. They're like a pack of hyenas. Vicious when one of them is threatened and they'll circle around you until they know you're sorted."

That sounded scary.

But I didn't tell Luke that.

"Okay."

"I'm glad you had a talk with Gordy. Next up is your brothers."

That sounded terrifying.

But I didn't tell him that either.

"I know."

"Proud of you, Shiloh."

"What?"

"So fucking proud, baby. I know that took a lot out of you and you still did it. My girl's tough as hell."

I wanted to blink, but I didn't want to miss a moment of the way Luke was staring at me. So I forced my eyes to stay open.

"You're not mad that I was irrationally mad at you and blaming you in my head?"

"No."

"I was really mad at you, Luke. I was thinking that you ruined me. That you vanquished Killer Frost and I needed her so damn bad to make Gordy shut up and go away. But she's gone."

Lord, what was wrong with me? Why was I trying to convince Luke he should be mad at me?

"I bet you were cursing my name. Pissed as shit you couldn't find it in you to turn Gordy away. Told you I was gonna make that stop. Told you I was digging it out. This is a good start. We'll build from here."

Luke did tell me and I never doubted he would do just that.

"Thank you," I whispered.

"You're welcome, Shiloh."

After he said that I was no longer looking into his beautiful face.

But that was okay, I got his lips on mine and his tongue in my mouth and that was even better.

21

"He's still in the wind?"

Carter's question pulled my attention from the white-board to Ethan prowling into the conference room.

"Yup." Ethan flung his big frame into the chair next to his brother.

The fact the chair didn't buckle under the force of Ethan's weight was a testament to its manufacturing. Ethan was madder than a motherfucker and I didn't blame him.

The cops in Montgomery had paid Jeff Shepard a visit. Instead of escorting Shepard to the station, they'd asked him to come in and speak to them. Of course, Shepard agreed then he ran.

That was two weeks ago.

Fourteen days and now the guy was a ghost.

Also, fourteen days of Shiloh in my bed or me in hers.

Two weeks of spending as much time with her as I could, getting to know her. Though, I was finding the getting to know her part wasn't all that necessary. What you see is what you get with Shiloh. I'm sure she'd disagree but she didn't hide who she was. From the first argument we'd had she'd laid herself bare. She might not have done it on purpose, but she'd let me in that night, and each day since, she gave me more.

Now, she was opening herself up to her team with Gordy leading that situation. Shiloh thought Gordy was pushing too hard. I disagreed. The man should've stepped up years ago. So he was making up for lost time, fully pulling her into the fray, guiding her to understand the true meaning of friendship. Shiloh bitched about this, but she did it in a way that stated plainly she was loving every second.

A week ago, Liberty had done exactly what I'd warned Shiloh she was going to do and reached out asking Shiloh out for coffee. Shiloh went and was met by not only Liberty but the entire women's brigade. That night, Shiloh was quiet and reflective through dinner. She'd asked me to take a bath with her and after we reenacted our first time in her tub—with a few variants that included me doing a whole lot more touching —Shiloh opened up and told me about her outing. This included Honor, Mercy, Tuesday, Delaney, Quinn, Hadley, and Addy all sharing their stories, and Liberty elaborating on what Shiloh already knew. Surprisingly, it was Addy who broke through. Shiloh didn't explain why beyond saying Addy "got it" and she was stronger than anyone she'd ever met. I couldn't deny Adalynn Walker's strength. Trey was a lucky sonofabitch to have Addy in his corner. The woman would stand by him through thick and thin. I figured that had a lot to do with the Walker loyalty that was ingrained but also because Trey hadn't faltered when the weight of most of her family came down on him. He stood strong and helped Addy heal from unthinkable hurt. So, maybe I wasn't all that surprised it was the shy Addy with her quiet strength who touched Shiloh the deepest.

"No word yet?" Brady asked.

"Nope. There's an APB out. Shepard hasn't used his credit cards. His car hasn't been spotted. None of his employees have seen him since the day before the cops showed. He hasn't called any of them. His ex-wife hasn't heard from him in years."

"Years?" I asked. "I thought he got visitation of his daughter. He doesn't speak to his ex during exchanges or to make travel arrangements?"

The details were fuzzy, but I distinctly remembered Jeff Shepard getting his daughter two weeks in the summer. I'd even checked the dates on the custody agreement to see if the time of the murder had taken place while he was scheduled to have his daughter.

"Apparently, he hasn't seen or spoken to his daughter in years. The ex-wife didn't sound upset by this. She actually said they were all better off with Jeff out of the picture," Ethan told me.

"Putting aside that Shepard's likely a murderer, I can see why the ex would say that," I began. "She filed for divorce but got nothing in the settlement because it was her that was cheating on Shepard with his business partner. There are three separate assault reports filed by the business partner. Not surprisingly, Shepard beat the shit out of the guy any time they came in contact. No charges were filed, but the reports are there. I'd think it would be a whole lot better if the ex you cheated on went away so she and her new husband wouldn't have to court a beatdown every time Shepard came to pick up his daughter. When was the last time Shepard visited his daughter?"

"I didn't ask specifically," Ethan returned. "I'll call her back and ask. There a reason you wanna know?"

"You *don't* wanna know?" I inquired.

"Oh, I'm gonna find out," Ethan stated. "I'm just wondering if we're on the same page."

"Shepard had his daughter for a two-week visit, and one week after he takes his daughter back to her mother and stepfather Becca Harper was murdered. I'd like to know if that was the last time he exercised his visitation rights. If seeing his daughter was the trigger. I'd also like to know if his ex-wife has more to say about why he stopped taking his daughter."

"And you say you're not any good at investigation work," Ethan mumbled.

"No, I'm damn good at it," I corrected with a smile. "I said I don't like sitting at my desk going over reports when I could be at the range blowing shit up."

"Now that sounds like an awesome day," Liberty said from behind me.

I swiveled in my chair and suddenly my day brightened.

Shiloh was standing next to her friend.

She was also smiling.

Though she was smiling when I rolled out of bed this morning after going down on her. And she was smiling when I kissed her goodbye before I left her bed to sleep in. And I could hear the smile coming at me over the phone when she called me a few hours ago promising me a thank you blow job. Something I was looking forward to collecting when I got home this evening. So by the time we'd hung up, I was smiling, too.

And right then seeing my woman happy I returned the grin and got up out of my chair and made my way to her.

"What are you doing here?" I asked right before I dropped a kiss on her forehead.

"Well, like Liberty said, it's an awesome day to blow shit up."

"We were stopping in to see if there was range time available," Liberty put in.

"Pistol's full right now. But the rifle's open," Brady answered.

"Perfect. That's where we were headed. Any classes out there today?" Liberty went on.

"What do you two have planned?" Ethan inquired.

"Planned? Why would you ask such a thing, cousin?"

Liberty feigned innocence, but Shiloh gave her away when she choked out a laugh.

"I ask because I *know* you," Ethan continued. "And your partner in crime over there is laughing."

"I'm not laughing," Shiloh lied.

"Babe?"

Shiloh tipped her head back and her smile widened.

"We're gonna blow shit up," she told me.

"What kind of shit?"

"The kind that explodes."

"Oh, I also need to use a Polaris," Liberty announced.

Carter's loud boom of laughter filled the room. It didn't take long for Ethan to join his brother.

"Woman, you own the joint. Why are you asking if you can use a Polaris?" Brady shook his head.

"Oh, right." Liberty waved her hand. "Come on, Sunny, let's load up."

"Hold on there, pyromaniac." I held onto Shiloh. "Not until you tell me what you're blowing up. I have a class tomorrow and I prefer not backfilling a crater."

"Just Tannerite," Shiloh beamed.

"Liberty," Carter groaned.

"What?"

"How much?" Carter pushed.

"Three pounds."

"Fuck no."

Shiloh giggled. Liberty crossed her arms over her chest. Carter scowled.

"Why not? As Brady pointed out, I own the place just like you. And we're shooting it from three-hundred yards so no worries," Liberty argued.

Three-hundred yards? Yeah, that won't work.

"You know better than that," Brady chided. "A two-two-three won't detonate Tannerite at three-hundred yards. The bullet needs to be traveling over two-thousand feet per second at impact. It's about—"

"Velocity, I know," Liberty snapped. "I'm totally offended. Next, you'll want me to sit in on your Bullet Ballistics101."

Shiloh's mouth twisted in amusement but she didn't interject.

What are these two up to?

"Then what are you shooting it with, a fifty cal?" Brady pushed.

"Nope. My brand new Sig Cross," Liberty bragged.

"No shit?" Carter stood and came around the table. "You have one?"

"Yep."

Well, damn. That was a sweet rifle. The last and greatest from Sig.

"And you're taking her out now?" Ethan got up but dropped his keys on the table.

I guess he was staying.

"Yep."

"I'm in." Brady started for the door then stopped. "How much ammo you got? We don't have two-seven-seven Fury in the armory."

"Just enough to show you boys how the big girls play," Liberty retorted.

"Seriously?" Ethan groaned.

"Naw. I'm just kidding. I wouldn't come just to tease you. But me and Sunny go first."

Brady took off like a shot and Ethan nodded.

"Deal."

"We'll meet y'all out there." I pulled Shiloh off to the side to let Carter and Ethan exit.

Liberty paused, turned, and smiled at Shiloh.

"I told you we wouldn't have to set up targets today."

"That you did," Shiloh returned.

"I'll have the guys load your gear. We'll see you out there."

"Thanks."

I waited until everyone was gone before I bent and gave my woman a proper greeting, one that included lots of tongue and my hands on her ass, and this went on until she moaned into my mouth. Unfortunately, that was my cue to break our kiss.

"How's your day been, baby?"

Shiloh did a slow blink before sadness crept into her eyes.

"River's going undercover."

"Shit, Shiloh, that's rough. He say what the assignment is?"

"There's a local gang with ties down in Pensacola. The local boys upped their game and are transporting. River's been working this case a year and finally flipped one of the guys he's been working. So he has an in and he's taking it."

There was something else working behind her eyes.

"What else?"

"Echo and Phoenix are working it, too. Not undercover.

But the crew here in Georgia is running drugs and guns. All three of my brothers are wrapped up in this. That's why Echo was here a few weeks ago talking to Jason. He was giving him the heads up the operation was likely to happen and if it did Echo wanted Jason in the loop."

No. Echo wanted Triple Canopy as backup. If shit hit the fan and there was blowback here in Georgia, he wanted his brothers and Shiloh covered.

"When we're done at the range, we'll find Jason and talk to him about what he knows. He hasn't mentioned anything to the team. Though he wouldn't until there was something to be mentioned. But I'm sure he already has contingencies in place should River need something."

"That'd make me feel better," she admitted.

"I know, baby, that's why we're gonna talk to Jason."

Shiloh fell silent and she did this studying me. Her eyes roamed my face and when they caught mine again the worry was gone. But there was something new at play. She did this from time to time—looked at me like she wanted to say something. Like the words were *right* there and wanted to come out but each time she held them back.

"I...um...thank you."

So close.

My hand went to her cheek. She leaned into my palm and my thumb stroked her jaw.

"You're welcome."

Sadly, we had people waiting on us.

"You ready to go blow shit up?" I continued.

"Do you need to ask?"

"Right. We better get on that before we miss the action."

Shiloh rolled to her toes, plopped a hard, fast kiss on my lips, and rolled back down.

"Lead the way."

"Ladies first." I swept my arm toward the door.

"You just like looking at my ass."

"Yep."

And that was all it took for Shiloh's smile to beam.

So damn beautiful.

"Good Lord!" Brady whooped.

My gaze didn't go to the fireball three hundred yards out.

I didn't share in the excitement of a target exploding in spectacular fashion.

My gaze was riveted on the shooter.

Her finger came out of the trigger guard, her hand came up and she ejected her brass, dropped the magazine, and finally, her cheek came off the stock.

Then her eyes lifted to mine and she smiled.

I swear at that moment the sun shone a little brighter, the heat of the day burned a little hotter, and I fell a little deeper in love with Shiloh Kent.

22

"I love the way he looks at you." Liberty nudged my shoulder. We were in the parking lot getting ready to leave.

Jason hadn't been at the office when we were done shooting, so Luke promised he'd get all the information for me when he got back from a site inspection.

"Drake looks at me that way," she continued.

"How does Luke look at me?" I asked.

Then I held my breath hoping Liberty saw what I felt. There had been occasions over the last two weeks when I'd caught him staring at me and I'd swear he was looking at me like he loved me, but he never said the words. And there were plenty of times when I wanted to tell him I was madly in love with him, but I chickened out.

"Like you're it for him. Like he's not sure if he wants to drag you into a closet and give you the business or if he wants to put you on a pedestal and worship you."

Liberty was correct in her assessment. I knew she was because oftentimes Luke went from "giving me the business" rough and dirty to switching it up and giving me slow and sweet in one session. I did not mind the change of pace. I actually loved that Luke could give me both.

"We've only been together a few weeks," I reminded her. "Do you think it's too soon?"

"Too soon for what?"

"For me to love him?"

In an instant, everything about Liberty softened and it scared the shit out of me. I was getting used to this friendship gig, but I was still in the early stages. I still had moments where I wanted to pull away. Times when Riddle, Chip, Gordy, or Mereno would ask me if I was still having bad dreams and I had to tamp down the urge to tell them to mind their own business. Which, by the way, I hadn't had a single dream about Penelope in two weeks. Not since Luke started sleeping next to me.

Then there were times when Luke would ask about my dad and push me to open up and I had to fight the panic. Only once did I slip and fall back into my old habit of shutting down and retreating. Luke simply reminded me he wasn't letting me hide. He did this firmly but gently. It took the rest of the night for me to apologize for being a bitch, but I was damn proud of myself for getting there.

I was a work in progress with a boatload of issues I'd yet to resolve but I was determined. Not for Luke—for myself. I wanted to be a better person. I didn't want to be selfish. I wanted the people I cared about to know what they meant to me. And I wanted to feel the fullness of their feelings for me. So, I had to let the fear go. I had to believe not everyone would abandon me. But mostly I had to learn to trust myself. I wasn't stupid. I had good instincts. I was surrounded by good people. I could be a good friend if I allowed myself.

"I've thought about this a lot—when was the exact moment I fell in love with Drake. And I think it happened in stages. But it started with three angry words shouted in my face, 'goddammit, *Liberty*, breathe.' I'll never forget Drake literally breathed life back into me. I was beat to hell, covered in blood and grime, and at my lowest. There was no farther down I could sink in my misery. Yet Drake never once treated me like I was broken. He reminded me how strong I was. I fell a little more in love with him because of that. So what I'm saying is it's never too soon to fall in love. I fell in love with Drake while my hands were cuffed, lying in the dirt after being tortured. And I did that before I even opened my eyes. Luckily for me, Drake is hot, or I'd be in love with an ugly dude."

Liberty stopped and made a funny face halfway between a grimace and a smile. I returned her smile thinking the friendship thing was pretty all right.

Like Drake, Luke had never treated me like I was broken even though I clearly was. Luke was strong, firm, unrelenting. But he was also patient, kind, and gentle.

"Haven't told him," I confessed.

"Why not?"

"Honestly? I'm scared. If he's not there yet with me I don't want to make things weird."

"Girl..." Liberty drew out the L and shook her head. "That man is gone for you. Totally and completely gone. And I'm not telling you this to be mean, but it's you who's gonna hafta put yourself out there and say it first."

Gah.

Liberty was right. Luke had done all of the heavy lifting in our relationship. He'd spent a lot of effort breaking through my barriers and every obstacle I'd put in his way, he'd found a way to smash those, too.

"And before you go thinking you need to find the *right* time to tell him, it's always the right time to share your feelings with the people you care about," Liberty finished.

And she was right about that, too, and it was high time I started doing just that.

"It means a lot to me, you taking the time to talk to me. I know I apologized—"

"Yep, you did, and saying you're sorry a second time means you didn't believe me the first time I told you I understood. So, let's leave that in the past, and let's get to the part where you promise to tell me and the girls all about how the Love Reveal goes."

"What does that mean?"

I asked the question even though I was fairly certain by the way Liberty was wiggling her eyebrows that I didn't want to know.

"You'll see."

"You know you say that a lot. Which reminds me, you still haven't told me your plans after the Army."

"Right. Who am I, if not a soldier?" Liberty shrugged. "I'm me."

"What?"

"I'm *me*. Just *me*."

"What does that mean?"

"It means you showed me the other day that being a soldier doesn't define who I am. It never did. Somewhere along the way, I forgot what "be all you can be" really meant. I was so busy proving to myself all the things I could do while in uniform I lost sight of something. Being all I can be to the people who love me. Being all I can be to a friend who is struggling. I don't need a uniform to do that. And saying that doesn't mean I'm not proud of my service or what I've accomplished. It simply means when the time comes for me to leave the Army I now know I won't lose what's really important."

I didn't think I actually showed Liberty anything but I wasn't going to quibble.

"I promise to call you and tell you about the Love Reveal if you promise to rally the girls and get them all to my house for..."

Shit, for what? What did a group of women do when they got together at each other's houses? *Did* women do that, get together at each other's houses?

Damn.

My gaze went over her shoulder and I felt my face heat.

"Sunny?"

"Huh?"

"Girl, stop. You look like you're ready to bolt, which is hilarious considering twenty minutes you were blowing shit up. You don't need an excuse or an occasion to call your girls over. You call, we come. Easy. You call and tell us you have snacks and wine, we come faster. You call and tell us you need us, we're there warp-speed. All you have to do is call. Unfortunately for you, you've come into the family at a time where you're gonna have to put up with a whole lotta talk about babies and weddings and I don't foresee that ending soon. Mercy and Laney are going to pop their kids out, then it will be Hadley and Addy's turn and right after them Quinn will be knocked up. Which is gonna be killer to watch Uncle Jasper have a freak-out with all of his kids back-to-back pregnant."

From what little I knew of Jasper Walker, Liberty wasn't wrong. The guy seemed rather protective over his children.

But I was stuck back on 'all you have to do is call.'

That easy?

I just had to call.

"And you and Drake? Are you planning on having kids right away?"

"Yes."

Well, alrighty then, that was firm.

Then Liberty did something strange, she busted out laughing. I watched her do this for a long time. And when she finally got control she smiled.

"You're fun," she declared.

Fun?

"Are you okay? Did the shockwave rattle your brain? Did you drink something when I wasn't looking? Because I think you're a little crazy and it's scaring me."

"Sober as a church mouse. Or is it sober as a nun?" Liberty waved her hand and smiled. "However the saying goes. I've never had a friend who's never had girlfriends before. Sometimes you look surprised. Other times you look stunned. We're friends, Sunny. And friends talk to their friends. Yes, I want to start making a family with Drake as soon as we can. Drake feels the same way. And I'll tell you something we haven't shared with the rest yet. Quinn's gonna likely be pissed but it's her fault for wanting to get married on Laney's due date like a crazy person so she can't be all that mad. Drake and I set a date. It's gonna be a surprise. We're gonna send out a text and give everyone one hour to show up."

"Are you serious?"

"Yep. No stress. No planning. Just family."

"And one hour to get there."

"And one hour to get there," she confirmed. "On that note, I gotta run."

We said our goodbyes, which included Liberty reminding me not to forget to call her, then I drove home.

I spent the rest of the day cleaning my house thinking it

was going to be great having friends. When I was done cleaning I spent the rest of the afternoon thinking I was all kinds of stupid for pushing anyone who tried to be my friend away.

"What's this?" Luke asked.

It was much later. Luke was home from work and I was at the stove pulling dinner out of the oven.

I glanced over my shoulder and nearly dropped the baked ziti.

Shit.

Goddamn.

I forgot to put the letter away.

But I didn't get to explain.

"Who the *fuck* is Clive Hutchinson?" Luke growled.

My stomach hollowed and the vibe of the room shifted to unhappy.

I didn't think any man would like to find a letter calling the woman he cared about a piece of shit. But a man like Luke, like my brothers, like the men I worked with, would like it less so. And I knew I was right because Luke looked like he was getting ready to blow.

Further, I didn't think Luke would ever understand those letters.

"Penelope's father."

"Come again?"

"Penelope Hutchinson. The hostage—"

"Babe, I know who she is. What I'm asking is why in the actual fuck is her father sending you a fucked-up letter."

Luke jerked the paper in his hand and it was confirmed

he'd never get why a grieving father, who blamed me, would send me letters.

"Because he needs to vent. He's in pain. I understand what that feels like. And if it makes him feel even a sliver better to send me letters—"

"Did you say *letters*?" Luke cut in. "This isn't the first?"

A dangerous current ricocheted around the room, bounced off the walls until the air was electrified with Luke's anger.

"Please stop cutting me off and let me finish. Clive is understandably upset. His daughter was murdered in front of him. His wife passed away years ago. Penelope was his only child. The man has nothing. He's lashing out. I get why he blames me. I understand the anger he feels. He'll burn out but in the meantime, I owe it to him, so I listen to what he feels he needs to get off his chest."

Luke might not have verbally interrupted me but that didn't mean he quelled the ferocity rolling off of him. If anything, it had magnified. His scowl had deepened, his posture went from alert to stiff, and his stare had gone from watchful to seriously pissed.

"Did you just say you understood why this motherfucker blames you?"

"Don't call him that," I whispered. "He lost his child."

Luke's eyes narrowed further and he took a step toward me.

"He did, Shiloh, but that doesn't give him the right to send you nasty letters tearing you down. He lost his child but through that, he didn't gain the right to call you a piece of shit. His daughter is dead and that's a tragedy but *you* didn't kill her."

The area around my heart tightened like it always did

when I thought about Penelope. A young girl whose life was stolen from the world. Snuffed out before she could do great things. A father left behind to mourn her loss.

I knew what it was like to be left, to mourn a loss—even if it was the loss of a dream. My father was trash, but that didn't mean when he went to prison I didn't feel it. My mother had been useless, but when she left I'd mourned that, too.

"Penelope left and—"

"No!" Luke snapped. "Penelope didn't *leave*, she was murdered."

"That's what I meant."

At this juncture, I was rethinking my stance on friendship. Rethinking why I'd allowed Luke in so easily. This didn't feel good. This was what I had avoided. I didn't want to talk about Penelope and Clive. I didn't want to discuss how I felt about what happened.

"You do not identify with Clive Hutchinson," Luke rasped. "What happened to him was not the same as what happened to you and your brothers. You're not anyone's punching bag."

I felt it, the panic, the cold. It was seeping into my bones.

Luke was right, it wasn't the same. But he was also wrong. I deserved to be called all the mean, horrible names Clive called me. I'd earned his anger. I'd failed his daughter.

I was a piece of shit.

And why shouldn't I be Clive's punching bag? I'd earned that, too, by being a bitch to so many people who had done nothing but try to be nice to me.

I was getting a taste of what I'd done to others.

I deserved that, too.

"Shiloh," Luke called.

Soft. Sweet. Gentle.

Hearing that, my vision turned watery.

"Baby."

More soft, sweet, and gentle.

"No."

My voice wasn't gentle. It sounded pained because it was.

So much pain.

"Baby, come here."

"No. I can't do this."

"Yes, you can."

"No, Luke," I rasped. "I can't. I cannot do this right now. Or ever. I can't do this *ever*. It is what it is. You don't get it. I fucked up and if he needs this I'm gonna give it to him. If he wants to write me a letter a week for the rest of his life telling me how horrible I am, I'm not gonna stop him."

"No, I don't get it. And it seriously fuckin' worries me you're all right with this."

"Why wouldn't I be? I fucking *deserve* this, Luke. He witnessed his daughter's head *explode!*"

Losing my balance I pitched forward, stumbled, but before I could fall, Luke was there.

His hands went to my waist and he hauled me up then wrapped his arms around me. I struggled to break free but his grasp tightened. I did my best in the small space Luke allowed to shove at his chest but he didn't budge.

"Let me go."

Silence.

"Luke! Let me go."

Nothing.

More silence.

More panic.

Please help her.

Clive's voice sounded in my head. I dropped my fore-head, hit Luke's chest, and I closed my eyes as best I could.

But I could still hear Clive's screams.

Nothing would ever silence those.

23

Shit. Goddamn.

My arms already tight around Shiloh got tighter when her body bucked and her legs gave out.

Shit. Fuck.

I shifted a trembling Shiloh and scooped one hand behind her knees. I lifted her into my arms and made my way to her couch while her body continued to shake. I sat down and she immediately burrowed in. Face to my throat, chest plastered to mine, hand fisting my shirt. She couldn't get any closer but I still locked my arms tight and held on.

I fucked up huge and lost it.

I should've found a better time to bring the letter up but each word I read had my blood heating. The sonofabitch was a goddamn motherfucker, grieving or not. The man had no business writing to Shiloh and he certainly had no goddamn motherfucking right to tell Shiloh she was the reason his child was dead. But that wasn't the worst of what he wrote. His closing sentence was what had set me on fire.

I hope you dream of my daughter's last moments on earth until you die a miserable death.

Not an outright threat but no less fucked-up.

It was no wonder Shiloh had nightmares. She was reliving that day over and over and not because her mind wouldn't put it to rest. Clive Hutchinson was twisting her head.

How many fucked-up letters had he sent?

Jesus, fuck me.

"I tried," Shiloh whispered.

Coarse. Tortured. Pain-filled.

"I know you did."

"It went downhill fast. Robbery turned into a hostage situation. We didn't know it then. Not until it was too late. The suspect was out on parole. He was facing the rest of a twenty-year sentence if he went back in. His mom was sick, MS. She didn't have twenty years waiting on her son to get back out. She also didn't have anyone to take care of her. Simon Abbot. That was his name."

Fucked-up situation all the way around.

"Shiloh, baby, even if you'd known the particulars it wouldn't have changed the outcome."

"All she did was go to work. Family business. A mini-mart. She worked there after school when she wasn't playing sports, and on Saturdays. No Sundays, that was her day off to spend with her friends. She was smart. Straight A's. Her friends loved her."

Something was seriously wrong with Shiloh knowing Penelope's work schedule.

"How do you know that?"

"He told me in his first letter. He sent me her report cards. Copies of condolence letters he'd received from her teachers, coaches, friends, neighbors. Everyone loved her."

That wasn't wrong—it was jacked-the-fucked-up.

"Shiloh, baby."

"Simon Abbot looked right at me. Right in the eye, Luke. And pulled the trigger."

Shiloh's body jolted and her face pressed deeper.

From head to toe, Shiloh trembled in my arms.

I said nothing.

Not because I had nothing to say, but right then with my woman shaking on my lap she was not ready to hear what I had to say. She wasn't ready to hear the truth. Simon Abbot killed Penelope Hutchinson and there wasn't a damn thing anyone could've done to stop him. And Clive Hutchinson's pain was not Shiloh's to bear and his fucked-up letters would be stopping.

But right then, I wasn't worried about Clive, Simon, or Penelope.

A person could only stand so much heartache.

And Shiloh Kent had been through enough.

Too fucking much.

In the silence, I thought about her nightmares. She hadn't had any since she'd been in my bed or I'd been in hers. But there had been times in the last two weeks when Shiloh had been called out in the middle of the night and by the time she got home I was gone. Which meant she'd slept without me. She had not mentioned if she had them then.

I thought the dreams were going away because she'd opened up to Gordy and the rest of the guys on her team. Shiloh was forthcoming about the conversations she had with the guys. They treated her no differently than they always had; there was just a layer of closeness Shiloh hadn't allowed in the past.

"You get nightmares when you get a letter."

Shiloh nodded into my throat even though I hadn't asked her a question.

"You know it's gonna happen. You know what the letter's

gonna say but you open them anyway knowing they're gonna give you nightmares. You do it to keep the pain fresh because you think you deserve it."

Again Shiloh nodded and a burn hit my chest.

"You're doing it to torture yourself."

She made a low, guttural, keeling sound and that burn slithered up into my throat. I felt the noises Shiloh made vibrating against my chest but I was wholly unprepared for the sob that tore from her. I flinched at the sound, jerked in surprise, and held on tighter when her body shuddered.

That burn that had ignited seared through me as pain leaked out of Shiloh. It streamed down her cheeks, it leaked from her pores, it filled the room until I couldn't breathe through the thick clouds of agony.

Body-wrenching.

Breath-stealing.

Excruciating cries of pain.

And I was powerless to stop it. There was nothing I could do but hold on. So that was what I did until my arms ached from clutching her close, then I held on longer until she cried herself to sleep. I waited a good long while until I carried her to bed and tucked her in.

Then I went back to the kitchen to turn off the oven and put the dinner Shiloh had made into the fridge. I turned off the lights, locked the front door, and got into bed next to my woman.

～

I felt the moment Shiloh woke.

It was nearing on midnight.

I'd lain awake for hours listening to her breathe coming up with a plan. My first instinct was to run roughshod over

Shiloh and take matters into my hands. I figured it would take a five-minute conversation with Echo and he'd shut Clive Hutchinson down. The problem with that was Echo would likely cause bodily harm while communicating to Hutchinson the letters were to cease. Not only would that put Echo's ass on the line but Shiloh would be worried about her brother. Gordy was an option. I doubted he'd take it to a physical level but the way he cared about Shiloh he might. Which again meant Shiloh would be unhappy. I considered them because I knew better than to seek out Hutchinson personally; there was no doubt I'd rip the man apart. And it was debatable after I held Shiloh while she exhausted herself sobbing in my arms—witnessing her pain and despair—if I'd have it in me to leave the motherfucker breathing.

So, I was out. Echo was out. Gordy was out. I had other options. My brothers would take my back, they'd go have a word and make sure Clive Hutchinson understood he was never to reach out to Shiloh again. I could make the letters stop.

But I couldn't make Shiloh heal. She had to do that for herself and the first step in that was admitting she did not earn the shit Hutchinson was shoveling.

Which meant *she* had to be the one who made him stop.

I didn't like this. I wanted to protect Shiloh. I wanted to stand between her and anything that would cause her harm. But I knew better. She'd twist my protection into something ugly. The irony of the situation was she wasn't strong enough to accept my help. She would view that as being weak instead of realizing it takes more strength to allow someone to help you than it does to push them away.

"Did you turn off the oven?" Shiloh asked groggily.

I smiled, something I didn't think I'd do with the memory of her tears fresh in my mind.

"Yeah, babe, I put dinner in the fridge, too. You hungry?"

"Did you eat?" she returned instead of answering.

"No."

I heard Shiloh sigh and she burrowed closer.

"You missed dinner because you didn't want to leave me," she said conversationally.

Shiloh was correct, therefore I didn't find it necessary to confirm. I liked her close, I liked what it said and I liked her turning to me for comfort. But I was uneasy about where her head was at after what happened.

"Don't get it."

The words were whisper-soft and even though her cheek was resting on my chest, her chin was tipped back, and her statement was uttered against the skin under my jaw I could barely hear her.

"Get what?"

"Why you don't leave me."

Before I could get a handle on my rising irritation she went on. Which only made it worse.

"I'm so fucked-up I'm a basket case. My job calls me out all hours of the night, it interrupts dinner, and it interferes with plans. I'm a total bitch. I pull away and hide because I'm a chickenshit. I mean, aren't you fed up with my shit yet?"

I took a moment to take a deep breath, then I exhaled and took another one. After the fourth one, I realized deep breathing wasn't going to work. Not this time. I also realized that the only way to get through to Shiloh was to say it straight.

So that was what I did and I pulled no punches.

"You love your job," I started with the obvious. "If you

didn't, you being called out in the middle of the night and rolling out of bed would seriously suck. If you didn't, you getting a call out while we're in the middle of eating dinner would get old. But you love what you do and I'd be a fucking dick if I complained about something that's important to you. I'm proud of the job you do. I'm proud knowing my woman rolls out of our bed, kits up, and goes out to protect and serve."

"But—"

"No buts, baby. That's it. I'm proud of you. Period. Now, we've discussed you pulling your frosty bitch routine. I know why you were doing it, you admitted you know why you do it, and we've moved on from that. And, Shiloh, as much as I love you and will stand next to you and help you through the rest of the junk polluting your head I won't allow you to keep dragging this shit back up. You explained, apologized, I told you I understood, and even though there was nothing to forgive I gave you that anyway."

"You love me?" she whispered.

"Crazy in love with you."

I felt Shiloh go solid. Her hand resting on my chest glided down and curled around my ribs and her fingers dug in.

"Why?"

"Baby, look at me."

I waited for what seemed like an eternity until she tipped her head back and caught my gaze.

"Why wouldn't I love you?"

Her eyes flared and the rest of the mask I hadn't realized she was still holding onto shattered. I watched it happen— all pretense fell away, and before me was the little girl whose mom left when she could no longer deal with the life she'd created. That being a life where she'd hooked her star to a criminal, made a family with that man, and when the repercussions of that life hit full-force she bailed.

Late one night, Shiloh had told me about her mother. A weak woman, who was tired of her husband being carted off to jail leaving her to fend for herself and four children. A weak woman who didn't wise up and use one of the many opportunities while Lester was in jail to pack up her kids and leave. A selfish woman who'd waited for Lester to be released, *then* packed her shit up, left her kids, and took off.

The Shiloh who was staring up at me didn't understand her worth. And I knew she didn't learn that shit from her brothers. They adored their baby sister. They all pitched in and took care of her and each other. They'd created the family their parents didn't. No, it was her parents who taught her she was worthless—easily tossed aside and left.

Fucking assholes.

My hand moved from her hip, pushing up the tee she wore, then I started gliding my fingers against her soft, warm skin.

"Tell me, baby, why wouldn't I love you?"

"Because you deserve something—someone—better."

"I deserve it?" I asked and Shiloh nodded. "First, no one *deserves* anything. No one is *entitled* to life's good offerings. Nothing in life is free or given. You have to earn it. And you should understand that better than most. You were dealt a shit hand, yet you *worked* to overcome the obstacles your father built around you. You worked to earn your place as a cop, then you worked and earned your place on SWAT. You worked and earned respect. Don't discount your accomplishments. You've struggled, fought, and preserved to earn every damn one of them.

"I know what I've done in my life to earn the love of a good woman. And make no mistake, Shiloh, I've worked my ass off my whole life to be the sort of man who can look at himself in the mirror and do it with pride. That's not to say I haven't slipped up. I have and my slip-ups were huge. The biggest one nearly cost me and Trey our lives. I put my team at risk. And I'm goddamn lucky I'm not blind. I lost my place in the Navy and spent way too much time feeling sorry for myself. But I snapped out of it. I worked to forgive myself and let go of the guilt. Hear this, Shiloh; I've earned you. I've worked my ass off to be the man you need. And I didn't start to be that man when I met you; I've been working at it my whole life, waiting to give it to you. There is no one in this world better for me than you. And I know down to my soul there is no one better on the planet for you than me. No one can ever love you the way I do because you are mine. Your insecurities are mine. Your imperfections are mine. Your strength, your loyalty, your humor, your beautiful eyes, your body, your intelligence, your heart, your love. All of it belongs to me. You can wrap that up in your bitchy attitude when you're scared. You can try to shut me out when you're afraid to face something. And that's okay because your fear is mine, too. I will not leave you. I swear it, Shiloh. I will love you through whatever life throws our way."

Her fingers digging into my side suddenly loosened and she clumsily scrambled to climb on top of me. My hands went to her hips to steady her when she pitched to the side in her hurried effort to burrow into me.

And for the second time that night, I held my woman while she cried.

Shiloh's body rocked with her tears. I slid my arms around her as tight as I could get them. And that was how we stayed. Her shaking and me absorbing her pain.

She finally broke the silence when she said, "Clive has to stop sending me letters."

Thank fuck.

"I should've stopped him after I got the first one."

Fuck yeah, she was getting it.

"At first I thought it was a grieving father's right. His way of healing after he lost his daughter the way he did."

No doubt Clive Hutchinson was grieving but that never gave him the right to hurt Shiloh. I didn't remind her of this. Instead, I remained quiet.

"And, yes, part of me thought I deserved to read what he was saying about me in those letters. Part of me welcomed the pain. You were right, I was torturing myself. I read every letter. Some of them I read twice. I gave myself those nightmares so I wouldn't forget her."

Shiloh lifted her head and sat up astride me. There was still plenty of sadness in those pastel eyes but there was something new and it looked a hell of a lot like hope. Her hands went to my chest for balance and mine went to her thighs pressing tightly against my hips. I said nothing as her gaze roamed my face. I stayed silent when she brought her right hand up and traced my jaw with her fingertips, then my lips, then over my stubble until she cupped my cheek like I did with her.

So fucking sweet.

"I know you won't agree with this because you love me. But if you think about it logically, like the warfighter you are, you'll understand. I didn't have all the information about Simon Abbot." With the mention of that asshole's name, my muscles tightened and I braced. "Information my team could've used. We would've responded differently if we'd known where his head was at. His mother was at the end stages of her illness, he was facing going back to prison, and knowing that, he was playing out a fucked-up scenario of suicide by cop. We might have been able to save Penelope from going down if we'd known. We didn't. And then I used Penelope's death as a reminder of how fragile life is. How important it is I'm the best I can be at my job. I didn't do that in a healthy way. I did it ugly, and twisted her murder into my personal failure. But the thing is, when there is loss of life, when we lose a hostage or an innocent civilian dies, it is a failure. And it has to be viewed as such so we can learn from it. I failed. My team failed. A young, beautiful, sweet girl with a bright future paid for that failure."

Most of what Shiloh said was good, she was untwisting shit in her mind. But she was still wrong.

"I get you." I gave her thighs a squeeze and continued. "And you're correct; each mission, each call out, every new situation is an opportunity to learn. What went right. What went wrong. And what adjustments need to be made. But, baby, they're only failures if your team doesn't learn from them. You cannot control every outcome. Your team cannot predict what a suspect is going to do with a hundred percent accuracy, a hundred percent of the time. It's just not possible. And if you keep looking at them as failures, keeping track in your head, and ticking a column every time you're called out, you're going to actually fail. You won't be effective. You'll second-guess yourself, you'll second-guess your team, and someone will get hurt because instead of following your instincts you'll be too busy overthinking the ending. The other option is you'll become ineffective in a different way, and you'll go off the reservation and become a maverick. And that only has one ending—*your* death."

Shiloh's gaze stayed glued to mine and I hoped to God she heard the last part. I'd seen it happen in the Navy. The heavy load of losing teammates. The feeling of failure that turns into a burn that leads a man astray. Helplessness that turns into a suicide mission to right perceived failures.

"I wish I had you when she died."

Christ, that felt good.

"I was struggling," she admitted. "I should've reached out to my brothers."

There it was.

"Yeah, baby, you should've. Asking for guidance and wisdom is a sign of strength. But that's in the past, too. Moving on from here, you'll remember turning to those who love you is not weakness it's the ultimate show of trust and love."

"What?"

"Shiloh, we all see it. We all know you got it going on, girl. You're tough, you're competent at your job, in your life. You got mad skills. We see it, we know it. So when a woman like you who's taken life by the balls, earned her place among the best, reaches out, it shows you trust the person you're reaching out to. You seeking their wisdom means you respect their opinion. It also shows your trust is shrouded in love."

Her head dropped forward and her eyes drifted closed.

"Thank you," she murmured. "Thank you for making it so easy to love you. For showing me the way and helping me stay the course."

"Eyes, baby," I rumbled, unable to keep the coarseness from my tone.

Shiloh's lids slowly opened and she looked at me from under her lashes.

"You love me?"

"Like crazy."

Two words. An affirmation.

That didn't feel good, it felt phenomenal.

So damn remarkable I couldn't speak.

But I could show her.

So I did.

Shiloh didn't protest when I hooked her around the back of the neck and brought her mouth to mine. She didn't complain when I started the kiss slow and sweet. Tasting and teasing with our tongues, building it for both of us until I tilted her head and deepened the kiss. Finally, when I earned her sexy-as-fuck noises I broke the kiss. That earned a new sound, a sexy whimper of disappointment.

"Luke."

Raspy, turned on, desire-filled.

Hell yeah!

"On my face, baby, I'm hungry."

I felt her body shiver right before she rolled off and tugged down her shorts. Shiloh started to climb back on when I halted her progress.

"Other way. I want your mouth around my dick while I eat you."

Another tremble.

Without delay or further encouragement, Shiloh threw her leg over my waist, her heart-shaped ass right in front of me and too sexy not to touch. My hands roamed her backside while she freed my dick from my boxers then I hauled her hips back, positioned her pussy over my mouth, and guided her down.

After that, I ate my woman until she was squirming, with her mouth working magic around my dick. Shiloh sucked and I licked. Her tongue ran the length of my cock and I used mine to tease her clit. She took me to the back of her throat and my hips came off the bed. I tongue-fucked her until she ground down on my face.

Both of us close.

I jerked her hips up, my cock slid from her mouth, and I swatted her ass, propelling her forward.

"Ride," I grunted.

Shiloh shifted, fisted my shaft, lined us up, and slammed down.

Christ, fucking A. So tight and hot and wet.

I lifted my head off the pillow and took in the magnificence before me. Blonde hair tumbling down her back. The sexy flair of her hips. Her ass jiggling with every bounce. All of it so fucking hot I had to clench my jaw.

"Lean forward. Hands on the bed by my knees."

Shiloh's hands glided down my thighs and then they fisted the sheets near my legs. In an effort not to touch her, I did the same.

The new position afforded me a new view. One that was arguably better than the first.

"Wish you could see this, baby. Your pussy taking my dick."

Shiloh slid up then slid down and the feel of it coupled with the visual was so insanely, unbelievably hot I was close to coming.

"Every time you're inside of me I think it can't get better, yet the next time you prove me wrong," Shiloh moaned on a downward glide.

Fuck.

"Faster, Shiloh. I wanna watch you fuck me hard."

Her pace picked up, her noises became louder and held an edge of frustration. And in a place deep inside of me, I loved she couldn't get off without me. I loved she could take herself to the brink but it was me who drove her over.

My tongue, my fingers, my words. Sometimes it was one or the other. Sometimes a combination of the three. Sometimes if I felt like it, I worked her up with my tongue and fingers, then finished off talking dirty to her while I fingered her. Any way I did it, she got off. But something I learned about Shiloh the very first time in her bathtub, she seriously loved when I talked her through her climax.

The filthier the better.

It was sexy as fuck.

"You close, baby?" I asked needlessly.

"Yes," she groaned and her head tipped back.

"Want me to help?"

"You know I do."

Yeah, I did.

"You want me to finger your clit or do you wanna hear about how fucking hot it is to watch your pussy stretch around my dick?"

"Both," she whined.

I jackknifed up, pressed my chest to her back, and my mouth went to her ear. I brought my fingers to her lips and tapped.

"Open up and get 'em wet."

She sucked my fingers into her mouth while my other hand cupped her breast, and my fingers found and then pinched her nipple.

"Enough."

Shiloh released my fingers and I dropped them between her legs and went to work on her clit.

"We're gonna make this fast, Shiloh. Watching your pussy wet my dick, feeling you clamped tight, you have me ready to blow."

I put more pressure on her clit and her body jolted. I pinched and rolled her nipple, pulling more desperate groans out of her.

"You have no clue how fucking beautiful you feel," I moaned against her neck. "Clenched tight, soaking my dick. The only thing that feels better is when you come around me."

"Luke."

Shiloh's voice hitched and her pussy spasmed and that was all it took for my orgasm to break loose.

"You feel that?" I grunted through the intense pleasure. "I can't hold back with you. Too good. Come with me, baby."

"Yes."

She lost her rhythm and her fast hard glides turned into jerks and shudders.

"Christ. Perfect."

"Perfect," she echoed on a long groan.

Before the last of my climax waned, I kissed her neck and whispered, "I love you, Shiloh."

"Love." *Tremble.* "You." *Another jolt.* "Luke."

It would be a long while before I settled us in bed. Side by side facing each other. Legs tangled. A sated, sleepy gaze coming from Shiloh. And I suspected I was giving her the same. I rolled, turned out the light on her nightstand, rolled back, and tucked her close.

It would be long after Shiloh fell back asleep when I realized I missed something. Along with the sated sleepy look, there was love shining in her eyes. A look that was not new but had been there from day one.

I might have missed it weeks ago, but I didn't miss it now, and I'd never miss it again.

24

It was five days after Luke found out about the letters. Five days after avows of love.

And a lot had happened but not a whole lot had changed. Luke and I were still Luke and me only with the added layer of commitment. What had changed was I'd told my captain about the letters I'd received from Clive Hutchinson. To say he lost his mind would be a blatant understatement. The man blew his stack. He yelled at me, ranted about Clive, yelled at me some more. All of this while intermingling creative curse words with promises of protection.

Obviously, my team caught wind of the letters. Gordy, Chip, and Valentine marched straight into the captain's office and demanded to read them. I felt this was a mistake. I knew I was right after the three of them passed the letters around and read each one of them. Gordy looked murderous. Chip looked perplexed. And Valentine looked concerned. All three looked unhappy. As in unhappy to the hundredth power.

This necessitated a team meeting—Reyes, Soloman, and Mereno took the opportunity to communicate their displeasure but also their worry. No one liked that Clive Hutchinson knew where I lived. I hadn't thought of that. I wasn't listed, I had no social media. It would be difficult for him to find my address unless he followed me home. That conclusion led to Gordy calling Luke.

Normally, this would've pissed me right the hell off. Especially when Gordy left the room to have a private conversation with my man about me. But after my last breakdown with Luke, I was figuring stuff out. This included me not pitching a shit-fit when the people who cared about me showed me they cared. And I knew this was Gordy's way of showing me he cared. He wanted to take care of me and the best way for him to do that was to make sure Luke had me covered.

After that things went back to normal with the guys. They didn't treat me like I was stupid for not coming to them sooner. They didn't give me more shit beyond that one day. They were just the guys. My team. My friends.

Now my brothers? *Their* response was unholy. Or I should say Echo and Phoenix's reaction was outrageously pissed. Echo made the decision as head of the family not to tell River until he was back from his assignment. So I got it from two brothers and would get it from my third whenever he got back. Luckily after two hours of ranting—yes, two hours—Echo burned himself out and turned back into my loving, but over-protective big brother. Phoenix on the other hand can hold a mean grudge. He was still pissed at me and had no qualms letting me know it every time he called me.

And right then Phoenix was sitting across the table from me, glaring. We were at Balls. Luke was sitting to my right. He'd pulled his chair close to mine and Echo was sitting to my left. They were all drinking beer while I was having a soda. Tonight was my last on-call for three days. My team was still pulling overtime. So much of it, my captain had demanded all of us got three days off. This meant if something went down Bravo would be called in and if they were busy a SWAT team from the next county over would fill in.

I could not wait to have three whole days off. No interruptions. No rolling out of bed—not that it happened every night but it happened.

"Any word?" That was Echo and he was asking Luke, not me.

Annoying. But whatever.

"No," Luke returned. "Gordy called earlier. He personally went to serve Clive Hutchinson with the restraining order and he wasn't home. He also cruised by the minimart and the man who was working the counter said he hadn't seen Clive in two days. And according to the store's schedule, he won't be in the rest of the week."

Gordy had told me the same thing this afternoon before we'd gone off shift. He and the guys were rotating going to Clive's house to serve him with the restraining order. I thought an official order was a tad overboard and we should've started with an unofficial visit to Clive's home asking him to stop contacting me. I was overruled by every man in my life.

I will admit, it had pissed me off and I slipped back into queen bitch. Unfortunately, this no longer had any effect. My team had basically laughed it off. Luke didn't laugh, he rolled his eyes. And when I continued to give him attitude he pulled me into his bedroom and commenced screwing my brains out. He'd done this muttering, "gonna fuck the sass right out of you, baby. You don't like it, don't be a bitch."

Sadly, I liked it. This didn't bode well for either of us.

Luke because it wasn't much of an incentive not to be a bitch if I got him rough and dirty. And me because I had zero chance of pulling out the bitchy attitude to get my way. He had my number, they all did. I'd pitched a fit but my heart hadn't been in it. I was mad but I couldn't begin to be mean to my friends. There was no ugliness when I told them to mind their own business and back off. And when they refused I had no recourse so I just gave in.

"Scheduled vacation?" Phoenix inquired.

"Not sure. Ethan stopped in this morning to give me an update on Jeff Shepard. Ethan's spread thin but he's gonna do some poking around tomorrow, go back to the store, see if he can get whoever's working to give us more information. Problem is Hutchinson's got no family, so his employees are all we got and they sympathize with him. They all worked with Penelope and loved her. So, getting them to talk about their boss is gonna be hard."

Phoenix's jaw was set firm and his posture read unhappy.

"Just to say, even if it takes a while before Clive can be served, Luke's checking my mail. It's not like I'll know if Clive sends another letter. It's all good, big brother. Stop worrying."

My brother's eyes narrowed and his mouth opened to say something but at that very moment, my pager shrilled.

Normally I would be grateful for the interruption before my brother went off on a tear. But right then, it sucked. I wanted to sit with the three out of the four most important people in my life and eat my burger in peace.

That wasn't going to happen. I silenced the pager and pulled my vibrating phone out of my back pocket. When I saw the nine-one-one message I closed my eyes.

"I gotta go," I mumbled. "Active shooter."

I heard both my brothers mutter curses but I ignored them and turned to Luke.

"Sorry."

Luke gave me a terse smile and leaned close to brush his lips on mine.

"I'll walk you out."

"No need. I gotta go, as in I actually have to run to my car."

"Be safe, baby, and come home to me."

God, I loved when Luke said that. And he said it every time I left.

"I'll always come home to you," I whispered.

"Go. My house when you're done," he ordered.

After one more lip touch, I stood and looked around the table.

"Love all you bossy men. Stay outta trouble while I'm gone."

My brothers called their goodbyes which included their demand I be safe then I was out the door running to my car.

My heart was thumping in my chest.

Too close.

Too damn close.

"This shit's gotta fucking end," Gordy growled from my right.

I had to agree. Being shot at wasn't my most favorite thing, even if I was mostly behind the ACP parked sideways in the shooter's yard.

I didn't get a chance to express this opinion to Gordy.

"Six-ten, you copy?" My captain's call rang in my earpiece from the command van parked three houses down.

"Six-ten, go," I returned.

"Take out those goddamn streetlights behind you."

"Copy."

Gordy dipped his chin and moved to cover me as I shifted and took aim.

My gloved finger slipped into the trigger guard, crosshairs dead center on the streetlight, then a volley of gunfire sounded off behind me and I flinched.

Fucking, *fucking*, shit.

"Get it, Sunny!" Gordy shouted.

On an inhale I lined back up, and on a natural, slow exhale I pressed the trigger. The light exploded and extinguished. As quickly as I could I took out the other three nearby and plunged the surrounding area into darkness.

More gunfire erupted as soon as I took my position and Gordy moved back to his original place.

It sounded like a goddamn warzone.

"Charlie team standby," Cap came over the radio.

"About goddamn time," Gordy grouched.

"Alpha team, that's a no-go on the front door. You have a fatal funnel and no eyes. Brake and rake A-side windows. Standby."

A moment later Valentine and Mereno were behind the ACP along with Chip and Riddle. Valentine's rifle hung by the sling at his side and in his hands was the long metal pole he'd use to rake out the window. Riddle and Chip each held the riot shields in case Valentine needed cover.

McCarthy, Soloman, Reyes, Watson, Guzman, and Jim were behind the second ACP in their own huddle waiting for the go-ahead.

"This is a mistake," Riddle muttered. "Two occupants and we only have eyes on one shooter."

No sooner had the statement left Riddle's mouth than a spray of bullets peppered the ACP. Thank fuck for the armor plating.

"It's only by a miracle he hasn't started taking out his neighbors' houses," Chip put in. "I don't like going in blind any more than you do, Riddle. But this shit has to end before someone gets killed."

"Alpha. Bravo." The captain's call cut off any further discussion. "In three, two, go."

Chip and Riddle took off in a full sprint, Valentine on their heels, Gordy close to Valentine's back, then I took up the rear. Gordy and I had our rifles up pointed at the window, covering the three men preceding us. Mereno hung back at the ACP with Reyes and they were returning fire as more bullets rang out.

I heard the glass shattering. In my peripheral Chip and Riddle were shuffling. To my far right, I saw Soloman raking out his window, Guzman and Watson holding shields.

Standard.

Textbook.

This whole scenario had been practiced a thousand times.

We all knew our places. We moved together as one.

But something was off. It felt different.

Dread hit my stomach and I scanned the yard, the windows, the front porch.

Nothing.

Everything went silent. No gunfire, no orders being called out, no loud hailer yelling to the suspect.

Calm.

Only my heartbeat and fast exhales.

Riddle was right. This felt wrong.

Valentine was through the window, Chip was almost through, and I scanned again.

Then the world around me exploded in a hail of bullets, grunts, and pain-filled shouts.

25

I was finishing up my third and final beer, watching Echo sink ball after ball, giving his brother no chance of winning. This was the second game Echo had won. And I was due to play the winner. It wasn't that Phoenix sucked, Echo was just that good. Phoenix had only had his cue on the felt twice.

"You mentioned Shepard earlier," Phoenix said from beside me. "Where's Ethan at with that?"

"Guy fled Alabama. Stayed under the radar but yesterday the ex-wife called Ethan and swears she thought she saw Shepard."

"She thinks?" Phoenix questioned.

"She hasn't seen Shepard in ten years. She was at the grocery store and the guy was at the end of the aisle wearing a baseball hat. She said she didn't get a good look but she was almost positive. Ethan's trying to get the store's surveillance footage but they want a warrant."

"Have that guy who works for you hack the footage."

My lips twitched and I chuckled.

"His name's Dylan," I told him. "Thought you cops frowned on breaking the law."

"This cop frowns on a killer walking the streets."

"I hear that. We're working on getting Ethan what he needs. But we're doing it in a way where his case won't get thrown out when the defense gets their hands on the evidence."

Dylan was being extra careful not to fuck Ethan's case.

Ethan had gone back to question the ex-wife and she confirmed the last time Shepard saw his daughter was the visit before Becca Harper's murder.

"Eight ball, side pocket," Echo called and missed.

My gaze went from the table to what had distracted Echo from his shot.

His eyes were fixed on the television playing in the corner. I stepped forward and turned to get a better view and my insides turned to stone.

Three SWAT officers shot in the line of duty. Scrolled at the bottom of the screen.

I didn't give any attention to what was playing on the TV and read the banner at the bottom one more time to verify I was reading that correctly.

Then I yanked my wallet out of my pocket and snatched out some bills. Not caring about the denomination, I tossed them on the table. Shoved my wallet back and pulled out my phone. I was tapping the screen to get to Shiloh's number while I was running through the bar.

Echo and Phoenix were right behind me.

The call connected when I hit the parking lot. It rang and went to voice mail.

Fuck.

I got to my truck and beeped the locks, hitting Shiloh's number again.

It was ringing when I heard Echo's voice boom from behind me.

"Where'd they take them?"

I got voice mail again, hit disconnect, and Echo was opening the passenger door of my truck.

"General," he barked.

Phoenix climbed in the back seat, doors slammed, and I tore out of the parking lot.

"Any report on who was hit?"

That was Phoenix. I assumed he was on the phone or talking to Echo. Either way, I was waiting for the answer.

"Fuck," Phoenix clipped. "Right. On our way."

My gut tightened and my chest burned.

"No word," he announced from behind me. "Three hit. One critical."

Adrenaline flooded and my ears roared.

One critical.

One fucking critical.

Please don't be Shiloh.

Silence filled the cab and maybe I should've said something to my woman's brothers. They were feeling this just like I was. Different but the same. They loved their baby sister. They couldn't lose her. Same as me. But radically different. I couldn't lose her, couldn't bear to think about life without her.

I just found her. We hadn't had enough time.

One critical.

Jesus fuck.

What felt like an eternity later I swung into the parking lot of General, pulled into the first spot I found, cut the engine, and was out of my truck sprinting to the emergency entrance.

The next several minutes were a blur. Thank God, Echo

and Phoenix were with me. A flash of a badge got information a lot faster than what I could've done. I followed Echo up the stairs to the third floor. Echo crashed through the door and I narrowly missed the heavy door swinging back and slamming into me. I held it for Phoenix and the three of us were waylaid by a crush of officers filling the third-floor lobby and hallway.

I scanned through the crowd and each face my eyes landed on that was not Shiloh felt like a kick in the balls. She wasn't there.

"Echo! Phoenix!" a voice shouted from across the room.

My gaze went to the uniformed cop waving the Kent brothers over. The man's face was grim, his eyes hard and glittery.

Fucking. Shit.

I followed close behind Echo, Phoenix dragging behind me.

Fuck. I should say something to Shiloh's youngest brother. But I couldn't find the words to reassure him when my insides were shriveled and my blood was boiling.

"Down the hall." The cop pointed but gave no further information.

"Jesus Christ, find someone who fucking knows something," I complained and ran after Echo.

We were halfway down the hall when Gordy stepped out of the waiting room. He looked pained. Not physically but emotionally. And there was blood dotting his arms.

Christ.

"Gordy!" I yelled and the man's gaze came up and landed on mine.

I skidded to a halt in front of Shiloh's teammate and he gave me nothing.

"Where's Shiloh?"

Before Gordy could answer Shiloh stepped out of the waiting room.

Time froze.

I swayed but at the same time, I did a top-to-toe scan. Blood in her hair but no injury.

No fucking injury.

Fuck yeah, I swayed. I could barely keep my feet as relief washed over me.

"Luke?" I heard Shiloh's voice like it was coming from far away.

Shiloh.

Her body hit mine, still in full kit. I grunted when her magazines dug into my chest. I welcomed the pain. Pain meant she was in my arms.

I wrapped her up tight, shoved my face in her neck, and finally took in a lungful of oxygen.

"Who was hit?" I asked, not lifting my face.

Shiloh's body bucked and she rasped, "Riddle's bicep was grazed and Chip took one to the shoulder. Valentine took two—neck and gut."

"Fuck. Any word on Valentine?"

"Surgery. How'd you know?"

"News was playing at the bar."

She hadn't been gone but two hours. That was all it had taken. Two fucking hours. We'd gone from dinner with her brothers to a hospital hallway.

The fragility of life.

Never forget from one minute to the next it can all be gone.

"Love you, baby," I whispered.

"Love you, Luke."

I had to give it to Echo and Phoenix. They'd given me a whole five minutes before they pulled Shiloh from my arms to do their own body scans. I didn't give the same. As soon as her brothers ascertained she was unharmed and had both given her a hug, I yanked her back and held her close while she told us what happened.

There'd been a second shooter lying in wait covering the downstairs. Valentine made it into the house, Riddle was on his way in, and Chip was in position when the man opened fire. Riddle had gotten lucky; not only did he get clipped in the bicep, he'd taken one to the vest.

Chip had taken out the shooter and another man, Soloman took out the second shooter as he came down the stairs. Neither suspect made it out of the house alive.

Shiloh didn't seem upset two men were dead, but the shock of the evening hadn't yet worn off.

"Alpha team! Call out!" a man shouted.

Shiloh went solid in my arms.

"Goddamn," Gordy grumbled.

"We're three down," the man continued. "I'm pulling from Charlie. Sixteen-year-old is being held hostage by her estranged father. Ex-wife might be in the house as well. Suspect, Jeff Shepard is wanted for questioning in the murder of Becca Harper. Staging area's been texted. No time's a good time, and I know we're all on edge after what happened tonight. But I need each of you to get your head right. If you can't do that, you let me know and I'll pull more from Charlie."

"Fucking shit," Gordy seethed and turned to Shiloh.

I missed what he asked her. My mind was stuck back on Jeff Shepard. The motherfucker tagged his daughter. I was reaching for my phone to call Ethan when I heard my name called.

"He's here, Cap," Shiloh answered.

I watched the man who'd been calling out orders walk in

our direction. He was weirdly taking in me and Shiloh. My arm curled around her tighter and his eyes narrowed.

Then he cut straight to it.

"Got a call from detective Lenox, he said you'd be here. He's requested you on scene. I gave my okay, but that was before I knew there was a personal relationship between you and Kent. I can't have—"

"I've been working on the Shepard case with Lenox," I interrupted him. "Ethan's requested me there, I'm there. Period."

"Sunny, why don't you stay here?"

Shiloh's head jerked toward Echo and her already solid frame turned to stone.

"Don't start, Echo. This is my job and you fucking know it. I will not stand down. Not tonight. Not ever." Her head whipped back and she stared at her captain. "I'm not standing down," she repeated.

It was then I wasn't sure if I was proud as fuck having Shiloh at my side holding her ground or if I wanted to beg her brothers to physically restrain her from going out again. I had yet to recover from the twenty minutes it'd taken from the time I saw the news to the time I saw her unharmed.

"Captain Thompson," the man introduced himself. "Lenox said you were a sniper and now work at TC. He also said you'd have your own gear. Is that correct?"

"Yes."

"Are you armed?"

"Yes."

Thompson took a long assessing look. Finally, he broke it with a nod.

"Kent, you're with your team. You do not break ranks. Whatever Luke and Lenox get up to, you remember your position on your team."

"Yes, sir," Shiloh said through gritted teeth.

"And, Luke, remember you're a civilian and this is Georgia, not Baghdad."

Without saying more Thompson turned and walked away.

"Call me when you're done." Phoenix broke the uncomfortable silence.

Echo yanked Shiloh into a rough hug and without a goodbye, he stood away.

"He'll be fine," Phoenix murmured. "Go kick ass, baby sister. And make sure your man here doesn't eat bullets. I think Echo's had enough for one night."

Well, that wasn't a ringing endorsement that Shiloh's brothers had accepted me into the family but it certainly fit with the Kent brand of humor.

"We'll be back as soon as we can," I told Phoenix and tagged Shiloh's hand. "You're riding with me."

Neither of us spoke a single word as we jogged down the stairs and through the main lobby, nor did we speak when I helped her into my truck. Not a word until we were pulling out and she gave me the address where we were meeting the rest of her team. Then we fell back into silence.

My mind was swirling in a million different directions.

Shepard. His daughter. Ethan. Valentine. Chip. Riddle. Shiloh. Bullets.

"I do not want you on scene," I choked. "I'd do fucking anything to have you back at the hospital waiting on Valentine to come through surgery. Safe in the waiting room with your brothers."

"Luke—"

"I've known fear. I've been captured, beat to fuck, and scared me or Carter, Drake, Trey, Logan, or Matt was gonna die. I've tasted it. I've breathed it. I've heard it. But never, not fucking once have I been so goddamn scared of losing something so special, losing someone I loved so fucking much I knew I'd never go on without them I couldn't function. I can't tell you how I made it to the hospital. I didn't know how long the drive was. I didn't even know what I was feeling because there was a hole forming in my heart not knowing if you were dead or alive or injured. I was numb. And now that's gone away and I'm feeling relief you're alive. But that fucking fear is creeping in, baby, and it's clogging my throat. It's choking me. And I didn't know how the fuck to push it down so I can let you do your job without me losing my fucking mind."

"Honey," she whispered and peeled my fingers away from the steering wheel.

Shiloh tugged my hand and rested it on her thigh palm up. She didn't hold it. Instead, she traced the calluses.

My hand curled around hers and I squeezed.

"I cannot lose you."

"You won't."

"I got twenty minutes that says otherwise."

I heard Shiloh sigh then say, "I don't know how to make this better for you."

That was because there was nothing that would make any of this better or easy.

Now that the reality of my woman putting her ass on the line and in danger every goddamn time she suited up for a job had smacked me in the face, nothing would ever make it easier.

I saw the armored vehicles and pulled into the lot and found a place to park away from the commotion. I got out and quickly rummaged through my gear in the back seat of my truck and pulled on my vest. I was adjusting the side Velcro when Shiloh stopped next to me.

"Probably not the best time to tell you this, but you look hot in a tac vest."

I shifted my gaze from my gear to Shiloh and I glared down at her.

"Probably not," I agreed.

"Too bad I'm telling you anyway." Shiloh glared back.

We didn't have time but I took it anyway.

My hands went to her neck and slid up until I was cupping her cheeks.

"You still have blood in your hair," I growled. "Do not fucking add to it."

She ignored me and issued an order of her own, "Be safe, Luke."

Then Shiloh rolled up on her toes and pressed her mouth hard against mine. Her tongue swiped my lips and she pulled away and ran across the parking lot.

26

My heart was jumping in my chest.

This was not because I knew Luke was somewhere lurking in the throngs of officers lining the street. It wasn't the red and blue lights that flashed up and down the block heralding police activity which would draw looky-loos and give the man—Jeff Shepard—a variety of civilian targets should he choose to take the barrel of his pistol from his daughter's ribs.

Shit night.

The worst kind of night.

Three teammates down.

One near dead.

Luke out of his mind with worry.

My brothers the same.

The rest of my team on edge.

And now we were facing down another crisis.

A teenage hostage.

A girl.

A father.

Logically, I knew this situation was different. Jeff

Shepard wasn't a loving father powerless to save his child. Shepard was the threat. So it was different but it was the same in all the important ways. An innocent girl's life was in danger. And seeing the familiar scene playing out again in front of me, knowing how the last situation like this—*just like this*—ended, made my heart race.

"Shepard, you don't want to do this," Ethan called out.

Jeff's body jerked at the same time he turned his glare to Ethan and the gun in his hand pressed deeper into his daughter's side. Even from the distance I was I heard the girl's whimper.

"Easy, Sunny," Gordy murmured.

I felt his hand on my shoulder halting my forward progress.

"He's gonna shoot her," I returned.

"Give Ethan time." That was Luke, in my ear on the radio.

What the hell?

"Lenox, you have two minutes to talk him down," Cap ordered.

This was because behind Jeff Shepard and his daughter, his ex-wife lay bleeding out on her front porch and had been for some time considering she was that way when we arrived ten minutes ago.

"You don't want Laurie to die," Ethan continued.

Wrong thing to say.

"That lying, cheating bitch is lucky I let her live as long as I did!" Jeff shouted. "Cheating, *cheating* bitch."

"There's still time. We can work something out."

Jeff's face twisted into an ugly snarl and he jerked his daughter's head back and forth. The poor girl cried out in pain and tried to lurch away.

Not good.

"Stephanie, right?" Her tear-filled eyes came to me. "Stay still, honey."

"Don't talk to her!" Jeff yelled. "No more talking. Everyone move back."

No one moved and Ethan continued to try to talk Jeff down.

"We know you don't want to hurt your daughter. Let her go and we'll move back. You can get into your car and leave."

"Bullshit," Jeff spat. "Bull-*fucking*-shit. Everything was fine. Everything was the way it should be then that bitch took my daughter. Lying bitches, all of them. They all think we're suckers. They think they can take our money, our houses, our kids. Stupid bitches. I gave that one time, hers had to be the worst."

"I've got a clear shot." Luke's voice came over the radio.

Without moving my head my eyes scanned the area. I couldn't see Luke anywhere.

"Mine's uncertain with the girl moving around." That was Soloman. He was perched across the street on a neighbor's roof.

"Does anyone else have a clear shot?" Cap asked.

"Best I got is thigh or shoulder," I radioed back.

The rest of the team called in their positions. None of them had a clear shot for a takedown.

I heard my captain mutter something under his breath then he begrudgingly ordered, "Marcou, you have the go-ahead on my command. Kent, standby."

"Copy," I returned.

"Lenox, calm him down now or we're ending this before that girl gets dead."

"Tell me about it." Ethan changed tactics. "I got a daughter, too. Bitch of a mother tried that with me."

That was a lie. Not Ethan having a daughter, he did.

Carson was a sweet little thing. But her mother hadn't tried to take her. The opposite was true. Carson's mother had signed over her parental rights to Ethan before he'd taken his daughter home from the hospital. Everyone knew he'd gotten his high school girlfriend pregnant. It was no secret he'd stepped up and raised her as a single, teenaged father.

"That stupid bitch was fucking her brother-in-law. Didn't even care I was in the house working. She just waited for Mac to go to work and Becca to get on the bus."

Mac Harper. Oh shit, Patricia Harper was having an affair.

"Just like that one over there." Shepard jerked his head in the direction of his ex-wife's prone body. "Cheating bitch took my money then turned my daughter against me. Now this one's gonna grow up thinking she can fuck around on her husband." Jeff shook his daughter again and I gritted my teeth when her head snapped to the side. "Now she's gonna know what it's like to lose just like the other one."

From there everything happened fast but at the same time, everything slowed. Jeff spun Stephanie around in front of him, lifted his gun, and Luke's voice echoed in my ear for me to take the shot.

Penelope's face flashed. Her father's wail sounded in my head.

I blinked to rid myself of the vision.

I blinked again. Drew in a breath. Exhaled and slowly pressed the trigger.

Jeff's torso jerked, his body pitched to the side, and he fell.

Gordy, Guzman, and Watson were on top of Jeff, rolling him over before I lowered my rifle. McCarthy rushed Stephanie, swung her up in his arms, and ran her to safety. Mereno and Jim hit the porch to help the mother and a dozen officers were skirting the woman's prone body to clear the house.

"Sunny? Hey, Sunny." Ethan shook my shoulder and my gaze went to him. "You good?"

"Yeah." I swallowed the lump that had lodged itself in my throat and nodded. "Yeah, I'm good."

Ethan studied me closely. His shrewd, intelligent green eyes took me in. He clocked my lie, but thankfully he didn't call me on it. Maybe he was going to but Luke came up from behind me and pulled me into a hug.

This was not professional. This was something that would've made the old Sunny's head pop off and spin around in circles after I kicked him in the balls for making me look like a weakling in front of my team. Luke's Shiloh however welcomed the comfort.

"That was a good shot," Luke murmured.

"Yeah."

"I know she was in your head," Luke continued.

He was talking about Penelope. And since he said he knew, I didn't think he needed confirmation so I didn't provide it. I just held on tight.

"You did good, baby. Kept your cool. I'm proud of you."

Luke was saying all the right things but I hadn't forgotten. Now that Jeff Shepard was neutralized, the situation was defused, and his daughter was safe, my head was filled with the memory of Luke running down the hall. Uncontrolled fear clear on his face. God, so much fear it hurt to look at him.

Stone cold fear.

Then on the drive over I heard it. I felt it down to my bones. Every word he spoke had been angry, full of agony, and possibly regret.

That was when the worry set in.

The fear that my job was too much. Too dangerous.

I had a sickening feeling in the pit of my stomach that Luke was going to leave.

And for the first time, I understood the true meaning of love. Real, true, deep love. I didn't ever want Luke to be afraid. Not ever. I loved him enough to let him go. I loved him enough to let him walk away and find someone who he'd never have to worry about. A woman who didn't leave their bed in the middle of the night. A woman who didn't have to promise she'd come home safe.

A woman who was not me.

That sickness in my belly roiled and turned to acid. My heart shattered into a million shards—razor-sharp pieces that pierced my soul.

Everyone always left.

27

Longest twenty-four hours of my life.

By the time Shiloh and I hit my house the sun was coming up.

She didn't protest when I took her into the bathroom and undressed her. She didn't make a peep when I pulled her into the shower and washed her. She was silent when I dried her off, helped her into one of my shirts, then got her into bed.

It wasn't until she was curled into my side and I was drifting off to sleep that her tired, dull voice broke the quiet. Her dead tone worried me. I'd never heard her sound so sullen. But I brushed it aside, chalking it up to Valentine being in critical care after he made it through surgery. Her reliving a situation that was eerily similar to the one that haunted her. I didn't need her to tell me she was thinking about Penelope and Clive while she faced down Stephanie and Jeff.

That was a mistake. I should've called her out on her tone. I should've asked what was in her head. Unfortunately at the time, I didn't understand how huge of a fuck-up it was. Like most lessons, I didn't know the true meaning until after I failed the test.

So, in the dark quiet of my bedroom when she finally spoke I didn't listen to my instincts. I just answered her question.

"Tell me about your tattoo. Why an eagle?"

Lifeless. Shallow. Sad.

Fuck, it hurt just listening to her broken voice.

I curled her closer and when I did she tucked her head under my chin.

"I was in Montana training and when we were done some of the guys decided to head to Yellowstone. We were on a day hike and caught sight of a wolf pack. Didn't see how it happened but one of the wolves had an eagle. We could hear it screeching, see it thrashing, but the bird was good as dead. I stood there watching thinking about how that wolf happened on an eagle. How the circle of life is a miraculous thing. Then all of a sudden there's this eagle flying, circling, getting lower and lower with every pass. I could not believe it when that eagle attacked the wolf. Talons out, screaming, total balls-out attack. Who would've ever thought a bird would attack a wolf? But goddamn if I didn't witness it."

"Were the eagles okay?" she whispered.

"Nope. The pack closed ranks and both birds went down," I told her. "But that's not the point. The first eagle wasn't giving up. He was fighting to the death. The second eagle swooped in like a warrior. Swear to God, it was the most beautiful thing I've ever witnessed. Can't say, I don't know if they were both males, male and female, parent and child. What I do know is that the eagle came out of the sky to help its fellow bird, uncaring it was going to battle a wolf. And right then, I understood the definition of a warrior. I had to ask myself when the time came would I be brave enough to answer the call? I wanted to be the eagle. I wanted to go into battle knowing I was brave enough to fight the wolf even if it meant certain death. And if I was the one on the ground, bloody and mangled, I wanted to have it in me to claw and screech and draw my last breath fighting."

I heard her suck in a breath, I felt the rush of air against my skin, and I still didn't press Shiloh to tell me what was wrong.

Big mistake.

"I love you, Shiloh."

I kissed the top of her head and her body went solid.

"I love you more than anything in the whole world, Luke. More than I ever thought possible," she whispered.

The words felt like velvet when they hit my chest. But they sounded off. Yet, I didn't push her to open up.

Big fucking mistake.

I woke up the next morning and Shiloh was gone.

I spent ten hours searching for her and when I finally found her I knew I'd made the biggest mistake of my life not pushing her to open up.

28

I sat and waited.

Thankfully, I didn't have to wait too long. I needed to get this done and get back on the road.

I'd been in plenty of detention centers, jails, and prisons over the years. If the building housed inmates I'd been in it. But this was different.

Vastly different.

This felt suffocating sitting in the large, sterile visitation room. With each inhale, I could smell the desperation and hopelessness. Disinfectant mixed with despair.

It was not a good idea, me being inside Georgia State Prison. And not because I was there to see Lester. For my safety, I was offered a private room. A police officer being seen by an inmate they'd had a hand in incarcerating could turn ugly. But I couldn't stomach the thought of being in a room alone with my father. This was bad enough—having to sit across from him in a huge, open space.

Finally, Lester was shuffled into the room by a corrections officer. I took the opportunity to study the man who had a part in creating me. And instead of doing what a father should do—that being love, protect, and nurture—he'd done the opposite. He'd crushed me. From a very early age, I knew he was mean. As I got older I learned he wasn't just mean, he was a total asshole. Quick to belittle, quick to yell, quick to raise his hand in anger. I couldn't remember a time when Lester had tucked me into bed, read me a book, kissed me goodnight, hugged me, or told me he loved me.

Before Lester Kent became a piece of shit cop killer he was a piece of shit father.

And watching him walk toward me, not having seen him for years, his hair fully salt and pepper—mostly salt—with his skin a weird shade of yellow, his face weathered and wrinkled, it hit me—Lester Kent was a broken man. He had always been broken. There was something inside of him that was not right. But whatever that something was, it was not my problem.

He'd made it mine. He'd forced it on me. He'd toyed with my brothers. He'd made us feel worthless. Lester had also found himself a broken woman and forced us to endure her as well. Together they made their children's lives misery.

"A reminder of the rules," the correction officer began. "You may embrace at the start and end of the visit. No other touching. No gifts. This includes letters. Hands must remain on or above the table at all times. Keep your voices low and do not disturb the other inmates and their guests. Enjoy."

The officer walked away leaving Lester's hands cuffed, and for some reason, I couldn't stop staring at the metal bracelets. How many suspects had I cuffed over the years? How many traffic stops had I made? How many calls of distress had I answered, accident scenes, domestic disturbances, home invasions? How many arrests? And now, with SWAT how many times had I put my life on the line to save someone else? What about my brothers?

All four Kent siblings were law enforcement. That was by design. That was a directive given by Echo. He was the eldest, he became the parent. The man of the house and he was determined to right Lester's wrongs.

Unintentionally, Lester Kent's actions had saved lives.

I liked knowing that. Nothing would ever absolve what my father had done. But the Kent family, led by Echo, was clean. We were a force of good and right.

"Well? Aren't you gonna give your old man a hug?" Lester asked.

I felt my lips curl with disgust. The thought of touching the asshole was vomit-inducing.

"Not a chance."

Proving himself to be the asshole I knew he was he laughed and sat down. The cuffs clicked against the metal table that thankfully provided distance between us and he launched right in.

"I take it Phoenix got my letter. Didn't expect to see you, though. Figured Echo would come."

There it was; he wanted face time with Echo who was his favorite person to fuck with.

"Yeah, we got it. Read it and tossed it."

His eyes squinted, his face got hard, and he leaned forward.

"Tossed it?"

Once upon a time, hearing that tone would've scared the shit out of me. Seeing his face hard and his eyes full of anger would've had me running for cover. All that was missing was the familiar way he'd cross his arms over his broad chest and stare down at me. My brothers came by their height naturally. Lester was tall and when I was a kid him hovering over me in a position of authority put the fear of God in me. But right then, sitting across from him I realized he could be standing looking down on me, we could be eye-to-eye, hell, I could be doing a handstand in a hula skirt and Lester would never, not in his lifetime, have any authority over me.

"I came here to ask you some questions, but sitting here, seeing you again, I realized I don't need the answers. Actually, none of us need a goddamn thing from you."

"I see my girl thinks she's something she's not. You and my boys—total disgrace. Four pigs. Never thought my kids would turn, especially Phoenix."

God, he was such a dick.

"First, I'm not your girl. And it's good to see you are exactly who I know you to be. No one else is coming. Not Echo, not River, and certainly not Phoenix. Take a long look, old man, this is the last you'll ever see of your family. You're gonna die alone in here. But before I go, I'm giving it back."

"Giving what back?"

Lester's sneer was as ugly as his soul.

"All the shit you gave me. All the shit you planted. I'm digging it up and giving it back to you. It's yours and I don't want it. Whatever broke you, fucked you up so badly that it made you into a worthless asshole, it is *yours*. It is not mine, it's not Echo's, River's, or Phoenix's. So I'm giving it back to you. I hope you enjoy it. I hope it knots your gut and gnaws at your insides until you draw your last breath."

"It's inside you, too, girl. You can deny it, but it's in your blood."

"Wrong." I stood and looked down at a pathetic, defective, tired old man.

A criminal.

That was all Lester Kent was.

That was his legacy—not mine.

I didn't say goodbye.

I didn't stop when he called my name.

It was me who got to walk out of that prison while he stayed locked away.

And I did it free.

Free of Lester's baggage, his filth, his weight.

It was about damn time I stopped carrying it around.

I knocked on the door and stepped back.

The neighborhood wasn't good but I'd seen worse.

When she answered the door I sucked in a breath.

I looked like her. Near identical. Same shade of blonde, same pale blue eyes. She was once beautiful.

Now my mother looked old and beaten down by life.

"After you left us did you have more children?"

Yep, that was the first words I'd spoken to my mother since the day she'd left us.

"Shiloh?" she asked.

And, yep, again, the woman had to ask if I was her child. This was my life. A father doing life and a mother who had to ask if I was her daughter.

This was the dysfunction I was putting to rest.

"Do you have more children?" I repeated.

"Will you come in?"

"Nope. I just wanna know."

"I'd like to explain."

There had been a time in my life when I wanted that explanation. But now I did not.

"There's not one thing you can say that would explain why you left us to him. There's not a reason good enough for leaving your children to live in hell. You knew who he was. You knew what he was doing. You knew it and instead of taking us with you to give us better, you saved yourself.

All I want to know is if there are more of us. If I have brothers and sisters I don't know. That's all I want from you."

"No, Sunny, I didn't have more kids."

"Thanks."

I turned and was halfway down the walkway when I heard her call out.

"I love you. You and your brothers."

"No, you don't. I recently learned that when you love someone you don't leave. Echo, River, and Phoenix taught me what family meant. But it wasn't until recently that I truly understood what love is. And what you did was not love. It was selfish. It was cruel."

"He threatened to kill me if I took you."

"Yeah, Ma, did he? He threatened to kill you. Well, guess what, you still should've saved us from that. You should've taken us and *saved* us! You should've risked your life to protect us. You should've been brave, and strong, and tough. You should've been a goddamn mother to your children. When you love someone you don't leave them. Not for anything."

I was back in my car when it slammed into me.

When you love someone you don't leave them. Not for anything.

Not for anything.

Not even if your job freaks the other person out.

You stay. You stay and fight.

Luke had not left me, not even when I was pushing him away. He stayed. He fought until he broke through every defense I'd built.

Now it was my turn to fight for us. I was not going to let him go.

〜

Four hours later I pulled into my driveway with a plan.

I needed a shower then I was going to call Luke. Or more accurately I was going to return one of his fifteen phone calls. I hadn't read any of the text messages he'd sent. I didn't need to, to know he was worried.

But not yet. I needed to wash away the stench of my parents first.

I pushed open my door and pain exploded at my temple. My hand went to my hip to reach for my sidearm but it was too late.

I shouldn't have waited to call Luke. I should've gone directly to him.

Those were my last thoughts as my world went dark.

29

My phone rang in my hand and my jaw clenched when I saw Drake's name.

I was on the verge of losing my goddamn mind. Fifteen calls to Shiloh and she hadn't picked up or returned a text.

Ten hours I'd been looking for her.

She was nowhere. And no one had heard from her.

"Yeah?" I answered.

"Fuck, Luke, *fuck*."

Hearing Drake's greeting I was instantly on alert.

"What's—"

"Nine-one-one call came in. Shots fired at Sunny's house."

No.

Jesus no.

"Team's been called, everyone's en route," Drake continued. I tagged my keys and was out the door with my phone still to my ear when I beeped the locks and slid in. "Not sure if we'll make it past the yellow tape, but we're sure as fuck gonna try. Ethan's been updated and on his way."

Oh, I was making it behind the police tape.

"Go in from the side," I told him as I backed out of my drive. "End of the block, corner house. They won't tape that far. Take the team and hop the fence. Shiloh's house is the fifth over. Her patio furniture is black and she's got a rock garden with a fountain. There's a faux rock, it says peace. The key to her side door is in it."

"Where do you want Matt?" Drake asked.

Matt, my sniper.

I rolled past the stop sign, pulled into traffic, and gunned it. I was ten minutes out.

Ten fucking minutes.

Ten goddamn hours.

And if I didn't cool my ass down, in ten seconds I was going to lose it.

"Next street over there's a brick house. I can see it plain from Shiloh's front yard. If he can get on the roof he'd have a shot."

"He'll get on that roof."

Yeah, he would. Matt was damn good getting in and out of tight spots.

"Gotta go, see you soon."

I disconnected and took a breath, then I took another, and when I realized there were not enough breaths I could take to sort my shit I gave up and made the call I didn't want to make but I knew I needed to.

The phone rang twice and Echo picked up.

"She's still not answering," he grunted.

I'd called Echo and Phoenix a few hours ago when I was out of places to look. It seemed he was just as worried as I'd been.

"Where are you?" I asked.

"Why?"

"Where the hell are you?"

"Home."

"No easy way to tell you this, brother—"

"Say it."

"Shots fired at Shiloh's—"

I got no further. Echo's very loud, colorful tirade sounded in my ear, then it was gone because he'd hung up on me.

She was fine. She had to be.

Matt's just a precaution I told myself.

Drake taking the team around the back of her house was a provision.

Shiloh Kent was a badass.

I stepped on the gas.

My fingers curled around the steering wheel and I drove.

I wanted to believe Matt was a precaution but I knew—I could feel it in my gut he wasn't. Shiloh was brave and strong and tough but she wasn't bulletproof.

My grip tightened and by the time I turned down her street and the flashing blue and red lights came into view my fingers were numb.

Visions of Shiloh filled my head and when they came they hit hard. So damn hard I had to suck in a breath. Shiloh next to me in bed—pressed close, her leg thrown over mine. At first, it had been me who positioned her like this, but now it was her. Every night she was in bed next to me, she got close.

Her sweet voice when she told me she loved me. The way her face got soft when I returned the emotion.

The fierceness of her loyalty.

Fuck.

Then further back to when she told me everyone left. When she'd refused to let people close. How far she'd come.

How hard she worked to open herself up to the people who cared about her.

And finally to last night. Closed off and cold.

I should've pushed her to talk.

I hopped out of my truck, not caring it was in the middle of the street—uncaring my keys were in the cupholder. If someone wanted it moved, they could fucking move it.

I had no idea where Shiloh had been for the last ten hours but I knew who was in her house. I knew with a certainty that burned a hole through my gut.

No one had been able to find Clive Hutchinson. His last letter to Shiloh was clearly a threat. Not that he actually told her he was going to kill her but he'd said she'd know his pain. I'd discussed this with Echo and Phoenix. I'd also shared my concerns that Hutchinson would go after one of them. Clive's pain was the loss of his child. The person he loved most. If he wanted Shiloh to feel that pain, he'd kill one of her brothers, not her.

"You need to move your truck!"

My gaze locked onto the uniformed police officer who had called out the order. Then I pulled my phone out of my back pocket.

One ring and Ethan was in my ear.

"Luke, brother—"

"I'm here. Tell 'em to let me through."

"Brother, fuck—"

"You got two seconds, Ethan. Tell them to let me the fuck through or I'm coming through and we'll sort out the mess I make later."

"Fuck."

I didn't know if Ethan meant to say more, and if he did I didn't hear it. I disconnected and found Drake's number. It, too, only rang twice.

"We're coming in through the side," Drake said.

"Matt?" I asked and glanced around but I was too far away from Shiloh's front yard to see the brick house I'd suggested.

"He's in position. Where are you?"

Too goddamn far away from my woman, that's where.

"Waiting for Ethan to get me through the barricade."

"Did he give you an update?"

My jaw clenched at his tone and I clipped, "No."

"Right, then you need to keep your head but you need to be warned. Hutchinson's got her."

My eyes closed and my head bowed.

Extreme anger ricocheted in my chest and pierced my heart.

Fucking shit.

"Brace, Luke, he's worked her over."

"The gunshot?"

"Unknown, but she's not bleeding, not from a bullet anyway, and neither is he."

Not from a bullet.

That should've quelled some of my anger but it didn't. That fucker had still made her bleed.

"He's waiting for one of her brothers," I told Drake. "He'll take one of them out or her in front of them."

"It won't come to that."

"You're goddamn right it won't."

I caught sight of Ethan running down the street.

"I don't care what needs to be—"

"You don't need to say it, Luke. You helped me pull my woman out of hell. I got your back on this. Hold your shit together and you'll have her back soon."

I got dead air. I shoved my phone in my pocket and ducked under the yellow police tape at the same time

Ethan made it to the cop who thought he was going to stop me.

"George, he's good." Ethan motioned in my direction.

George stepped to the side and fell in step with Ethan as he started to jog back to Shiloh's.

"Hutchinson got the drop on Sunny. She's alert and she's pissed. Hutchinson is demanding to see River. I don't know why he picked that brother but seeing as he's not available that's not gonna happen."

If Hutchinson gave her the option of which brother she wanted there to watch her execution she would've chosen River knowing he was in another state.

I didn't explain this to Ethan.

"Is someone going to be able to lock down Echo and Phoenix?"

"You're fucking kidding, right?"

Shiloh's house came into sight and my steps faltered.

Not even twenty-four hours ago, I'd witnessed the exact same scenario. Only last night it hadn't been my woman with the gun to her side.

"Jesus fuck."

"Luke, lock it down. If you give Hutchinson the slightest indication she means something to you, he might use you as a substitute for one of her brothers. You gotta play this cool."

Shiloh's head turned and I sucked in a breath. Blood was trickling out of her nose, skimming her lips before it dripped from her chin. It had obviously been bleeding away, her shirt was dotted with red stains. There was a gash on her temple that was bleeding as well. My gaze dropped to her torso, then down to her legs.

She was standing.

And Ethan was correct. She looked pissed right the fuck off.

Her eyes found mine and I watched her clench her jaw.

Oh, yeah, she was mad.

Not scared.

Not afraid.

Furious.

I didn't know what to do with this knowledge.

I knew what I was going to do when I got my hands wrapped around the motherfucker's throat.

But at that moment, after having Shiloh in grave danger twice in under twenty-four hours I was emotionally paralyzed. Fear had manifested into enraged fury.

"And how are you playing it?" I ground out, my gaze snapping back to Shiloh's.

"The negotiator is on his way," Ethan told me.

"Shiloh's not gonna wait for a negotiator to get here."

"She's—"

"Look at her, Ethan. Hutchinson didn't bind her wrists or legs. How long's she been outside?"

"He just brought her out five minutes ago, if that."

"And how long's that guy been yelling at Hutchinson to let her go?"

"He's been here fifteen minutes."

"So my take—she couldn't get close enough to him in the house so she waited for him to bring her outside knowing he was gonna use her as a shield. She will not let her brothers watch this. If you think she looked pissed before I hit the scene, look at her now. She's gonna make her move and she's gonna do it soon."

My hand went to my hip and yanked my gun clear of the holster. Ethan stepped closer, his body going tight, and he issued an unmistakable order. "Holster your weapon, Luke. You're surrounded by cops."

I held Shiloh's eyes and I felt it. The air around us went

wired. Hutchinson shouted something but I was beyond comprehending what he'd said. Ethan must've felt it, too, because his head turned from me and he shuffled until he was fully facing Hutchinson. Shiloh's eyes flared then she winked and dipped her chin.

She fucking winked.

After that everything blurred. Shiloh's right arm swung up, hitting Hutchinson under his armpit. Her left hand hammered down, hitting the wrist holding the gun. A shot rang out and the gun dropped. Shiloh sidestepped and dipped her hip, pulled Hutchinson forward using his right arm, and flipped him over her body.

The whole thing lasted three seconds max.

Hutchinson was on his back, Shiloh was on top of him, and they were grappling.

I wanted to go into battle knowing I was brave enough to fight the wolf even if it meant certain death. And if I was the one on the ground, bloody and mangled, I wanted to have it in me to claw and screech and draw my last breath fighting.

Jesus Christ.

Shiloh was shouting something and beating the absolute fuck out of Hutchinson. I took off, Ethan right behind me, and about a dozen cops descended like vultures to pull the two apart.

But not me.

If I didn't want to check for myself my woman was safe I would've stood by and proudly watched.

But my need to hold her won out and by the time I hit the grass Shiloh had already been pulled to her feet.

Her face like granite, her eyes glittering with fury.

And that pride grew ten-fold.

Tough as fuck.

That was my girl.

Those gorgeous blue eyes came to mine, and before I could demand she come to me she ran directly into my arms. I took the brunt of the impact and wrapped my arms around her.

"You good?"

She nodded and wiped her face on my shirt. Then her head came up, as did her hands, and she grabbed my face.

"I'm not giving you up," she declared.

"Come again?"

"It might be selfish, but I'm not letting you go. I'm not letting you walk away."

"Not letting me walk away?"

What the hell is she talking about?

"I know my job freaks you out. And right now's probably not the best time to talk about this but I've thought about it and I changed my mind. You deserve someone who won't get called away and you deserve to have the sort of woman who won't worry you. But I don't care. I'm not letting you leave. No matter what, you're stuck with me."

"What the fuck?" I couldn't stop the growl and if I wasn't careful I'd start frothing at the mouth. "Told you, Shiloh, I'm not leaving you. So I'm un-*fucking*-clear what you've changed your mind about but you're goddamn right you're not leaving me."

"I have a lot to tell you," she stated the obvious.

"Yeah, you do, and just a warning—I'm pissed as all hell you've been dodging me all day. And you're lucky you're standing here instead of bleeding on the grass like that asshole."

Shiloh's eyes narrowed dangerously and her head tilted to the side.

"Aren't you gonna ask me if I'm all right?"

"Baby, I asked you if you were good. Your response was

to tell me you weren't leaving me. And before that, I watched you disarm then kick Hutchinson's ass. I know you're all right. Though you wiped your blood all over my shirt. Yours is a mess and you need some fucking ice for your eye. So we're gonna do that, then I'll sit with you while you give your statement and after that, I'm taking you home."

"Home?" She smiled.

My eyes dropped to her bloody lips then went back to hers.

"Home. Our home."

"Are you asking me to move in with you, Luke?"

"No. I'm telling you, you no longer live here, Shiloh."

"So you're telling me I'm moving in with you?"

I figured I was clear that was exactly what I'd done, therefore I didn't answer.

"Okay, I'll move in with you."

I didn't respond to that either, seeing as not only hadn't I asked, I wasn't giving her options.

I had no clue what had taken place in her house or how Hutchinson got the drop on her. I did however know what happened on the front lawn. I also knew I'd hear the story when she gave her statement and I wouldn't like it. And since I knew that to be the case there was no chance in hell she was living in this house. Further, it would be a complete waste of time and money for her to get another place and for us to continue to bounce back and forth from one house to another when she'd be wearing my ring and soon.

Tomorrow, if I could pull it off.

"I love you, baby."

Shiloh's face planted into my chest and she mumbled against it, "I love you, too, Luke."

30

I would've laughed if I wasn't so damn tired.

I would've laughed if Luke didn't look like he was ready to commit murder and if Echo and Phoenix didn't look like they were ready and willing accomplices.

So even though I wanted to bust a gut when Luke pulled onto his street and found carloads of people standing in his front yard, I didn't.

I even bit my tongue when Luke got out and growled at everyone to leave.

No one listened. Not a single person who'd been waiting for our arrival cared that Luke sounded as annoyed as he looked.

But it was Liberty—bold as brass—who stalked right up to Luke, put her hand on his chest, and gave him a sad, sullen look accompanied with a soft smile.

"Payback, Luke" was all Liberty said and *poof*, all the irritation slid from his features.

Which I thought was a miracle. The kind of miracle that someone should notify the Pope about considering Luke's mood had seriously deteriorated when I sat with Ethan, my captain, and officer Frank Nigma while he listened to me make my statement.

There wasn't much to tell, really. Clive had broken into my house and was waiting for me to come home. I had to pause my retelling when Echo ranted for five minutes about how he's told me twenty-million times to get an alarm. That was a slight exaggeration but I wisely didn't call him on it. Then I paused again when I explained Clive had shot the family picture I had on my bookshelf in the living room. I was forced to pause because it was Phoenix's turn to go off on a tangent. His didn't last as long and was basically him making up creative curse words to call Clive.

Luke hadn't interrupted but he did give Ethan a knowing look when I explained why I waited until Clive had taken me outside before I attempted to escape. While we were in my house he was prowling around like a caged animal. He gave me no opening to get close. And the way he was swinging the gun around worried me. I didn't want him to shoot me. I figured one of my neighbors would've called nine-one-one when they heard the gunshot but I couldn't be sure. And when the police rolled up, lights and sirens, Clive ordered me out of the house.

Throughout the time I was in the house with Clive he didn't say much. But what he said broke my heart. He missed his daughter and he blamed me. However, as much as my heart hurt for him and I understood why he blamed me, I wasn't going to let him kill a member of my family as payback. So when he asked me which brother I wanted to die I immediately said River knowing he was safely in Florida undercover. I just needed to buy time.

I might've lost it for a minute and gotten a few good hits in after I disarmed Clive but I was relieved the standoff ended without him being killed. Seeing Luke on scene had actually motivated me to make my move sooner than I'd planned. I was going to try to talk Clive down, but once Luke was there and I saw what he intended to do, I knew I needed to make my move or Luke would end Clive.

Now it was hours later. I'd had the worst two days of my life and I really wanted to lock the doors, turn off the phones, and crawl into bed with my man but I couldn't because there was a house full of people.

And by that I meant, a house so full people were milling about in the backyard because there was nowhere to sit or stand in the living room, dining area, or kitchen. I was on the loveseat, Luke beside me. My brothers on the couch, Drake in an armchair with Liberty on his lap, and Ethan was standing next to the chair where his wife Honor sat tucked to his side. Ethan's daughter Carson had her brother Hudson and cousin Emma in Luke's bedroom and they were watching TV.

Every Triple Canopy employee was there and each of the men I worked with had been by. Some just came by to give me a once-over and make sure I was okay, then left after hugging me but Gordy and Chip had come and stayed. They were currently in the backyard. Mereno had come and stayed for about ten minutes but wanted to get back to the hospital. Valentine had woken up and everyone was taking shifts to sit with him so he wouldn't be alone. I promised I'd be by to see him tomorrow. Luke had stepped in and told Mereno I wouldn't be around until the day after. I'd started to argue until Luke cut his eyes at me. I'd promptly clamped my mouth closed and nodded my agreement.

I had a lot to say and my energy was waning so I figured it was time to get on with it.

"I went to see Dad today," I blurted.

My brothers' angry stares pinned me in place and Luke's fingers curled into my shoulder.

"It will come as no surprise to you he's still a dick. I informed him that none of us would be visiting him."

"Sunny—"

"That's it," I cut Echo off. "It's done for us. I made it clear his shit was his, it is not ours. It never was. We've been carrying his burdens around for too long. Especially you, brother." I looked at Phoenix and waited. I knew what was coming. Anytime my father was brought up Phoenix closed down. I understood this. But it was time for it to stop. "After I left the prison I drove to Mom's."

"You did what?" Echo seethed.

"Don't try and bullshit me, Echo. I know you've looked her up, too. All of us have but none of us wanted to tell the others we knew where she was because that would mean we'd have to talk about her. In case either of you was wondering, she didn't have more kids after she left us. That was all I wanted to know from her."

"Thank God," Phoenix muttered.

I agreed, totally. That was something I'd thought a lot about over the years, wondering if I had other siblings and if they were being taken care of.

Now, the hard part.

"My whole life I felt worthless. Mom left. Dad didn't love us. And what he left us with, the mess he'd made, weighed me down. Echo, brother, I knew what you were doing when you became a cop, I understood it, and we all gladly followed you. You held us together. You guided us. We all know what you sacrificed for us. But no more. Today, I gave it back to Dad, all the shit he piled on us—I gave it to him and none of us are taking it back. It took until I saw Dad today to understand it was never me who was worthless, it was him. I did nothing wrong. And, Phoenix, neither did you. He didn't love us because he doesn't know how to love."

"Sunny."

That was all Phoenix said but his meaning was clear. He didn't want to discuss his feelings about our father in a room full of people. I totally got that. So I let it go.

"And about today. I'm fine. Completely fine. And after a good night's sleep, I'll be even better."

Luke curled his arm around me tighter. Something about this felt good beyond the obvious. It was a silent form of encouragement. No, that wasn't right, it was more than encouragement. Luke was by my side—not because he thought I needed his strength but because he was proud to be there.

I wasn't sure how I knew that, but I did.

He was proud of me and I felt it.

I let that feeling sear through me.

"I'll take that as you kicking us out," Echo reluctantly mumbled.

"I promise you I'm all right and if I wasn't Luke would make me that way and so would you, River, and Phoenix. I know that now, too. Needing people in my life and turning to them for support doesn't make me weak."

Echo jerked in surprise and Phoenix smiled.

"Wasn't sure he was good enough for you," Phoenix started and I rolled my eyes. "Wanted to not like him. Wanted to offer to kick his ass out the door. But now I'm seeing he's a goddamn witch doctor or miracle worker or some such shit. Whatever he is he's welcome to stay."

I rolled my eyes again.

"Good to know because I hadn't planned on leaving."

Apparently Luke didn't find Phoenix amusing like I did.

"Just to say, I've already washed the blood out of my

clothes once this week and I'm too exhausted to do it a second time. So if we can dial back the alpha male tendencies it would be appreciated."

My joke fell flat and I knew it when Luke grunted. "Tomorrow I'd like a word with both of you. River should be there, too, but I'm not waiting until he's back so he'll just have to deal."

"Why do you need to talk to my brothers?" I tipped my head back to look at Luke.

"Because I can't ask you to marry me without their blessing. And since I plan on doing that soon..."

Luke's lips were moving. I was sure words were forming but I heard no other sounds. The room as a whole ceased to exist for me.

How was it possible that yesterday had started great, went to shit then turned even shittier, I'd gone to bed last night heartbroken, woke up with dread filling my chest, I'd faced off my father, saw the woman who'd pushed me out of her womb but gave me nothing more, had been attacked in my house—all of that making for the worst two days of my entire life.

Bar none, the worst.

All of it so bad I wanted to get into bed and sleep for a week so I didn't have to think about any of it.

Yet with a handful of words Luke wiped all of it clean—save Valentine still being in the hospital; I was still worried about him. But the rest? Gone. Vanished.

"You want to marry me?" I whispered.

"Asked you to move in with me a few hours ago, baby."

"Um, no. You told me I was moving in but that doesn't answer my question."

"How many times do I have to tell you I'm not leaving you? I've promised it. I've sworn to you I'm never leaving.

And I'm gonna make that official and I'm gonna vow it to you."

I was finding it hard to breathe so I wasn't surprised when my next question came out breathy.

"But you promised me that the first night after the bar."

"Yep." Luke smiled. "But I knew before that."

"You did?"

That came out breathy, too.

"When you asked me if I was letting you walk in front of me because I wanted to check out your ass. That's when I knew you were it for me. But it started when you told me you would kick my ass if I offered to carry your rifle case."

"But that was—"

"The first time I met you? Sure was. And if I remember correctly I fought the pull of you for about three days before I gave in and committed myself to the task of breaking you down."

I heard someone clear their throat and I was suddenly reminded we had an audience.

"Don't need to have that talk, brother."

"Welcome to the family."

The first statement was Echo, the second, Phoenix.

And it wasn't until that moment that I found it was possible to feel so much love it hurt. The pain was extraordinary. It was exquisite. It hurt so good I knew I wanted a lifetime of it.

31

"You're an asshole."

At Logan's declaration, I kept my eyes on the ceiling but let go of the bar I was getting ready to lift off the rack.

"Why am I an asshole?"

"Matt's dating," he spat out.

"And that makes me an asshole?"

"No, you're an asshole because you're shacked up with Sunny. And so now Matt's trying his hand at dating. That leaves Dylan."

Logan was not pissed because Matt was dating. And seriously, dating was not the word for what Matt was doing. It was more like Matt was trying his hand at sleeping with a woman more than once. And Dylan was a good-looking guy, smart as fuck, and could arguably pull more tail than Logan, but that still wasn't what had crawled up Logan's ass.

It had been four months since Shiloh had moved in with me. Four seriously great fucking months. And we weren't shacked up, we were engaged—or we would be by this evening. I'd waited as long as I was going to wait for River to get done with his assignment before I asked her. However, the one conversation I'd had with him when he called to check in after he'd heard what went down with Hutchinson he'd given me his blessing as well. So I was no longer waiting for all of her brothers to be present when I asked.

I'd waited far too long as it was.

No, Logan had a thorn up his ass because *Lauren* was dating.

We all warned him the woman was not going to wait for him. He repeatedly stated what he'd said since the day I'd met him—love wasn't real.

But it seemed to me and to Drake, Carter, Matt, and Trey that Logan was full of shit. But due to what happened between his mom and dad—the experience so horrific that it shaped his opinion about relationships, family, and love— we never called him on it.

Maybe that had been a mistake. He knew Carter loved Delaney. He'd had a front-row seat to Drake falling in love with Liberty. He watched it happen to Trey with Addy. And now with me. I didn't hide how much I loved Shiloh.

"If you're pissed Lauren's—"

"I'm not pissed about Lauren. Though I will go on record to say the guy's a douchebag and all wrong for her."

Unfortunately, I had to agree. There was something not right about a guy whose name was Guy. Not to mention he gave off a weird vibe. I couldn't place it. He wasn't overtly asshole-ish but he was for sure hiding something. I just hoped Lauren figured it out before she was in too deep.

"Alright, Logan, I'm still not sure why I'm an asshole but if Dylan's cutting into your action now that he's the only single one, ask Echo or Phoenix to go out."

Logan huffed a sigh so I sat up from the weight bench and gave him my full attention.

"Tell me what's really crawled up your ass."

"My mom's coming to town."

"So? You're a total mama's boy, you should be happy."

Logan flipped me a rude gesture and his face twisted into a snarl.

"She's met someone."

Oh, fuck.

This was not good. As far as I knew, Logan's mom hadn't dated anyone since her husband died.

"And my sisters like him. They say he's the shit. He has no kids. His wife had cancer early on in their marriage and couldn't have any. He stayed until it finally took her. Then he waited ten years after she died before he started dating. My sisters say he's serious about Mom and they think he's gonna ask her to marry him."

"Logan—"

"He beat the fuck out of her," Logan growled. "He beat *us*. How the fuck can she trust another man? Why would she even want to invite a man into her life?"

There were so many reasons why she should, could, and would want to. So many I didn't know where to start to explain them all. The problem was, Logan wouldn't be receptive to hearing any of them. And part of me understood. His father was a sonofabitch. And when his mother had taken her last beating she'd shot and killed her husband. Though it wasn't her husband beating her that made her snap that night, it was her husband taking a knife to Logan.

"Brother—"

"Never mind. Forget I mentioned it."

"But you did. We should talk about this."

"There's not enough hours or enough whiskey to talk about that motherfucker."

Fuck.

Logan was prowling toward the door when I called his name. He didn't bother to turn around when he answered.

"Just not right now. Not here. Not now. I can't think about this."

"I'll drop it only if you promise to come by the house one night this week. If you want I'll ask Shiloh to find a night to hang with her girls."

"Name the night and I'm there."

Then he was gone.

Fuck.

We should've worked this out of Logan years ago.

My phone beeped with a text. I picked it up off my desk, opened the message from Drake, and smiled.

It was an address and a time.

I closed the text and pulled up Shiloh's number.

It rang once.

"It's go-time!" she squealed.

"Where are you?"

"Home."

"I'm leaving work now. I'll be home in ten."

"Kay. Drive safe."

I heard another happy squeal then she hung up.

I walked into the house and the first thing I thought was we needed a dog. Maybe two so they didn't get bored while Shiloh and I were at work.

My next thought was we also needed children but before

that happened I needed my ring on Shiloh's finger and her to have my last name.

Yeah, I wasn't waiting any longer for River to come home.

I entered the bedroom and stopped. It looked like a bomb went off. This was not unusual; Shiloh wasn't a slob but she was messy. She dropped her clothes where she took them off and only picked them up when it was time to do laundry. The rest of the house was clean, but our bedroom was a total disaster. What was unusual were the dresses strewn on the bed. Shiloh was a jeans-and-tee type of woman. Shorts and tanks if it was hot outside. I'd been with her nearing on half a year and I hadn't ever seen her in a dress or skirt. And the closest she got to high heels were wedge sandals.

This was not a complaint. Shiloh in cargos and boots was hot. Shiloh in cut-off shorts, a tank, and flip-flops sexy as all get-out. In shorts, a tank top, and wedge sandals that made her ass look even better than I thought possible —outstanding.

"We need to hurry, Luke. They only gave us an hour and the botanical garden is thirty minutes away. That's without traffic."

I peeled my eyes off the piles of clothes and sucked in a breath when I caught sight of Shiloh. Blonde hair down in straight, shiny sheets that fell over her shoulders. Big, pastel blue eyes. Flawless tanned skin. The dress was low cut and showed a good amount of cleavage but on Shiloh, it looked classy instead of trashy. It was some shade of blue—not dark but not light, somewhere in the middle. It stopped at the knee and the only adornment was the fabric knotted between her breasts, cinching the material before it flowed down. It wasn't tight, it wasn't showy, but it was sexy as hell.

And on her feet were a pair of silver high heels. One strap across her toes that were painted pink with sparkles. Another strap at her ankle.

"Jesus."

"Is the dress not okay?" Shiloh asked and smoothed down the fabric at her hips. "Liberty said casual. I didn't own any dresses so I bought a few but now I don't know."

"Christ, you're gorgeous."

"Luke," she whispered.

"Serious as fuck, baby, you're so beautiful sometimes I look at you and I wonder how in the hell I got so lucky."

"Luke."

I loved, *fucking* loved when she whispered my name. It never failed to hit my chest and ignite a burn.

"I want to get a dog," I said.

"Okay."

"I want kids."

Shiloh's eyes flared and she nodded.

"Okay."

"You want kids?"

"I want to have your kids."

Christ, I loved her.

"Come here, Shiloh."

"No way, Luke. I know what that look means and we can't be late."

"Baby, we're gonna be late."

"We're not gonna be late to Liberty and Drake's wedding."

"We are if you don't strut your fine ass over here and keep arguing with me instead."

"Why am I always walking to you?" she snapped.

Cute as fuck.

"Because I like to watch you move. I like knowing a

woman as sexy, as beautiful, as smart, as strong as you are, is walking to a man like me."

"And what kind of man are you?"

"The kind that's proud as hell to have you at my side."

Shiloh didn't walk, she moved quickly, then her arms were around me and her lips were on mine. I gave her approximately thirty seconds to control the kiss before I took over. There was one thing I knew I'd never get used to. Not in five years, not in ten, not in twenty. The feel of Shiloh when she gave herself over to me. So strong. So tough. The woman could and did take care of herself, but the second she was in my arms everything about her softened. She trusted me to take care of her every way a man could take care of his woman.

I reluctantly broke the kiss but didn't go far when I demanded, "Turn around. Hands to the bed."

I spun her around, kept my hands on her hips to steady her, and didn't wait for her hands to hit the mattress before I was kneeling behind her skimming my palms up her thighs as I went. I hooked her lacy panties, yanked them down, and tapped her ankle.

"Spread."

Shiloh started to lift her foot but I stopped her.

"Leave 'em, I want them stretched."

I watched as she spread her feet in those sexy heels as far as she could with her lacy panties still hooked just above the silver strap.

Once I took my fill of her ankles bound, my hands went to her calves and started their journey upward, bunching the material of her dress until I exposed the curve of her ass cheeks. Then I buried my face between her thighs. My tongue speared into her pussy, my hands squeezed her ass, and my dick twitched in my pants.

"Oh, God," she moaned and pushed deeper into my mouth.

I licked, I nibbled, I tongue-fucked, and I lapped up her excitement until Shiloh was making those needy, hungry noises indicating she was close.

I was on my feet with my cock freed and lined up.

"Tip your ass higher."

Shiloh stretched out and tipped.

I pushed her dress around her waist, then I slowly pushed inside. I savored the feel, the heat, the squeeze of her pussy. Silky wet. Hot. Tight. Heaven.

"Every time, Shiloh. Every damn time I'm inside of you. Nothing more beautiful than feeling you take me."

"Now who's making us late?" I asked as I watched Shiloh fix her hair.

"I can't go to a wedding with sex hair."

Sure she could. It would match the pretty glow on her cheeks.

I stepped into the bathroom and slid behind her. Once I had my hands on her hips I dropped my lips to her shoulder but kept my gaze fixed on her face.

"You look perfect."

"You always say that," she said and placed her brush on the counter then declared, "Ready."

"Almost. You're missing something."

Shiloh frowned and I watched her eyes in the mirror roam from her face down to her dress then back up to lock onto mine.

"What am I missing?"

Instead of answering I took my left hand from her hip,

reached into the pocket of my slacks, and found what I was looking for.

I held the ring out in front of her.

Shiloh's chin tipped down and I heard her suck in a breath.

"Marry me, baby."

In the mirror, I saw her eyelids drift closed.

"Never thought I'd be this happy. Never thought I'd have this. Never in a million years did I think this existed." Her eyes opened and came to mine. "We're gonna get married."

"Yeah, we are."

Jesus.

"You're gonna be my husband," she whispered, and that burn in my chest blazed. "I'm gonna be your wife."

"Yeah, baby, you're gonna be my wife."

Shiloh held out her left hand and wiggled her fingers. The gesture was so unlike Shiloh I smiled.

I slid the band on and she moved her hand farther away and stared.

Then she started bossing.

"As soon as River gets home. I don't want to wait. I'll wear a dress but it won't be white. And I want to get two dogs. One would get lonely. He'll need a friend to play with. And four kids. My brothers are a pain in my ass but every girl needs big brothers."

"Whatever you want."

"If we weren't already late I'd take you back to bed and show you how much I love my ring."

"You'll show me when we get home."

I gave her hip a squeeze and started to back away but stopped when Shiloh's gaze came to mine. Even looking into her eyes through the mirror the pastel blue sparkled. One day she'd give those pretty eyes to my daughter. One day I'd watch her give to our children everything her parents never gave to her.

"If we weren't already late I'd take you back to bed and show you how happy you make me." Shiloh dropped her left hand and found mine at her hip. Once she had her fingers twined with mine she continued, "Thank you for not giving up. Thank you for breaking down the walls and not letting me rebuild them. Thank you for loving me."

I swallowed the blockage that had formed in my throat and pulled her closer.

"You're welcome, baby."

"No one else would've ever been able to do it. Just you. Every day—I'll show you how much I love you every single day. I promise every day to show you how thankful I am you never gave up on us."

My eyes drifted closed and I let my future wife's promise sink deep, and I did this with the platinum band inlaid with diamonds I'd slipped on her finger digging into my fingers.

32

Logan Haines

"Rolling Rock," I ordered.

The cute brunette behind the makeshift bar flashed me a broad, flirty grin.

"Sure thing, darlin'."

The woman pulled a bottle from the bucket of ice, popped the top, and placed it in front of me making sure I got a good look at her cleavage between the popped buttons of her white blouse. I took a moment to take in the sight that stirred not a damn thing. Not even a twitch of appreciation.

What the hell is wrong with me?

"Thanks." I placed a tip next to my beer and lifted the bottle.

The next smile she gave me was one of understanding—I wasn't interested. Which was a damn shame.

I turned to face the crowd of well-wishers. As weddings went, Drake and Liberty had done it right. No muss, no fuss. Just family and close friends. The ceremony had been short and simple, the party afterward the main focus. A big celebration.

My gaze scanned the happy faces and immediately I found Lauren. She was holding Shiloh's left hand, staring at her ring and smiling. That was Lauren; always smiling, always happy, always upbeat and so goddamn chirpy. She was also seriously pretty in a girl-next-door way. If the girl next door had a rockin' body, double Ds, a smile that warmed from the inside out, and a voice that was cheery and playful. A voice that made a man want to worship her body just to hear her moan his name.

I was about to look away when *Guy* came up beside Lauren and put his arm around her. Fucking dipshit. Without my permission my jaw clenched and I forced myself to watch the couple. Lauren went stiff before she relaxed. What she didn't do was slide her arm around him or show any interest in being close. This shouldn't have made me happy but it did. Nearly as happy as I felt yesterday when I overheard Lauren telling Addy she hadn't fucked the asshole yet. Of course, Lauren hadn't used those words, but had said that she wasn't ready to "go there" with the man she'd been dating for three months. Proving irrefutably that Guy was a total shmuck.

"Thanks for coming." Drake gave me a bone-jarring pound on the back and I barely contained my wince.

"Wouldn't miss it, brother. Been waiting a while for you to make it official."

"Right." Drake chuckled. "We all know you think love's bullshit. But I'm telling you, when you meet the right woman she'll make you a believer."

It wasn't that I thought love was bullshit. Okay, I did, before I saw Carter with Delaney. I still had my doubts, then I watched Hadley Walker work some sort of voodoo magic and turn Brady into a love-sick puppy. After that, I came to realize that there were people in the world who had the capacity to love. Real and true love, but it was rare. And even though Drake had found it with Liberty and Trey with Addy and fuckin' Luke of all people with Shiloh, I still knew with a hundred percent certainty that I was not one of those people who could love.

"I think Liberty makes you happy, but more importantly *you* make *her* happy. Which is a damn good thing, brother. Her dad and uncles would have no issues putting your ass down, you fell down on that particular job."

"No chance of that happening. Dinner will be served in about an hour. You're staying, right?"

"Of course I am. Don't be a dick."

"Lauren's—"

"Not mine. Will never be mine. And I don't *want* her to be mine," I quickly interrupted.

Drake gave me a look that told me he didn't believe me. Seeing as it was his wedding day and his wife would be unhappy if I busted his lip, I didn't call him on the look. I should've been used to Drake, Trey, Matt, Carter, Luke, and even fuckin' Dylan giving me that same look at least once a day since Lauren started dating her *boyfriend*.

Fuck. Even the word gave me hives.

"I'm going to find my wife," Drake beamed.

And with another pound on my back, Drake did just that; he left to find his wife.

Fucking hell.

They were dropping like flies.

Matt would be next. He seemed to be determined to find a woman.

I felt her presence before I heard her sweet voice.

"Two Millers, please."

I did another scan of the crowd and found Guy lounging back in a seat, his eyes glued onto Quinn's ass as she bent to talk to her niece, Emma. If Brice caught the fucktard eyein' his woman's ass like that Guy would be blind.

"Idiot," I mumbled.

"What?"

I turned to find Lauren staring at me.

"Your boy, he's an idiot."

"Why are you always such a jerk?" she asked.

She sounded genuinely perplexed, like she really wanted to hear my answer. Maybe even cared what my answer was.

"Why is it you're up getting drinks and your boy's sitting his ass down?"

"Stop calling him that, Logan, he's not a *boy*," she seethed.

I took a step closer and fuck me, the little spitfire stood taller and squared her shoulders.

"A man doesn't let his woman get her own drink and he sure as fuck doesn't let her get his. He makes sure her ass is sitting and enjoying herself then he goes and gets *her* a drink. A man doesn't check out another man's woman. And a fucking man doesn't let weeks turn into months before he makes a woman his."

Lauren huffed out a humorless laugh.

"Funny, you talk a big game. You talk like you know how a man behaves. Yet you have no clue."

I closed the remaining space between us, tilted my head down so my mouth was inches away from her ear. I inhaled her fresh scent then I promised, "Sweetness, I guaran-*damn*-tee I'd have you beggin' to be mine before the night was up and I wouldn't be wasting a second of it talking a big game. You know it and I know it, so don't give me shit about not having a clue."

I'd miscalculated my play.

I'd gotten too close.

I felt Lauren shudder, and when she sucked in a lungful of oxygen her chest expanded, and at the same time she pressed her chest against mine, got up on her toes, and hissed:

"Prove it."

With that, she nabbed two cold Millers off the bar and strutted her ass back to her date.

I watched the sway of her hips, not feeling a twinge of remorse.

I also did this with my heart pounding in my chest, my blood burning through my veins, and my skin electrified.

If there was ever a woman I would prove anything to it would be Lauren.

If there was ever a woman who could make me a believer it would also be Lauren.

But being the son of a man who religiously beat his wife and children, being the son of a woman who had been forced to kill her children's father, I knew better than to let my guard down. I knew he was in me. My hand automatically went to the scar on my stomach and as it happened every time I saw what my father had done to me, I remembered I wasn't meant to have a family.

I had to find a way to let her go. I had to stop taunting her, and in doing so torturing myself.

Lauren Saunders was everything I could never have.

She was the type of woman who would dig her claws in until I was in so deep I'd never let her go.

Then my demons would rear up and ruin her.

It was time I faced the truth—I couldn't be trusted. Not with something as precious and beautiful as Lauren.

Up next...Lauren and Logan. A man who doesn't believe he can love and woman who's looking for forever.

Grab your copy of Tarnished

ALSO BY RILEY EDWARDS

Riley Edwards

www.RileyEdwardsRomance.com

Romantic Suspense

Gemini Group

Nixon's Promise

Jameson's Salvation

Weston's Treasure

Alec's Dream

Chasin's Surrender

Holden's Resurrection

Jonny's Redemption

Red Team - Susan Stoker Universe

Nightstalker

Protecting Olivia

Redeeming Violet

Recovering Ivy

Rescuing Erin

The Gold Team - Susan Stoker Universe

Brooks

Thaddeus

Kyle

Maximus

Declan

Blue Team - Susan Stoker Universe

Owen

Gabe

The 707 Freedom Series

Free

Freeing Jasper

Finally Free

Freedom

The Next Generation (707 spinoff)

Saving Meadow

Chasing Honor

Finding Mercy

Claiming Tuesday

Adoring Delaney

Keeping Quinn

Taking Liberty

Triple Canopy

Damaged

Flawed

Imperfect

Tarnished

The Collective

Unbroken

Trust

Standalone

Romancing Rayne

Falling for the Delta Co-written with Susan Stoker

BE A REBEL

ACKNOWLEDGMENTS

To all of you – the readers: Thank you for picking up this book and giving me a few hours of your time. Whether this is the first book of mine you've read or you've been with me from the beginning, thank you for your support. It is because of you I have the coolest job in the world.

Made in the USA
Middletown, DE
23 April 2021